The Chosen...Two

Michelle Summers

Charming Lil Penny

For my J: Thanks for putting up with yet another dream of mine.
I think this one is going to stick.

For my girls: I love you more than you can possibly know. Hopefully
by the time you're old enough to read these you'll think it's cool, not
embarrassing, to have an author for a mom.

Contents

Chapter 1

MIRANDA

I look into the beast's benevolent eyes, which are roughly the size of my head, and pity him. Teardrops the size of my fist fill them as he tries to pull his horned head into his multicolored and domed shell, dark green with flecks of orange, red, and white, in an attempt to hide from me. The red hair framing his green head is fluffed out like he just stuck his tongue in an electrical outlet. His nostrils flare wildly. Fear is not the emotion I would expect to elicit from a monster roughly the size of my house, yet here we are.

He is as disoriented by the current situation as I am. The fact that dragon turtles originated in China isn't what has me confused. Over the last six months, I've learned no matter where people create or most widely believe in a creature, that critter can still turn up here, in the good ol' U.S. of A.

What is baffling, to both my current rival and myself, is he *should* be hanging out in a large body of water, not wandering around the fourth floor of a science museum, browsing the fish tanks of the Hudson Bay exhibit like he's wandering through the grocery store deli. And if this dragon turtle and his family are anything like goldfish, based on his size this particular dude came from a *very* large body of water.

"Hey, Buddy," I call to him sweetly, similarly to how I talk to Sammy in fact, "Can I call you DT? Let's see if we can get you back home, okay?"

The whine he responds with is somewhere between a whale's song and the chatter of the triceratops at the theme park we took the kids to last summer. The long moan comes to me on a stream of foul breath that smells like the fish he slurped from the tanks. Thankfully that snack of his kept him busy long enough to give the security guard the opportunity to track down who, or what, had triggered his alarms.

No one knows why the dragon turtle is here in the first place. And by "no one", I mean the League of Docents (think, council of men in charge of my life as the Guardian even though they are completely out of touch with the realities this life comes with), the security guard on their payroll, George, and myself. (I recently learned that the League of Docents runs all of the biggest security companies in the tri-state area for just such an occasion as this.) Luckily, as of now, we're the only ones who know about this big fella.

But that luck is going to change if I can't get him over to the Hudson River soon, before tourists, science enthusiasts, and buses of school kids start to fill the parking lot I have to get him through.

But first, I have to get him *to* that parking lot.

I look at the big chunk of pyrite, "fool's gold," the security guard grabbed from the mineral exhibit for me when I told him I'd need some kind of treasure. Hopefully it will fool my new friend– dragon turtles are, after all, dragons, and dragons love treasure.

It's slow going to get the beast to follow me to the stairs–there's no fucking way I'm getting in an elevator with him. He has to be over the weight limit, if he's even fit inside. He plods along, I think happily, at least if his tail is any indication. He takes up so much of the room that when his tail swishes from side to side it crashes into the fish tanks, leaving dusty white patches and cracks in the glass in its wake. I'm impressed by how gracefully he slides down the staircase, not to mention the fact he even can *fit* on the staircase.

As we approach the third-floor landing, I know I have to keep him on target so he doesn't wander over to the "Wild About Animals" exhibit and accidentally break something loose. I shudder thinking about Sammy's fascination with the hissing cockroaches and how badly Natalie wanted to bring home a naked mole-rat. Weirdoes…

Once we hit the second floor, I have to lure him around a corner and down a short hallway. His full attention is on me until the giant breathing ball hanging over the stairs we need to descend. The silver sphere is made up of thousands of scissor-like hinges, opening and closing to expand and contract the ball rhythmically. I don't know if it's the shiny metal or the movement, but DT is mesmerized. He sits down, staring at the ball as it grows and shrinks and grows and shrinks, a lopsided goofy grin on his face. I run down to the gift shop and grab a bar of gold the size of my forearm and way faker than even the pyrite I've been using as a lure so far.

But fake or not, my new souvenir gets his attention. He closes his mouth and tilts his head. He looks like a puppy who is totally focused on the juicy treat his owner is coaxing him with. Of course, this puppy is green and the size of a tractor-trailer.

With more speed than a creature of his size should be capable of, he pushes himself to his feet and begins charging down the stairs. Thankfully, the main entrance is right behind me so I turn and run as fast as I can.

I push through the double doors, entering into the all-glass hallway we need to navigate to get outside. I've always loved the trippy effect the incandescent bulbs set in the dark ceiling above make when they hit the reflective metal strips across the floor, but I have no time for that admiration today. I can't forget that I'm on a mission. And if I *could* somehow forget, then the crash of glass shattering as my pursuer follows me into the fragile vestibule would certainly remind me.

I run through the second set of double doors, my eyes scrunching shut against my will. It's a lot a brighter out here than it was when I arrived in the wee hours of the morning. I forgot my watch as I stumbled out of bed when George called, so I don't know the exact time, but when I got here the sun was only peaking over the horizon.

Shit. I really hope Jake was able to get everyone up and ready for school on time. He's never had to do that alone before. Does he even know whose lunch box is whose? Focus, Miranda! I look around frantically as I keep running at a pace I know I cannot sustain much longer. What am I going to do with this thing? Facing off with demons and monsters that I can fight and kill is, in a way, a lot easier than dealing with this guy. But I'm a protector, the Guardian, and that means my job isn't simply "kill everything." I need to protect humans, and sometimes that lines up with protecting a mythological creature, even if only from himself.

He's not trying to hurt anyone. He's just giant and clumsy. And really fucking terrifying to behold. Behold? Where'd I pull that one from? I am grateful for the brief but sage advice George gave me when he called at four in the morning to tell me I was needed.

I believe his exact words were, "It's a dragon turtle. They're a little scary looking, but they're good guys. Try to remember that. Don't kill him! They originated as good luck charms."

Sure they are. This guy definitely compares to the rabbit foot I kept on my backpack in second grade. That is, before I found out it had once belonged to an actual rabbit and threw up.

I glance behind DT to the pile of glass shards that was formerly the bridge between the real world and that magical place of science. I really hope I don't have to pay for that. But then I remember, George can probably afford it, and he definitely owes me for waking me up so early today, so I breathe a little easier for a moment.

But it's only for a moment. Because now that we have cleared the solar-panel-covered parking lot, I can see just how far I still have to lead him before we reach the water's edge. At least, in the direction I was planning to go. I stare at the immense park, so thick with trees I can't even see the playground that I know is on the other side. And all of it lay between us and the bay. I would have to lead this thing a solid three-quarters of a mile through a dense grove if I steered it in that direction. I'm exhausted just thinking about it.

From all our lunches on the terrace outside the museum restaurant I know the piers are up the road to my left. I turn back to the creature, once again considering his size. Can he get around the boats docked there without damaging them, or attracting too much attention? I think this particular marina is mainly private sailboats and therefore I would think the area is pretty desolate this time of weekday. I don't have time to give my limited options any more consideration, so I start running to the left.

I turn back to my colossal adversary and wave the fake gold bar in the air.

We've halved the distance to the piers, and I know chances are there will be other people there when we arrive. Oh well. Still less attention than if I had to march him across Liberty State Park. Something tells me we couldn't pass for a girl walking her Great Dane.

The closer we get to the water, the longer the distance between him and me becomes. He's slowing down. Come on, Buddy. I stop, not wanting to lose his interest completely.

"Hey, what's up big guy? Don't you want to go back to your home in the water?"

Again, his sad roar reaches me. He squints his giant black eyes closed and shakes his head, the way an enormous dog would shake away water droplets from its ears. His neat little orange beard shakes open, ruffling his tidy tuft. He ducks his head low and looks up at me, a ginormous puppy cowering. He lets out a high-pitched whine.

"What is it, boy? Is Timmy stuck down a well?"

He snorts foul puffs of air through his dinner-plate-sized nostrils. He is not amused with my mocking tone. Oops.

I move toward him a few steps until I can catch his eye with the gold bar again. His eyes begin to trace its movement as I wave it around in front of his nose.

He snorts again, happily this time, and droplets of dragon snot hit my face and chest. You would think I'd be used to being covered in snot after raising four kids. And you'd be wrong. It takes every bit of my self-control to not throw up right here.

"Lovely. Okay, Buddy, time for you to go home." When I am sure I have him focused on the bar, I turn, keeping it behind me, and run as fast as I can for the piers.

He plods along behind me, because that's all he has to do to keep up at this point, as I pant and hold my side. I bring myself to a skidding stop at the edge of the water and throw the golden brick into the bay, before turning to check on his progress. Unfortunately, I had completely misjudged our distance, both from the water and each other, and he's too close for me to effectively dodge his charge after the gold.

Not being known for their jumping abilities, the dragon turtle knocks into me on his way after his quarry, and we fall into the water together. I'm grateful the fall isn't too far because he lands on top of me and immediately swims away, with unbelievable speed. He grabs the bar of gold in his wide mouth and turns his head to wink his thanks at me before swimming off, past the boats docked in the basin and out to the bay.

I'm happy to have fallen in far enough from the boats that we didn't land on any, until I realize that my only exit from this heavily polluted, likely toxic waterway is one of the ladders on the docks, the closest of which is about twenty feet away. Not an Olympic swimmer on my best day and already not at my freshest, I flip onto my back and do a lazy backstroke.

I heft myself out of the water with the ladder. Feeling like an express train slammed into me instead of another living being, I start toward my car. I wish I could ignore the stares of the few people working on the docks, but I probably should address their concerns over the beast they just saw dive into the Morris Canal.

"Uh, nothing to see here. He was just, um, an animatronic. From the science center. He got a little out of control so we had to put him down over here. All this new AI is going to be the end of the world, am I right?" I end with a forced snorty laugh.

Their eyebrows scrunch down, and they stare at me a bit longer, but soon they break off into their own conversations, some with a shake of their heads, as they return to work. Just a typical Friday morning for them.

I shrug. It's New Jersey. I guess there are far stranger sights than a dragon turtle knocking a middle-aged woman into the Hudson.

I resume trudging to my car, my sodden feet smacking against the pavement with every sloppy step, and daydream of the hot shower I will take when I get to my docent's house. My husband should be heading there right about now, also.

We're supposed to train together today. But as I collapse into the driver's seat and feel the watered-down dragon mucus drying all over my front side, it occurs to me that I might need a nap first. Well, shower first, then nap, *then* maybe I'll be up for training.

It's rush hour now, but thankfully George lives in the opposite direction of morning traffic from the science museum. I'm barely through the door when he sits me down in his living room so he can question me about the panic attack I had the day before, at the mere discussion of training outside, in the unpredictable wild, instead of safely in the dojo.

"Do you have any idea what freaked you out yesterday?" His blue eyes penetrate mine, looking for an answer, for hope.

"Nope. I already left Maria a message though. Hopefully, she can see me sooner than later, and I can figure out why I was triggered and get over it." I'm staring at my thumbnail and bouncing my leg impatiently. Maria is the therapist the League of Docents assigned to me–to *us*. She is technically the marriage counselor for Jake and me, but since I'm not exactly at liberty to share most of what I encounter on this job, if I want a therapist to talk with about other issues, issues not relating to Jake, she covers that too. "This conversation is making me uncomfortable," I look down at myself. "You know what? That may just be all the dragon boogers I'm coated in. Can I go shower now?"

He stares into my eyes a second longer before nodding and walking back toward the dojo. "Jake and I are in here when you get out."

I climb the stairs to the guest wing of the house, slowly, walking more than a touch like Frankenstein's monster to the room where I have a small dresser with emergency clothes in the bathroom. This bathroom serves as my own little headquarters inside George's house at this point.

It's been six months since I found out I am The Guardian. While nothing has so far compared to my first big battle, having to rescue my own husband from a handful of horny muse goddesses, I have had to keep up with my training. And fighting slimy, mucous-ejecting beasties is part of the job. Add in not wanting my kids to see me come home covered in all those lovely bodily fluids, and it made sense for me to keep some clothes here so I can get cleaned up before going back to being Mom.

I've peeled off the clothes, which I'm not sure I'll ever want to wear again, and have just turned the water to scalding when my phone rings. It's Maria.

I look at the hot water spraying into the shower stall that is already filling with steam, but I shut it off so I can hear my therapist. "Hi, Maria. Thank you for calling me back."

"Hey, Miranda. What's going on?" Her voice is peaceful and patient on the other end of the line.

"So, um, I've been having these panic attacks lately. I had one yesterday, after our session, and I was hoping we could try to unearth why I was triggered?"

"I'm sorry to hear that happened to you. Do you know what the trigger was? Was it from the exercise I assigned to you and Jake, where you're supposed to look into each other's eyes? That would not be unheard of, if it was that."

I flinch at her words. That sounds so bad. Also, we completely forgot we were supposed to be doing that. "No, not at all. George told me he wants to start training outside. As far as I can tell, I believe the idea of training outside kicked it off."

For a moment, I hear nothing but her breath. Then she starts to speak again. "Okay, that's a little strange. I think we should discuss this in person. As luck would have it, I have the rest of the afternoon free today. Can you come in now?"

Again, I look at the shower. "Sure? Not right now though. I'm about to wash some creature goo off myself. We should be able to be there in about an hour though, if that's okay." I hope Jake accepts the olive branch I'm extending when I invite him along.

"Eww. More blood?"

"No, wow, you know me so well already. This time it's monster mucus," I answer unaffectedly, which makes a nice contrast when I think I hear her gag over the phone.

"Oh God. Of course. Please, take your time. See you soon."

"See you soon." I tap the red button to hang up the call, place the phone on the counter, and turn the scalding water back on so I can finally get clean.

Twenty-five minutes later, I walk into the dojo, smelling much better and no longer encrusted in phlegm.

Jake is fighting a platform punching bag, and George is correcting his form. They are playing so nicely together, much better than when Jake first came to train and didn't bother to hide his contempt for George or the fact that I am the Guardian. I almost don't want to interrupt them—almost.

"Hey guys," I call as I approach.

They both turn to me, but neither speaks. George looks annoyed I interrupted, and Jake looks like he can barely breathe, much less speak.

I continue to cross the room to them while I convey my discontent with the morning so far. "I'm good, thanks for asking. My new buddy, that dragon turtle thing, didn't hurt me too badly when he knocked my ass into the Hudson River. Oh! That reminds me. George, are you sure this dude is supposed to live in water? Sure, his feet looked like giant flippers, but he did *not* look like he wanted to get into that river."

George furrows his brow. "Really? Are you sure?"

I widen my eyes in response. "Yeah. Pretty fucking sure. He cried when he realized I wanted him to go back in."

George crosses his arms and studies the floor. "That's fascinating. I'll have to look into it."

I nod, "Sounds great," then look at Jake. "Hey Babe. I'm going over to Maria's to talk about the panic attack yesterday. Want to come along? I would love for you to be part of this."

His jaw is set, and his eyes squint with skepticism. "Am I allowed to be there? I mean, are you sure you don't want George to come instead, seeing as how he's known about the attacks longer?"

That may have been remotely deserved. Jake only found out I've been having panic attacks yesterday. George, who has been with me when most of them hit, has known about them for weeks. Jake was less than thrilled when he learned both of these pieces of information.

I want to tell him to grow up, but I know that will be counterproductive to the work we're trying to do for our marriage. Especially since he's not entirely wrong to be angry. Instead, for once in my life, I swallow my pride.

"Please come with me, Jake. I want you to be a part of this process with me."

He sulks for another minute before nodding his agreement. "I'll go change quickly, and we can go." He disappears into the back hallway toward the bathroom.

As soon as he's gone, George clears his throat. "So, if you're both going to be done for today, I'm going to get cleaned up for my date tonight."

My eyes almost pop out of my head. "I'm sorry, a date? I didn't know you were seeing anyone!"

He rolls his eyes. "I'm not. It's a first date. My first date since Evan, in fact. I doubt it will go anywhere though." He looks away, shaking his head.

I rest my hand on his shoulder. "Hey there, now who's being hard on himself? You need to believe in yourself. You're a catch! I'm proud of you for putting yourself out there. And even if it doesn't go anywhere, that doesn't diminish what a huge step this is for you."

"Yeah, well, I've been pretty lonely here." He's looking down at his feet.

I try to ignore the unintended sting of that statement. After all, he's here only because he had to give up his life with Evan in Colorado to be my docent. But I'm not supposed to be his friend, just his Guardian, so I get it. Still, I give him a quick hug anyway. "Well, have fun!"

Jake walks back into the room, and I turn to him while speaking out of the corner of my mouth to George. "Don't do anything I wouldn't do."

George looks confused and mutters back, "Says the woman who slept with an incubus."

I smack his arm, but I do allow myself a smirk when I realize Jake didn't hear.

"All ready?" Jake asks politely with a tight-lipped smile.

I nod, and we head out to Jake's car, leaving mine behind to pick up on the way home. We already have one strike against us for breaking Maria's drive-to-your-appointments-in-the-same-car rule.

I'm glad he agreed to come with me. I am sure I will need his help to get through these panic attacks.

Chapter 2

JAKE

Maria is a stickler about her marriage counseling patients arriving to appointments together. Because of this, she has no waiting room. At our first session she told us that, when we arrive each time, we are to stand outside the thin white metal storm door, and wait. While we stand at the door this time, anxious for Maria to let us in, I am suddenly aware of my hands. Leaving them hanging at my sides feels heavy and oafish, so I clasp them in front of me. That feels ridiculous. I cross my arms and am just remembering what a gift that body language is to therapists, when Maria appears behind the silver mesh screen set into the top half of the door.

I let my arms fall back to my sides and place one hand on the small of Miranda's back as we cross the threshold. There is not enough pressure to push her, but I want her to know I am standing behind her, in every sense. This is where my hand should have been all along, of course. Afterall, I am here to learn how best to support her.

I look around the room as we enter the office, at the bookshelf full of psychology texts and self-help books, as well as the framed photos of gentle ocean waves and dew on blades of grass. I'm sure those pictures are supposed to be calming, but I notice Miranda shudder slightly as she walks by. It was so slight that most people probably wouldn't have even noticed. But I know her tells. Or, at least, I thought I did until all this shit with George, being Guardian, and this new appearance of her old panic attacks.

I follow my wife and wait for her to sit, which she does slowly, with a hint of hesitation she didn't even show our first session here. She's been so self-assured and confident lately. But now...not so much. As she sits, she perches at the edge of the beige couch cushion, looking as if she wants to be able to jump to her feet and run for the door. Her hands are clasped on her lap, the tip of her right thumb trembling against her left.

I lower myself beside her, absorbing her anxiety and feeling it multiply in my chest as my own heartbeat quickens. I want to give her space, to let her stand on her own, so I force myself to sit on the opposite end of the sofa, resting my elbow on the arm, trying to look calm and collected, pretending to be the rock I need to be, for her.

There is so much that makes this feel different than our last time here. But one thing is the same: the heavy silence in the room. We have no idea where to start.

Miranda is the first to break the silence with a heavy sigh. "So."

"So." Maria smiles, and that's all she has to do for Miranda's posture to relax. Maria's smile glows with eternal patience as she watches Miranda melt back into the couch. Once she is settled, I grab her hand so she knows I am here for her, and Maria continues. "On the phone you said you had a panic attack while training? Let's talk about that."

I can't help but get distracted, lost in my own mind for a moment. Just hearing the words *panic attack while training* scares the shit out of me. What happens if she has one of these episodes and passes out while she's in a fight? As long as she's having these attacks, I'll be worried that her life is in even greater danger than it already was.

When Miranda squeezes my hand, I focus back on my wife. She glances at me, quickly pulling the corners of her mouth up in an imitation of a smile, before looking at Maria to begin.

"Um, okay. George was saying that he thinks we should start training outside. He thinks it will help because of the extra distractions in the environment. I'll have to learn to ignore them, which will make me stronger." While she speaks, she lets go of my hand to tuck hers under her thigh, which has started to bob up and down as she bounces her knee frenetically. Some deep, sleeping memory gets poked when I see the movement.

"That makes a lot of sense. So why did that make you panic?" Maria looks at the pad and jots down notes.

I stare at the tip of her pen as it moves back and forth across the page. There is an electric jolt in the top of my chest. I want to protect Miranda. I want to know what this woman is writing about my wife. I suddenly want to jump up and grab that notepad from Maria. But I don't, because I know that is not what Miranda needs right now. I tear my eyes from the pen and take a deep breath.

Miranda looks up at the ceiling. She hates feeling weak, and it's really hard not to when you're unloading all your emotional baggage on someone. I know this first hand. My body still convulses with guilt every time I watch her train. My mind instantly goes back to Vegas, to when I was in bed with those muses. Thinking about how I even enjoyed it, how I almost stayed there with them instead of coming home to the kids, to Miranda, to our life. When those images come into my mind it's all I can do to keep from vomiting on the dojo floor.

Miranda has decided her fingernails are completely fascinating. She is picking at one with another when she starts speaking. "I don't know. I've hated being outside for as long as I can remember. Although I did enjoy it as a kid, I think. I know my family used to go camping a lot, and I don't remember ever having a problem with it."

Tapping her pen on the pad and looking up, pulling a memory into the present, Maria looks at Miranda, carefully choosing her next question.

"Okay. When we had our initial phone call, you told me a little about your family growing up, that your father in particular had many shortcomings as a parent."

I can't help but let out a snort that draws all eyes to me.

Raising her brow Maria addresses me directly. "Do you have something you'd like to say about her father, Jake?"

As I run my fingers through my sweaty hair, I lock eyes with Miranda, raising my own brow to ask her permission to speak freely. When she shrugs and crosses her arms, sinking into opposite end of the sofa, I take a deep breath to begin.

"Well, you *could* say all that crap about his shortcomings a parent. But, another way to put it, is to say he was a drunk, deceitful, abusive piece of shit."

Maria blinks rapidly at my blunt words. In my periphery, I see Miranda press her fingertips to her forehead, just above her eyebrows.

My heart pounds in my chest. Maybe I shouldn't have spoken out, but it is instinctual for me to protect my wife. It has been since the moment I met her father.

We were at her college graduation party, a small affair at a local restaurant, especially small if you compared it to the catered shindig my parents threw for me. Miranda was off talking to her cousins. I was at the bar getting a beer. A good-looking older man in front of me ordered a glass of scotch. He looked familiar, even though I was sure I'd never met him.

A second bartender asked for my drink order. When I gave it, the man joked, "Put it on my tab!"

The woman pouring my beer winked and said, "Oh, Mr. Jones! The whole place is on your tab tonight!"

I squinted and looked at him, "Mr. Jones? Are you related to Miranda?"

He squinted back at me and smiled. "I sure am, Son. I'm her dad. Who might you be?"

I smiled back, "It's so nice to meet you, Sir. I'm Jake, Miranda's boyfriend."

"Well, hey there, Jake. Nice to finally meet you. I've heard so much about you." He clapped me on the back like we were old friends. I thought it was a good sign that he had heard so much about me, since I had heard nothing about him.

We talked for a minute and then I saw Miranda standing alone, looking around. She smiled and headed to me when I caught her eye and waved. Her father had already disappeared into the crowd.

"I just met your father," I told her proudly. "He said he'd heard a lot about me. I hope only good things," I added with a wink.

Miranda blanched. No, it was more than blanched. She turned so pale I thought her heart may have actually stopped beating. "My, father?" She was suddenly having a hard time taking in air, like a kinked air hose. "I, I need, I'll be right back." She turned on her heel and made a bee-line for the door.

I followed.

Outside, she paced back and forth on the top stone step, muttering to herself, ringing her hands together. She didn't notice I was there at first. She saw me and jumped. "Oh, Jake. What are you doing out here?"

I raised an eyebrow, "You're out here."

She smiled at me but it didn't reach her eyes. She turned around but even from behind I could see her head duck down and her hand go up and knew she was brushing away tears she didn't want me to see.

I put my hands on her shoulders and leaned in to whisper to her, "You don't have to hide. I'm here for you. You can talk to me."

She turned back and buried her face in my shoulder. Through her sobs her words tumbled out. "I didn't know he was going to be here. I haven't seen him in years. He's horrible. He's a horrible person, a horrible father, a horrible husband. I don't understand why he's here."

"Hey, it's ok. I'm here. You're safe. I have you. I always will." That was the moment I knew I was in this for real.

And now, twenty-years later, I'm still in this for real.

After a moment of silence, stunned at the tone I took on when I'm normally so casual, Maria again smiles sweetly. "Okay, thank you for that insight, Jake. Let's talk about that a little more." She shifts her hips in her chair to make it clear to me that now she is addressing only Miranda. "How often did he drink?" She looks down at her pad to take more notes. I think it's also to give Miranda some privacy to gather her thoughts, thoughts she has lived her life trying to scatter to the far corners of the world just so that she *can* live her life.

"Oh jeez... I think it may be easier to say how often he was sober."

The therapist's eyes stay focused on the pad as she tries to open up her patient even more. "That bad, huh?"

Miranda nods and bites the inside of her cheek. "It was pretty bad."

Pausing her notetaking, Miranda looks up with just her eyes. "Did he ever drink while you were camping?"

The deep breath my wife draws in appears to physically pain her as her eyes get squinty and her mouth grimaces. "I can't remember. I can't remember him *not*, though. I think I was just so accustomed to his drinking that it doesn't stand out in my memories. You know?" Maria nods, yes, she knows, so Miranda continues, "So, yeah, I guess he probably did."

Maria presses the end of her pen to her pursed lips while she thinks. She looks away while she forms a hypothesis. "How often did you take these camping trips as a kid?"

Miranda shrugs. "I dunno. A lot." Her body sinks into the couch as the discussion continues. She bends her spine, so the cushion can't support her lower back to hold her up straight, like it should be doing. I want to reach out and hold her up with my own hands, but that would definitely be distracting, if not enraging to her. She's going through something right now and I need to let her.

Maria's brow furrows slightly and flicks her eyes to my wife's crossed arms and back to her face. "Are you okay?"

Miranda raises her eyebrows and nods. "I'm totally fine."

Uh-oh. I know that "I'm totally fine." That "I'm totally fine" has started many long, drawn-out screaming matches between us.

"Okay then. So, what kind of things do you like to do outside now that you're an adult?"

I flinch. This is a dangerous line of questioning. I'm not very into the outdoors myself, but Miranda is in a foul mood after fifteen minutes in our own yard with the kids.

With a shaky smile, Miranda jokes, "If I had to pick a favorite thing? Probably walking from the house to my car, but only when it's a really nice day!" She shakes her head slowly when she realizes we aren't laughing. "Honestly? Nothing. If I can avoid being outside, I do."

Maria sits herself up straighter in response to Miranda's ever-worsening posture. "Okay, well if you can't avoid it, how does it feel?"

I subconsciously lean into the arm of the couch while looking at Maria with wide eyes. I'm worried my wife may explode if she's forced to continue discussing the outdoors. I have always known her to hate being outside *that* much, although before now I never considered a deeper significance.

"I hate it," Miranda snaps almost as soon as Maria's words have left her mouth. My wife's tone is way more abrupt than either of us are used to hearing in this room. Again, I flinch.

Ever the professional, Maria seems unaffected as she continues to prod, albeit in a slightly more guarded tone. "But how does it feel physically?"

"Physically? Sweaty, cold, or itchy from bugs and plants and nature. I really am not a fan of nature." Miranda's arms are crossed tightly across her chest. I think she's giving herself a hug for comfort. I hope this conversation proves to be worth the trouble it's bringing up.

Maria's smile is back. "Well, nature is kind of an important thing."

Miranda reminds me of Jessie as she rolls her eyes. "I guess."

"You're acting very different than you have in the past when you're here. Different even than you did at the beginning of this session a few minutes ago. Do you feel that?"

She shrugs and stares at her feet. "I don't know. Maybe."

Out of the corner of my eye, I see Miranda's knee start to bounce. My heart is beating as fast as those bounces.

Maria, keeps her eyes on the movement while she speaks. "Are you uncomfortable talking about this?"

I know I am. I want this to end. It feels like I am watching a medieval torture, seeing my wife squirm the way she is. I am going to need to get her a really big coffee when this is all over.

Miranda licks her lips, furrows her brow, and leans her elbows onto her knees. "Which part do you think is making me uncomfortable? The physical discomfort I feel whenever I have to be outside for longer than thirty-five seconds, or my abusive father?"

Maria leans back in her chair in response to Miranda's leaning toward her.

Then Miranda jumps to her feet and blurts out, "I don't think I can keep talking about this right now. I need to get something to eat before we have to pick up the kids." She starts for the door as I sit stunned in her wake.

I am not used to her walking out of an unfinished conversation like this. I'm not used to her having an outburst with anyone outside of our immediate family, her safe people, as she calls us when she tells the kids it's ok to lose your cool sometimes and we'll always been there.

I know all about her dad. I didn't know about him until that graduation party. But then, it all came out, fast and furious.

We went back inside together, and I asked if I could get her a drink. Never a big alcohol drinker, she wanted a Shirley Temple. I ordered two. As I turned around to bring them back to I almost slammed into him.

"Whoa there, Jakey! Oh hey, whatcha got there?" He examined our drinks before chuckling out, "Shirley Temples, eh? That silly daughter of mine still can't drink grown up drinks, huh?" He elbowed me playfully. "And you too? What, are you a sissy? Why are you having that kiddie drink?"

My mouth was dry as I took him in. I scrunched up my eyes. "Well, sir, we're perfectly happy with our drink choices and I'm not sure why it matters much to you." I looked at Miranda who had gone pale again on the other side of the room. "And as for your daughter, she's the most amazing woman I have ever met. I love her, and I'd appreciate it if you wouldn't speak about her in such a deprecating way."

He stood slack-jawed, unsure how to respond to someone who didn't immediately melt into his hand like everyone else seemed to. He shook his head and walked away.

I brought Miranda her drink and we stood there, shoulder to shoulder, observing the people who were supposed to be there to celebrate her, but were clearly just there to see her illusive father.

I didn't bother looking at her when I told her, "If you want to cut him out of your life, I will support you. One-hundred percent. You are my priority. I just need you to be okay."

I felt her head lean down to rest on my shoulder and heard a faint, "I love you, Jake Gold."

Maria clicks her pen closed and lays it on the notepad, showing she is open to receive whatever Miranda wants to share, and speaks softly so Miranda has to stop and turn around to hear. "Miranda, I need five more minutes. Please?"

Surprising both Maria and me, Miranda comes back to the couch, dragging her feet the whole way. Another new behavior I've never seen. I wonder what the rest of the day is going to be like when we walk out of here together.

Maria speaks with measured patience. "I'm not going to bullshit you. I think that something seriously traumatic happened to you on one of your childhood camping trips, and I don't think you're going to be able to get over it unless you let me help you to access your memories. And I can't do that if you're going to cross your arms, sulk, and close yourself off to my help like you're still a teenager."

Miranda furrows her brow and snaps, "What are you talking about?"

I'm on the edge of my couch cushion now. Something traumatic? I could name half a dozen traumatic things she went through because of her father. But I know about them because she remembers those. And they're pretty bad. But this is something so bad she doesn't even remember it. Even if Miranda doesn't want to know what it is, I think she has to. *We* have to. I want to move forward together and I don't know how we can with this hanging over us.

Maria looks her right in her eyes when she speaks. "You just had a trauma response when we actually got into it just now. You regressed into a teenage-like state of defiance. It isn't your fault, but you need to be aware of it. And we need to have more sessions on these issues so we can get you through it. Only then will you be able to make some real progress. Okay?"

I recognize Miranda's apologetic, ashamed nod.

"Good. I know this is a lot and I won't make you stay and dig into your blocked memories now. However, before you leave, I want to go over a couple techniques you can use to calm down when you start to feel panicked. That is, when you start to feel your heart race, start breaking out in a sweat, feel like you just want to freeze and at the same time run like hell. Yeah?" Maria turns to me, pulling me into the conversation more than I have been so far. "Jake, I'm glad you're here. I want you to remind Miranda of these techniques when you notice her start to get anxious."

The idea that I need to remind her of anything when she's anxious makes my gut clench. Afterall, she punches me when we train so I know how hard she hits. I have the literal bruises to prove it. I bite back the remark I want to make about how Maria obviously doesn't care if *I* survive these panic attacks. but I know this isn't the time, and I do want to be there for Miranda. She has always been my rock. She's helped me through so many of my own breakdowns, and near breakdowns. She is always there for me. Now that it is my turn, I want to rise to the occasion for her. So, I simply nod in agreement.

Maria continues once I've taken my phone out and opened the notes app. I really don't want to forget anything. "Okay. First is a breathing technique. It's called four-seven-eight breathing. Start by putting one hand on your belly and the other on your chest. Good. Now, breathe in, two, three, four, hold, two, three, four, five, six, seven, and exhale slowly, two, three, four, five, six, seven, eight. Good. When you do that four or five times, the pattern will help your amygdala realize you're not in danger."

Miranda raises an eyebrow but only says, "I really need to go. Was there anything else?"

"Of course. The next one is called five-four-three-two-one grounding. You're going to look around yourself and name, out loud, five things you can see, four things you can touch, three things you can hear, two things you can smell, and one thing you can taste. This grounds you in reality so your mind can't run away with your fears."

Miranda stares at the woman who is trying so hard to help her. "I promise you I will not be able to remember any of that."

"Well, luckily, I have a present to help you!" Maria opens the drawer of the end table next to her chair and pulls out a small, white box, which she hands to Miranda.

Miranda opens the package to find a silver bracelet, an open cuff about three quarters of an inch wide. When she picks the bauble up, I can see words are engraved on the inside.

She reads, "Five see, four touch, three hear, two smell, one taste."

Maria smiles. "Now you can remember. Use that as a talisman. Grab it when you need to remember what to do."

My eyes squint as I look at the silver band and wonder if my part in this is still so important, now that she has shiny new jewelry to remind her about her new coping strategies.

Miranda takes a purposeful breath and calmly replies, "I'll call you tomorrow to book my next session."

Maria smiles to show there are no hard feelings from what transpired this session, which is good, because she wouldn't be much of a therapist if there were.

I hold the door for Miranda as we leave and walk out to the parking lot. I want to hold her hand, but I feel as if someone hollowed me out with an ice cream scooper every time I catch a glimpse of her fancy new bracelet. So, I shove my hands into my pockets instead.

Miranda is still shaking when we get to the car. Wordlessly, I get into the driver's side. I don't want to be her passenger in her current state.

The silence in this car may crush me so I know I need to break it, even though I don't want to draw attention to myself. "Thank you for letting me tag along."

"I'm sorry for not telling you earlier. About the panic attacks, I mean. I didn't want to worry you." She's staring down at the bracelet that she's now rotating in her hands.

I reach over and put my hand on her thigh, giving it a gentle squeeze of affection before my voice cracks alive. "Hey, this isn't my work to do. And if you ever want me to stay out so you can have some privacy with her, I'll understand. Just say the word."

With one hand she lets go of the bracelet and squeezes my hand. "I love you, you know."

I pull hers to my mouth for a kiss. "I know."

Chapter 3

MIRANDA

Fifteen minutes after leaving Maria's office, Jake and I enter our favorite diner and slide into a booth. The whimsical décor of jewel-tone paisleys against black-and-white stripes and checkerboards always makes me feel like I've fallen down the rabbit hole on my way to an absurd and eccentric tea party. But today I feel more as though I'm hitting a croquet ball with an uncooperative flamingo in a fruitless attempt to keep my head attached.

Jake and I spent most of the car ride over in silence, still processing Maria's declaration about a traumatic event in my past. A friendly-enough-but-not-overly-chipper server comes to our table. She breaks the awkward silence we've been trying to pretend was due to studying the menus that we've each ordered from a hundred times before.

I eye the pancakes at the table across the aisle, but I know that protein is a better choice for me, so I begrudgingly order an egg white omelet with vegetables. I do order the rye toast though. George can pry that from my cold dead hands. Jake gets an omelet as well but opts for whole eggs and cheese. Which is fine, because he's not the one who needs to get into prime fighting condition.

When she retreats to the kitchen, taking our menus with her, she leaves us without an excuse for the silence. We each take a few more moments to glance around the room, looking at the employee lowering the window shades after too many complaints about the sun, the black-and-white porcelain pendant light above our table, the yellow flowers in tall silver vases flanking a group of chotchkes in the same black and white theme as the lights. That is to say, we each take a few moments to look everywhere but at each other's faces. Eventually, my eyes travel in a lopsided spiral inward and finally land on his. We give each other a half-hearted smile, the one where the corners of your mouths only twitch up and our lips bunch in on themselves.

Just then, the server brings my coffee. I take a moment to add the creamers, all four that I asked for, and watch them swirl like mystical clouds as they turn the dark brown liquid into golden-brown manna from heaven, which also brings it dangerously close to the rim of the mug.

I have to break the silence.

"So." I have always been the bigger chatterbox in our relationship, so it's weird to not have anything more to say.

"So." Jake looks right into my eyes.

I wish I could read his mind, or that he would just tell me what he's thinking. That would be even better. I wish I knew if we are ever going to fully heal, ever go back to how we used to be. I know going to Maria together is helping, but can it be enough?

"Hey Miranda, I was thinking..." He looks down at his hands. The nail of his forefinger is tapping at the table rapidly, almost sounding like Morse code. "I know I travel a lot for work, but we haven't been away as a family in forever."

"Right...well...I don't know if I get any vacation time if that's where you're going." My words drip with spiteful sarcasm I didn't intend to use. I'm not sure we can go away for a multitude of reasons right now. In fact, I don't know that I even want to go away. But my Guardian role seems the easiest way to deflect the idea, even if it's also the most likely to start a fight.

"Well, I talked to George about that. He said it's okay."

I am floored. "You...talked to George about it? Without asking me? What, is he my keeper now?"

"I mean, isn't he?" he blushes.

I shake my head and feel the slight breeze the movement causes across my flared nostrils. "You should have talked to me."

He looks confused. "Isn't that what I'm doing right now?"

I shake with the boiling anger I am trying to keep a lid on, for the sake of the rest of the diner patrons in the very least, since I don't care if my husband sees me angry anymore. "You should have talked to me first, Jake. I'm not some damsel that needs the men in my life to *decide* my life. I don't know that I even want to take a break from my training right now!" I feel the heat invading my face with every word. Even if I would have otherwise agreed, there's no way I will now. I'm way too stubborn for that, and he should have known that. "After all these years together, you still didn't think better than to leave me out of the conversation."

He looks at me with cold empty eyes. "Like how you included me in the conversation about your panic attacks, you mean?"

Pressing myself back in my seat to put as much distance between us as I can, I shake my head and respond quietly, "That's different and you know it."

He stares at the table as he indifferently utters his next words. "Besides, I thought you liked guys who take charge now."

I have no response but a sharp gasp. He slams his fists on the table, making the silverware, and some of our fellow diners, jump. He glares into my eyes. "I don't think *any* of our previous years of experience can be called upon anymore. This is a whole new sport, much less ball game. Everything has changed." His tone shifts from anger to desperation. His eyes soften. "I am just asking you for next weekend, Memorial Day weekend. We're going to stay with the Danes. I already talked to Eliza.

We'll meet her, Rory, and Tabitha at her family's place. One weekend at the shore. One weekend in our old, happy getaway place. You don't even train on weekends anyway. Other than being pissed at me for not asking your permission first, what reason do you have to say no?"

As I look into my husband's pleading face, the idea hits me that if I say no to this request, I think we could be done. I think this is his final plea. He needs to know if we can even *be* a normal family anymore, even for a weekend. And I realize, I need to know also.

I nod and squeak out the one word that he needs so desperately to hear. "Okay."

His eyes widen. He was not expecting my concession, especially not so soon, or so easily. Something inside me hurts at that knowledge.

Jake, on the other hand, relaxes his shoulders, possibly for the first time since this all began. He has a satisfied grin on his face that I would normally want to smack off, but today it is the first genuine, not-offspring-induced smile I have seen from him in months. "We can go over all the details tonight..."

He continues to talk, but his voice fades as other voices move into my mind over his. Voices I have not heard in months.

Did you hear that? They are going to go away! She will be away from her docent.

Yes. We need to tell them.

"God. Damnit!" It is my turn to hit the table. At this point, more of my coffee has landed in the saucer than my mouth.

Jake stops talking mid-sentence and looks at me with a lot of concern. "What did I miss?"

"Fucking imps!" I hiss as quietly as possible while I look around frantically, not caring that I am making a scene in our most frequented diner. "Where are they?"

Jake's eyes are practically crossed in confusion while he lowers his voice too. "What are we looking for?"

I look back at him and smile, happy he's on my side. "Little red bat-demon looking things. They would probably look like birds to you. That's what I thought they were the first time I saw them. They're probably outside. I can hear them as if they're right in my head." The shades are down in front of all the windows in the dining room. My guess is they're right on the other side. I mouth, "I'll be right back," then look into Jake's face and say out loud, "I think that trip is exactly what we need!" before I jump to my feet to run outside.

The other customers are looking at me like I'm a lunatic as I almost knock over two servers on my way through the dining room, around the corner, past the cash stand, and out the doors. I slow down as I round another corner, this time on the outside of the restaurant. I slide against the rough brown bricks and arch my neck to see ahead of me.

The little fire-engine-red dumbasses are still sitting on the window ledge with their ears pressed to the glass. Their eyes are squeezed shut, probably to focus on their eavesdropping; I don't think they have enough brain power to put toward using two senses at once. Whatever the reason, it works for me. I'm able to sneak up silently and grab one in each hand, before they get a chance to see me and escape. They screech little screams into the air and clearly are trying to get away, but their faces scrunch up and cheeks puff out as they struggle, reminding me of the faces my kids made when they were pooping as newborns.

"Hey guys! Fancy seeing you here. What's up?" I act like we're old friends.

"Ummm, hi? Guardian lady?"

"Yes. Hi?" Their actual voices are so much quieter and higher pitched than when I hear them in my mind. It's bizarre. I mean, it's all bizarre, but, yeah. This? This is beyond.

"Whatcha guys doing out here? Spying? On little ol' me?" I squeeze them a tiny bit tighter as I interrogate them.

"Uh, Jerry, why can't we teleport away?" The slightly shorter and rounder of the two asks.

"I don't know, Cliff... It must have to do with her powers."

I make a mental note to ask George if my powers can block Imp magic, like a lead shield blocking X-rays.

"Jerry and Cliff? Your names are Jerry and Cliff?" Such every day, average-Joe, human names. I stop myself from laughing, but only barely. They do not look amused. Actually, they look pretty terrified. "Listen here, Jerry and Cliff. Here's what we're going to do. I'm going to let you go."

They both breathe out puffs of brimstone-smelling air in relief.

But I'm not done. "*After* you tell me who you are spying on me for, *and* after you *swear* to work for *me* now."

They look at each other with just their eyes and shrug the best they can under the pressure from my fingers wrapping around their wings and arms. At the same time, they say, "Okay. Sounds like a good deal."

I blink and turn to look at them out of the corner of my eye. That seemed way too easy. I am trying to decide how to know if they're being honest when Jake comes jogging up behind me.

"Hey, Miranda. I wanted to check and see what's taking so—Oh. Holy god in heaven, what the hell are those?" My big, strong, beating-up-our-twenty-five-year-old-trainer husband hides safely behind me, peeking down into my hands from over my shoulder.

"These," I hold my new friends up a little higher so Jake has a better view from his foxhole, "are imps. They were just about to tell me who they are working for and swear their allegiance to me so we can have spies inside whatever network of baddies they're a part of."

They smile and nod over-enthusiastically. Cliff answers, "We do. We swear. We will do whatever you want. We will tell you what she wants to know about you and what she has others doing."

My eyebrows go up in surprise. "She? Who is she?"

Jerry doesn't want to be left out and promptly answers next. "Calliope."

At that name, Jake lets out a groan, and I involuntarily squeeze harder. "Calliope is still keeping tabs on me? *Why?*"

Both tiny demons swallow hard. Jerry is the one to answer again. "She...can you just...loosen your grip a touch? Ah, thank you. She wants to make sure you don't try to interfere with the Muses' popularity. That's all. She doesn't want you, or *you* for that matter, anymore," he uses his chin to point at Jake. "She just wants to make sure you don't get in the way of her fame and fortune again."

Now I am raging. "Oh, well, you can tell that little goddess wannabe that I wouldn't have gotten in her way the last time if she hadn't kidnapped *my* husband and kept him for her, her, her...sex plan!"

I'm disappointed in myself for tripping over my words. My snark is usually much more on point. Damn, I'm really off my game. But whatever. Cliff and Jerry work for me now.

I shake my head and take a deep breath. "Here's what you're going to do. You're going to fly back to wherever those skanks are and tell them whatever you were planning to tell them before I grabbed you. Because I don't really care about them as long as they're not fucking with me. Got it?" They are nodding so fast that they look like two bright-red bobble heads. "Good. Do *not* forget to keep me in the loop about anything you hear that you think may be the slightest bit relevant to me. You *swore* allegiance to me. I take that very seriously."

"Yes, mistress," they say in unison.

Oooh. Mistress. I like the sound of that.

I nod and loosen my grip on them both. "See you soon, boys." I release them the way I always picture my kids releasing their class butterflies to the wild after they have raised them. As they fly away, I mutter, "Fly away, little ones. Fly away."

Jake's brow is furrowed when I turn to him.

I don't have time to guess why he's confused so I just ask. "What?" I suppose he still has a lot to get used to.

He shakes his head. "How do you know they'll stick to their promise?"

I shrug. "I just have a hunch. I'm powerful. They're weak. I think they're probably too afraid to cross me, even if the magical binding isn't real. But for all I know, it is." I shrug again and turn to head back inside the restaurant.

"For all you know?" He runs a hand through his neat dark brown hair, mussing it, and paces a couple of steps. "Shouldn't *you* be the *one* to know? What the hell kind of trainer is George if you're still out and about saying things like *for all I know*? You know what? It doesn't matter. I'm out."

I freeze where I stand; it is suddenly hard to even breathe. "You're...out? Out of what, exactly?" Tears fill my eyes. "Out of our marriage?" I am starting to hyperventilate.

Jake concentrates for just a second with a furrowed brow before he realizes how his words came across, how I took them. His eyes get wide, and he shakes his head quickly. "Oh, Miranda, no. I just meant out of the training. I can't be a part of that anymore. Since we can't do anything to change this whole situation and since I'm going to kill George one of these days, or would, if he wouldn't kick my ass for trying, I think I should stay out of that part of your life. At least for now. But for *us*? I'm here for us. Forever."

I didn't know how badly I needed to hear him say that until I heard it. I collapse against him, sobbing. His arms wrap around me without hesitation for the first time since Las Vegas. We are a team again, at least for this moment. And knowing that the possibility of us being a team still exists is everything right now.

Chapter 4

GEORGE

I close the door behind Miranda and Jake and pull out my phone from my back pocket. As luck would have it, I have a message from Andrew. The corners of my mouth rise into a subtle smile while I tap my thumb on the black and yellow icon to open our chat. The gray bar of text says,

> I can't believe there are still six more
> hours before our date!

My smile spreads into a goofy grin when I write back,

> Sry for late reply. was w a client and
> didn't have my phone. At least it's only 5
> hours now ;)

My stomach is turning somersaults as I look at my reflection in the foyer mirror. "Get it together, George. You have no idea if this guy is even going to be worth your time. What the—" I peer closer into the mirror, then run upstairs to the master bathroom because it has the best light and mirrors in the house.

And there I see it. Them. Worry lines.

"Goddamnit," I murmur to myself while trying to flatten out the deep creases running across my forehead.

It's not enough that I had to give up the life I was building when the League of Docents made me move home, that I had to say goodbye to the love of my life; that I had to watch my boyfriend not even consider moving with me. No, none of that was enough. Now I'm also prematurely aging from the stress of this job.

"Okay. Just relax. Maybe he'll think they make me look distinguished."

I heave out a sigh as I drag myself to my bed, where I collapse. I'm not normally one to nap, but I'm completely exhausted, and I have no idea why. I obviously can't show up to a first date with worry lines *and* bags under my eyes, so I set an alarm and try closing my eyes for a bit.

The sun is settling into a nest of pink and purple clouds when I pull up to the very trendy restaurant Andrew picked. In fact, it is too trendy for me. I feel the music bouncing in my car before I get out.

I hesitantly hand my key to the valet while starting to doubt if my date is the guy for me. I've always been a homebody, not really a party guy. But being a homebody has left me lonely, so it's time for me to try something else.

As I push through the club doors, I note what an odd place this is for a first date. I guess he didn't want to talk much, or at all. No ice breakers or deep conversation can possibly be heard over the blaring sound system.

I look at the people sitting at the bar. That's where he said he'd be. I check my watch. 7:03. Perfect. Not on time, but not so late as to be held against me. I wonder which one is him. As the music fades off, like I'm on a plane taking off and my ears haven't popped yet, recognition clicks in my mind when I scan the row of barstools. The person with the black hair perched on the last barstool, that's my date.

But as I approach, my date's hair changes under the club's hyper neon lights. The dark hair looks lighter, reddish now. Right before my eyes that hairs grows longer, fuller. Now the lush mane almost reaches their slender waist, the center of a perfect hourglass figure, which is currently wrapped in a tight red satin dress.

This is not Andrew. Yet I feel like this is who I came to meet. When I'm close enough to reach out my hand and touch her, I take a deep breath. A strong but pleasant smell invades my nose and mouth, cutting right through the sweat-and-alcohol odor of the club. This new scent is floral and citrusy with a sweet earthy undertone that tickles my nose. My hand lowers of its own accord while my senses bask in that scent.

But I don't want to get kicked out for just standing here and breathing on a customer, so I finally tap the shoulder of my date. "Hey, what is this place? I thought we were meeting at that restaurant I told you about. My mom's favorite place. Remember?"

As she turns slowly in the seat, I can make out the line of the slope of her breast. I tear my gaze away and let my eyes slide up toward her face. But right as I see the chin and think *This isn't Andrew's face,* the fire alarm shrieks, and everyone runs to take cover from all-encompassing cascade of the building's sprinklers. In all the chaos, I lose my date. Someone pushes into me, and I fall back.

As my butt hits the floor with a thud, my eyes open. I don't think I have ever fallen out of bed before. My ass hurts now. I groan and turn off the alarm on my phone. It's a good thing I set it because I slept for over two hours. It's now five; only two more hours until my date.

I turn on my shower so the water's as hot as I can stand and jump in, using extra body wash so I can be sure to smell my best when I arrive at the restaurant. When I'm dried off, I apply a little foundation. Obviously, I need to make sure my skin looks good. And I put gel in my hair.

I move to my closet and peruse the racks, eventually landing on a black button-down shirt that I wear untucked over dark-wash jeans. I leave the button below the collar open to show a triangle of white tank top underneath.

I look at the finished product in the mirror. I think I look decent, but I'm not sure it's enough, so I take a picture and send it to Miranda.

How do I look?

Miranda barely hesitates before responding.

HOTTT!!!! Go get him!

I smile. She often makes me smile. Too bad she's not a guy. We could have a Joanna-Ben thing if she were. I mean, except for the part that if she were a man, she wouldn't even be The Guardian; I wouldn't be her docent; and we'd never have met. But there's no point thinking about what-ifs. That path leads only to remembering what I've given up. And tonight's date is all about moving forward.

Contrary to my dream, I did in fact choose the location for our date this evening, a fancy Italian place in a swanky nearby town. This restaurant was my parents' favorite date night spot. I haven't eaten here since I was little. I barely remember the food, but when I called my mom and freaked out that I had a real date to plan and couldn't think of where to go, she told me to pick this place. So here I am.

As the valet gets into my car, I glance at my watch. 7:03. Not perfectly on time, but not so late as to be held against me. But the number makes me stop and think for a second. It's familiar, but I don't know why. I shake my head and walk through the front door of the colonial-era house that is home to one of the best restaurants in the state.

After giving the hostess my name, I read the typed transcriptions above framed originals of General Washington's letters from his time in this town during the Revolutionary War. The hostess comes over to inform me that the guest I'm meeting has not yet arrived. I agree to be seated rather than waiting around the host stand. Just as I sit down and cross my hands over the menu to wait, I see Andrew enter.

His dark hair is kept short in back but longer in the front. It's a sexy reverse mullet swept to the side so I can see his big, brown eyes from across the room. He likely gets whatever he wants, whenever he wants it, with those puppy eyes.

Time seems to slow for a minute. While he talks to the hostess and smiles, his confidence shines like the rays of the sun. I feel my heartbeat quicken, and I'm suddenly aware of how ridiculous I look with my hands folded like a school boy of yesteryear, waiting patiently for directions from my teacher. I disentangle my fingers and consider picking up the menu to attempt to look casual when I realize he's on his way over to me, and hiding behind my menu would look rude.

I run my fingers over my (hopefully) perfectly coiffed hair and twirl a short lock near my neck. It's a stupid habit I've had forever. Evan always thought it was adorable. My mouth is insanely dry, so I take a long swig of water when Andrew finally gets to the table. I hurry to stop drinking while pushing my chair out to stand, and water splatters down my chin.

Andrew chuckles. I feel heat rise to my cheeks. I'm not sure what to do next, but Andrew reaches down, picks up his napkin from the table, and uses it to dab the water from my chin. Our eyes meet, and his smile widens.

"Hi, George. It's nice to meet you, in person anyway. And if I may say, you're absolutely adorable when you're nervous."

The heat radiating from my face intensifies as I smile shyly and look up at him with only my eyes. "It's nice to meet you too, Andrew. And if *I* may say, you're too kind."

He rewards my remark with a full belly laugh. Such a loud laugh, in fact, that some of the other diners turn to see what is going on. I'm surprised I don't care. I gesture to his chair, and we both take our seats.

We sit in silence for a few minutes. My silence is the awkward kind while his is the comfortable-enough-in-his-skin-that-he-doesn't-have-to-make-small-talk kind. I almost remember a time when I radiated confidence like that. Miranda's self-doubt must be contagious.

Wanting to break the silence, I try to think of what people say to each other when they first meet like this. "Did you have any trouble finding the place?"

He smiles and raises an eyebrow. "Nope. I just put it into my GPS and got right here."

I flinch, feeling as though I was smacked right between the eyes by my own stupidity. "Oh. Right. Because it's not the twentieth century, and people don't need paper maps and printed directions anymore. Sorry." I'm doing great tonight. I pick up my menu as if I'm perusing the options, but really, I'm just hiding myself away behind the leather book.

Andrew sees through my ruse and places his hand on top of mine, gently pushing it down so that I have to lower the menu. "George, please relax. I like you. You don't have to worry about trying to impress me."

I take a deep breath and tell myself that when I release it, I'm going to release all the tension that's causing me to act like a moron. I exhale. "Can we start over?"

Again, Andrew flashes that glowing smile my way. "We can, but we really don't have to. You're doing fine."

This is of course the moment our server chooses to come over and introduce himself. After we listen to the specials, Andrew orders a glass of merlot, and I ask for a whiskey sour. Then the server walks away, and we begin to look over the menus in earnest.

"Do you come here often?" Andrew asks. He is actually curious, not just using a line on me. I think.

"Not in years. It's my mom's favorite. It used to be my family's go-to place, but I wasn't home much after I went away to school. After my dad died, I think it was too hard for my mom come back here." I realize how quiet the table has grown and hesitate before I look at Andrew, afraid of what I'll see in his face. "That, that was too much for a first-date conversation, right?"

With his brows high, he presses his hand to his chest, over his heart. "No, that was not too much for a first date! Thank you for sharing such a big piece of your life with me." He moves his hand to rest on my shoulder in a comforting gesture. I feel the weight and warmth of it through my shirt. It feels nice that he cares. Actually, better than nice. It feels delightful and comforting and phenomenal to be cared for.

Our server returns with our drinks and to take our orders. The menu is prix fixe, so we have to order every course now, even the desserts. When he walks away to put our order in, Andrew leans toward me and speaks out of the corner of his mouth. "Little presumptuous of them to think we'll enjoy ourselves enough to still be here for dessert, isn't it?"

When I look at him confused, he winks. I chuckle softly before moving along our conversation. "So, Andrew, what were you doing on that cesspool of an app? Your profile said looking for long-term, so is it safe for me to assume you're not just going to hook-up with me and never call?"

It is his turn to blush. "I mean, I wouldn't necessarily be *opposed* to a hook-up. God knows it's been a long time since I got any. But yes, generally speaking, I'm looking for something long-term. How about you?"

"I think the same? It's been a long time for me too."

As we look into each other's eyes, the server sets a plate before each of us. Both plates are bare but for one fancy, lonely looking shrimp in the center.

Once the server walks away, Andrew gives a low whistle. "You'd think in a joint like this they could at least remove the tail." He winks at me so I know he's joking.

"Well, if they did that, the plate might look too empty," I counter sarcastically.

He laughs that belly laugh again. A tingling warmth starts in my heart and spreads throughout my body at the sound.

The rest of the evening passes in a similar fashion. Both the food and company are beyond reproach. I laugh easily, and I think he does the same. We hold hands while we wait for our cars at the valet, and when I look at him I picture waking up to his smile. *I could definitely fall in love with this man.*

"Well, this is me," he says, squeezing my hand and looking so deeply into my eyes my breath catches, as a black Ioniq pulls up to the door. The fact that he has an electric vehicle makes me like him more. "I'll call you tomorrow, George Keating." Then he kisses me softly on the lips before walking around to the driver door. He raises his eyebrows at me and does an adorable little wave as he lowers himself into his seat. I return the wave as he drives away.

I feel so light I worry my feet won't stay in contact with the ground. I have not felt this flutter in my chest since early in my relationship with Evan. I have a giant, goofy grin on my face, but I can't seem to care.

As I wait for my own car, another group arrives in a stretch limo. Even absently looking at them feels like I'm invading their privacy, so instead I turn my face to the sky and think about how brilliant the moon is tonight. I take in a deep breath of crisp night air. Night air that smells distinctly of flowers, citrus, and woods. The scent makes my brow furrow. I turn to look at the people who emerged from the limo as they enter the restaurant. A tight red satin dress and long, dark auburn hair disappears into the building.

Chapter 5

MIRANDA

I could barely contain myself while I got the kids ready for school Monday morning. I usher them all out the door in record time before filling my travel mug and heading out the door. I am excited to get to George's house so I can hear all about his date Friday night.

I pull up his driveway and find him sitting on his front steps, elbows on knees, head in hands. Oh shit. That can't be good.

"What happened?" I slam my car door and run over to him. Okay, I don't actually *run*. I *mosey* over to him, but quickly.

He shakes his head and lifts his brow while closing his eyes and running his fingers through his blond locks, which are not as orderly as I am used to seeing them.

"Oh no... Did you get catfished? Wait! Do you still have both your kidneys?" I paw at his back to make sure his body is intact, that he didn't have any organs stolen to be sold on the black market. Also, I hope to make him laugh. Luckily, it works.

"Okay, okay, stop!" He stands, smiling. "Andrew was amazing. Wonderful. The date could not have gone better. Well, maybe I could have stood to, ya know, get some." He waggles his brows in a very un-George-like way. "But that's fine. I can wait for that. He was very sweet and respectful and is worth waiting for." A big, pearly white smile takes over his face.

As he tells me all the great things about Andrew, my insides vibrate with excitement. But even as I bounce on my toes, anxious to hear the next line of conversation, an ache begins in a corner my heart for something I can remember from long ago. There's nothing quite like the feeling you get when a relationship is just starting. When you only think of *them* and your day doesn't truly begin until you hear from them. That's a feeling I'll never have again. Which is okay, really. It's been replaced by the kids' laughter and morning snuggles. I just wish I still felt some of that joy with Jake.

Maybe that's what Maria meant when she said we have to go back to the little things. Except that was about feeling safe. The feeling I'm talking about is anything but safe. New love is like freefalling without wanting to land, like skydiving and waiting as long as possible to pull the rip cord. It's your palms sweating and your stomach flipping when you enter a room and your person is there. And it's recognizing their scent on your shirt for the rest of the day after they've given you a hug.

What Jake and I have to figure out is if a couple who has been together for two decades, who has been through so much and seen it all and then some, can even get back anywhere near that place. Sure, we made love the other day, and it was nice. But it wasn't the kind of rip-each-other's-clothes-off-the-second-we're-alone-sex we had when we were first together. If that is what Maria meant when she said to try to get back to the beginning, I just don't know if it is possible. I don't know that we could have even gotten back to that point *before* everything that happened in November. Adulting is hard, and it makes it impossible to keep things fresh and exciting in your love life.

George's smile lingers just a moment after he finishes talking, but then he looks apprehensive again.

I scrunch my eyebrows together, and the rest of my face follows due to the force of it. "So then, what? What's wrong?"

Again, his fingers tangle in his hair. He looks at his feet as he kicks at the dusty driveway with his toe. "You're going to think I'm crazy."

We stand in silence for a moment. I look at the man who showed up on my doorstep one day, telling me all about the Chosen One and that she's me, and he's worried I'll think he's crazy *now*. "I'm going to think you're crazy? Hasn't that ship sailed, sank, and had a replica built, which then also sailed and sank?"

He finally locks eyes with me but stays silent. His jaw is still as if carved from rock. His entire face looks like it belongs in a hall of ancient sculptures.

I'm starting to get worried. Shifting around under his gaze, I slowly raise one eyebrow as I turn my head slightly to angle my ear toward him. Finally, I raise my hands in annoyance. "Spill it."

George lets out a breath that I think he's been holding in for hours. "Okay, so, well..."

I run my fingers through my curls, grabbing fistfuls in frustration. "George, I've gotten to the point faster tracing my finger around a circle."

He sighs and rolls his eyes before continuing, "Well, *Miranda*, before the date, I had this dream about the date itself, I guess. But I wasn't meeting Andrew. It was a woman, in a red dress, with long dark hair. I didn't see her face. But I could smell her. Don't say anything, okay! Just let me finish!" When he saw me open my mouth, he must have thought—okay, knew—I was going to make a smart-ass comment. He puts his hands up and raises his voice just enough to be sure I stay quiet. "Okay. So I went on my date, the real date I mean, and when I was waiting for the valet to bring my car around afterward, this group arrived at the restaurant in a big limo. I was kind of on cloud nine, so I didn't look at them until they were past me, but then I smelled the same smell as in my dream. When I turned to look, I saw a woman in a red dress with long dark hair walking into the restaurant."

We sit for a moment, and I nod, absorbing everything he said. "Okay, so let me get this straight. You had a great first date with Andrew. Wonderful conversation. You seem to like the guy. And then some chick shows up and gives you déjà vu, and *that's* the part you're focusing on?"

He shakes his head and walks up the stairs to the front door, spitting his words at me. "You know, I knew you would react like this. You don't understand. I was raised to notice this kind of thing. I was raised to know when something isn't just a coincidence."

I shoot back, "Or you're just afraid you like someone new and won't be able to keep moping around about Evan if it turns out maybe he wasn't the love of your life!"

He stands in the doorway, one foot over the threshold. I can't see his face because I'm still on the driveway behind him, but I imagine he's shaking his head and biting his lip in frustration. But I can't bring myself to believe there's more to this. I need to believe George can go out on a date without our work following him there. Because if he can't, that says a lot for the likelihood of *me* having any kind of normalcy in *my* life.

He studies me for a minute. I feel like a kid waiting for the teacher to decide my punishment for not turning in an assignment.

Finally, he speaks. "Okay. Whatever. Let's go do some research." As we walk to the library, which looks like it belongs in a university and not some dude's house, he explains the situation at hand. "There's some weird stuff going on in my woods. I need your help figuring out what is happening out there." His eyes are stormy today, matching the atmosphere in here.

"Wait, *your* woods? Is this the real reason you want me to start training outside?" My chest is suddenly so tight, it is hard to breathe. Damnit. I stop where I am, close my eyes, and breathe in, two, three, four. Hold, two, three, four, five, six, seven. Exhale, two, three, four, five, six, seven, eight.

I repeat it twice more and my body is relaxed again. Well, shit. It really worked!

When I open my eyes, George is in front of me, his eyebrows close together, lips pursed. "Are you okay, Miranda?"

I force a smile. "Of course. Maria gave me a breathing exercise for when I feel stress coming on, so I did it, and it worked, and now we can move on." I gesture with my hand for George to keep walking. As I follow him deeper into the library, I worry my bottom lip. I didn't realize when he mentioned training outside soon that he meant *this* soon, or involving something so personal to him. I know I'm being cheeky in an attempt to distract myself, but at the same time, I do realize that it's time to step up my Guardian duties. "Anyway, can you be more specific? Or is *weird stuff* a technical term with an exact definition in docent speak?"

He spins around so abruptly that I run into him. Then he stares down at me. "Can you keep the jokes to a minimum right now, please? This is my family estate. It's important to me."

I step back, instinctively retreating, as I nod. If I had a snappy retort, it flew from my mind the moment I saw his expression.

We dig into our research at separate counter-height tables in his library. I'm looking into creatures that prefer to live in the woods, and he's looking into creatures responsible for crop circles because the *weird stuff* is a lot of underbrush and flora dying off in unusual patches. We plan to regroup and cross-reference. My mind is having a hard time focusing, so I glance at him. It's just a glance to give my eyes a different focus for a moment, the equivalent of a weight lifter shaking out their legs after a set of difficult squats. But when I look at him, something else in my mind clicks. I watch him for a minute, my eyes squinting.

"Hey, George?" I call to him with a sweet, sing-song tone.

"Mmm-hmm?" He answers back without looking up. "Did you find something?"

"Oh, lots of things. Lots of things live in forests. Also, I find it interesting that you gave my husband permission to take me away on a trip."

At this, his eyes snap up, though not to me, just straight ahead. He doesn't move as he thinks about how to respond. I bet he hoped I wouldn't bring this up at all. He probably figured I'd never find out about my arranged vacation. Now that he is caught off guard, he doesn't know what to say.

He glances my way and finds me looking at him, head cocked to the side, eyebrows raised. I'm not angry per se, but I'm obviously not happy. I cross my arms, trying to act casual but also intimidating, and he starts to fidget under my gaze. This could almost be considered fun.

Finally, he clears his throat and squares his shoulders. "Look, Miranda, Jake came to me. I never told him he had to clear stuff like that with me. I *knew* you'd be pissed."

My brow furrows. "And yet you still *gave* him permission? Honored his request?"

"What was I supposed to say?" His voice cracks a little in his exasperation. "I was trying to be supportive of your stupid husband!"

There is silence for a beat as my brows shoot up, and then for a beat more. He quickly realizes what he blurted out and at least has the courtesy to close his eyes in shame.

"My...*stupid* husband? You think Jake is stupid? What is with you two? Why is it always a pissing match between you?"

He looks at me again, the blue of his eyes set on fire. This may be the most worked up I have ever seen him. His arms gesture wildly as he attempts to explain himself. "Maybe Jake isn't stupid, but he *is* irritating. In many ways. But for some unknown reason, you love him, and I want to support *you*, so here we are."

We look into each other's eyes from across the library for what feels like hours but is probably more like five seconds. My eyes narrow. My mouth is suddenly dry. Ultimately, I decide to act like a grownup and put this all behind me. When I speak, my tone is steady, too steady, behind my forced smile. "Well, thanks, I guess. For giving us permission to go away." But I still roll my eyes while I say it.

Outwardly, I appear to go back to my research, but internally I toss around the words we just exchanged until I snap my head up again. "You really don't think Jake is good enough for me, do you?"

A silent glare is all that I get back.

I try to go back to researching in earnest, but now too much tension fills the room for me to be able to focus. I snap my book shut, making George jump. "I say we go out, and you show me what has you worried in your woods. I can't find jack shit based on what you told me. Maybe I'll have some kind of Guardian epiphany if I see it all firsthand." I put the book on the stack of other books I've finished leafing through and glare impatiently at him where he stands, the book still open before him on the counter. "Well? You coming?" My foot is tapping, and my tone is sharper than I intend.

"Umm, yeah." He sounds hesitant but follows behind me as I walk with a pressing urgency, though not a run, to the front door.

We exit the mansion into the bright mid-day sun, and I realize I have no idea where to go on his expansive grounds. I stop abruptly with my hands on my hips and ask without looking at him, "So where to?"

He moves in front of me. "It will be easiest if you just follow me." And off we trudge into the trees.

Ten minutes later, we've lost sight of his house, which is no easy feat given its size, as we trek through the woods surrounding it. We hike in silence, aside from my grunts and gasps as I stumble and begin to regret that I didn't bring a bottle of water along. The ground has a thick coating of brown leaves in various stages of decay, returning to their literal roots and giving back to the earth they've hidden beneath them.

I smack a mosquito that's having my arm for lunch and wipe the blood smear onto my gi. "Yuck. I really should have used some bug spray." I feel my pulse pick up. Really? Bug spray is a fucking trigger? I instinctively touch the bangle wrapped around my wrist. "I see trees, stones on the ground, George, leaves, those boulders. Now, touch? Oh, my bracelet, my shirt, tree bark, my hair. Hear...leaves crunching, my heart beating, bird chirping. Smell, George's excessive cologne and—" Ew. What *is* that smell? Fully grounded even though I didn't finish the exercise, I open my eyes.

There's a patch of ground directly in front of us, about as large as a king size bed, completely devoid of trees and flora. Instead of grass and leaves, the slimy black ground smells like the salad mix I always buy and never eat before it all turns into mush in the bag at the back of my fridge. Behind the nasty clearing is a freestanding row of five of the largest boulders I have ever seen, each with a four-foot gap in between them.

Six feet behind the boulders, the ground slopes upward, creating a rocky hill that tapers off a little above my head before receding into the rest of the woods. Ferns and other plants grow between smaller rocks and larger trees.

"See where the plants were burned?" he says, holding his nose with one hand and pointing to the decimated plant matter at our feet with the other.

But his nose is no match for that of woman who has super-smelling abilities. "Those weren't burned. They've rotted. I can smell the bacteria."

He looks at me doubtfully, one eyebrow cocked. "You can smell bacteria? How can you smell bacteria? Is that one of your abilities? I've never heard of a Guardian having super-smell before."

"Well, as you've said, there's never been a mom Guardian before. My sense of smell got stronger with each pregnancy." I look at him, but he is still confused. I secretly relish when I have to momsplain something to him though, so I remain patient, and only a little condescending. "During pregnancy, a mom's sense of smell is heightened to protect the mom and baby. In some cases, it sticks around after the baby is born. I'm one of those cases. I always said it was my superpower. You know, before I found out that I have *actual* superpowers."

He still isn't sure he believes me but decides to give me the benefit of the doubt. "So, we have our own personal K-9 unit?" He smiles playfully, and when I shoot him a glare, he lets out a boyish laugh. "That's pretty awesome, actually. So, what do the rotted plants mean?"

I look back and forth along the rocky hill in the distance. Something pops into my mind from what I read back in the library. "Any chance there are caves somewhere along that hill?"

He studies the wall himself, from our distance, "Um, maybe cave-like structures. I don't think there's space for extensive caves. You in the mood for some spelunking...or...?"

"I think you have a troll problem. We won't find them in the daylight though. They'd turn to stone. We should come back after the sun goes down." I look up at the sky. We have some time to kill.

He responds with a shrug. "What's a few more hours, I guess. But I think I'd have noticed some giant oafs on my property. Shall we?" George tilts his head and holds out his hand toward the direction we came from, asking me to follow. "Why do you think it's trolls?"

I take a long slow breath, trying to force myself not to hyperventilate as I hike and talk at the same time. This definitely is a different kind of exercise than training in the dojo. "Well, they rot food with their breath. It makes sense that they'd rot vegetation in the forest also."

He raises an eyebrow at me. "Aren't trolls largely galumphing idiots who mainly keep to themselves?"

I point at the sludge where there used to be plants. "You want all your woods to look like this?" When he shakes his head, I continue, "We can probably convince them to leave. Maybe I won't have to hurt them."

His face is full of concern, but he's nodding. "Yeah sure. Let's go back to the house. We can do some more research to see how we can talk—"

My daily "Go pick up the kids" alarm cuts him off. "Sorry. Time's up for today." I grimace but then divulge other insights I had read as we walk back to my car. "They need a place to hide from the sun, so I think that big hill must have some kind of cave in it somewhere."

He murmurs a bit to himself as he thinks before letting me in on his revelation. "Now that you mention it, an old fox den used to be in there. I don't know if it's still there or if it would even be big enough for a troll, but we can look for it next time."

"You'd be surprised. The myth of their size is purely conjecture. They're pretty close to human-size in actuality. They can even disguise themselves to look more human."

"I had no idea!"

I smile. "I know, me neither! I just read it today in your library. You learn something new every day, I suppose."

As we approach my car, a thought comes to my mind. It's probably reckless, but I don't care anymore. "I have a crazy idea." I say this as if it's a throw-away line, but his raised brows tell me that I've piqued his interest. "Want to come over for dinner? Meet my kids?"

He rocks back and forth from one foot to the other, hands fidgeting, looking uncomfortable in his own skin. "Wha, what will you tell them?"

I shrug and look down at the ground, acting as if I haven't thought about this exact scenario a million times. "I'll tell them you're my personal trainer. That you've been working with Jake sometimes too. And since you're becoming a bigger part of our lives, you might be around sometimes now." In response to his apparent hesitation, I add, "That is how I met Eliza. She wasn't my trainer, but we *did* meet at the gym. So, it's not like there's no precedent here."

He looks off into the distance before he looks into my eyes and responds, "This is going to be interesting. What time?"

We agree on a quarter to six, since my family's routine pretty much dictates dinner at six o'clock sharp. Then I head off to get the kids, my stomach flipping with nerves.

There is a definite chance this is going to piss Jake off, but George is a big part of our world now, and the two men in my life are going to have to learn to play nice together. The last six months have been torturous, keeping my kids in the dark about this whole Guardian thing, hoping they don't notice when I come home wincing after a particularly grueling sparring session. So far, I've been successful in my deception. But it doesn't make lying to my kids any easier because I know they're not picking up on the deception. I'm not ready to tell them tonight, but I think that time is coming fast, and maybe it will soften the blow if they know and like George.

Chapter 6

JAKE

At my desk, I tap my pen, hoping that if I can move that little end up and down fast enough, I won't lose my shit on my biggest client's useless agent. Just as we finally get into the meat of our conversation, my phone lights up with Miranda's face and starts buzzing. It's four forty-five, so I'm technically not late, especially for a Monday night. She's probably just calling to see when I'll be home. Whatever it is, it will have to wait.

"Yeah, I hear you, Dave. But the thing is, he doesn't care. You know he's been looking for more serious roles. Why aren't you getting him the auditions?"

I don't listen to the hemming and hawing this guy fills his end of the conversation with, as Miranda is calling once again. I should probably get it. "No. No excuses. Just get him in the room, okay?"

And that's when I get the text that snaps me right the hell out of work mode. "Dave, I gotta go. Yeah. You're the best. Thanks."

> FYI, George is coming over for dinner. I'll
> tell the kids he's our personal trainer.
>
> Oh, and I have to go back to his place later
> to hunt some trolls.

Real trolls, not the internet kind…

Thanks for understanding. Love you.

Umm, what now? I thought I made it clear that I want to spend less time with George. I can't imagine she took that to mean I want the guy over to our house for dinner. And I don't understand why she would want to bring this Guardian shit home to be around the kids. On some level, of course I realize that she had no choice in being The Chosen One. But it still scares the hell out of me that she has to be involved in this stuff. I hate that she is in so much danger at all times. And after what happened to me with the muses…I'm terrified of any part of that world coming near our kids. I don't know how either of us would handle it if one of them was kidnapped or hurt.

I need to find out what could possibly be going through her head, so I put my office phone on do not disturb and call her back from my cell. My pinky taps on my desk like a hummingbird flapping its wings while I wait through three rings before she finally picks up.

"Hello?" Her voice lilts, questioning who's calling as if her phone doesn't display my name *and* picture when I call.

"Hi. What the fuck?" Perhaps my words are a little harsh for a greeting. But seriously, what the fuck?

"Wow. Okay then. Nice to hear from you too." Her tone is dry and not nearly as offended as it should be. A piece of my brain thinks maybe I've made her nervous, but how could she expect any other reaction from me?

"Nope. Sorry. You don't get to make me feel bad for how I respond to that text. Why is George coming over for dinner? Where did he get that idea?" The word "he" drips with vitriol.

Quietly, she answers, "I invited him," as if she's afraid of what I'll say next.

My tapping pinky is no longer an adequate outlet for the energy pulsing through me. I roll my chair away from my desk and spin it around so I can stand up and pace. When I speak it's through a clenched jaw. I want to scream but I know that won't make anything better. I know she needs me to be supportive. I know when I yell, she feels like she's ten again, dealing with a narcissistic father who doesn't care about her emotions. "Okay. So. You invited him. Why?"

"I just figured, since he's going to be a part of my life for a while, I mean, forever really, right? Well, isn't it better the kids know him on some level? Better they meet him as our personal trainer, rather than noticing some random, weird guy following me around somewhere some time."

I pace for a full minute while I think about what she's saying. I remember back to when I came out of my muse-induced haze on the top of that mountain. I remember the confusion, and having to wait until we could be alone so we could talk about what the hell had happened to me–to both of us–and why. George was pacing at the bottom of the mountain as we descended, and when I found out who he was I just felt betrayed that this kid knew more about my wife than I did. All of the emotion inside of me, everything I hadn't been able to deal with yet, focused into a laser beam of anger, at him.

Now, I wonder if I would have felt differently about George in that moment, and all the moments since, if I had known him before everything that happened in Las Vegas.

The family picture we took on the beach last summer catches my eye. It doesn't matter how *I* felt or if *I* would have felt differently. It wouldn't keep them safe to keep them ignorant of...everything. I have to admit that she's right about this, that it makes sense to have the kids get to know George in one way or another now. I stop in the middle of my office, pinching the bridge of my nose with my thumb and forefinger.

Finally, I sigh and manage to speak with a softer tone, hoping I sound understanding. "Yeah, I get it. Fine. But I'm not happy about it." Still, my voice is scratchy from a long day and a life I have little control over now. "I just would have liked for you to ask me first before you made these plans."

"Well, I guess we're finally even then."

Touché, wife. Touché. I can't help but chuckle. "Yeah, okay. It will be fine. Jessie will know we're lying immediately, of course. But hey, maybe we'll have *some* time before she calls us out on it."

Miranda laughs nervously. She knows I'm right. Hell, I wouldn't be surprised if Jessie *already* suspects something. She's too smart for her own good—and ours.

"We okay?" Miranda asks.

"Always. I'll be home around five thirty."

"I gotta run then. I need to check on the chicken, stir the barley, and finish setting the dining room table. I know the rest of the dining room is a disaster, but I can't possibly make it look neat before George gets here. Hopefully my housekeeping skills don't make him doubt my ability to protect humanity. Or, at least, not more than he probably already does."

"Listen, if he ever doubts you, that's his loss." Then before I hang up, "I love you."

I hear my wife smile through the phone, "I love you, too."

After hanging up, I sit back at my desk to finish up some loose ends before I leave for the night. I look again at the framed family picture. We were all so blissfully ignorant a year ago. But really, that doesn't mean we were any safer. Maybe it's time I try to look at George a little differently. Maybe he's not the one that brought this into our lives. Maybe he's just the messenger. But maybe he's the only one who can keep us all alive.

Chapter 7

GEORGE

As I drive to Miranda's and Jake's house, the little metaphorical angel on my shoulder tells me that I've made a horrible mistake. These two need their time away from me. They need time together, with their children, as a family. Sometimes Miranda needs to put her Guardian gauntlet down and just be Miranda.

But the devil on my other shoulder reminds me that in this role, she is never off the clock. I need her to keep our responsibilities at the forefront of her mind, no matter how much of a burden and inconvenience they may be. And, as much as I hate to admit this, I also miss her when we're not together. She's fun, and funny, and I enjoy who I am when I'm with her. I'm obviously not romantically interested in her, but she has a magnetic personality. She's able to light up any room she walks into. If only she could lighten Jake up a little.

I'm not sure what his deal is. I don't know if he's jealous that his wife is a superhero, annoyed that she has responsibilities outside their house, or if he's genuinely just scared for her. Whatever is behind his behavior, his presence at our training has been stifling her. There is a difference, clear to me anyway, of how she acts and reacts and fights when he is at the dojo versus when he is not. I hope Maria helps him to remove whatever stick is firmly up his ass before he really gets in Miranda's way.

I pull into their driveway at 5:43, two minutes early. Well, I've always thought it's better to be early than late. Both her and Jake's cars are here. Hopefully, Jake can behave himself and pull off pretending that I'm his personal trainer as well as hers. I look into my rearview mirror to make sure my hair is properly coiffed but stop when I realize I have no one to impress, and laugh at this nervous tic of mine.

I grab the bottle of wine from the seat next to me and push open my car door. It took a bit of a drive to find a store that had the 2008 ice wine she said was one of the only kinds she likes, but I could not bring myself to buy the eight-dollar glorified sparkling grape juice she said was the only other option. I've never bought an eight-dollar bottle of wine before, and I didn't want to start today. So, since I had the time to get this one, I figured, why not! I actually bought the store's entire stock of it, since the vineyard doesn't produce it anymore. I mean, if it's the Guardian's favorite, it can't hurt for me to keep a stash around for emergencies. Plus the alcohol can be a nice antidote for all the caffeine she consumes if she's ever too hyped up.

I focus my energy on taking deep breaths so I don't have my own panic attack as I walk up the stone path running through their perfect suburban yard. I take one final, deep, shaky breath and ring the doorbell. The circumstances are so different from the last time I rang this bell, the day I told Miranda she was the Guardian. It's hard to believe that was only six months ago. However, it's also hard to believe that six months have already passed since that day.

The door flings open, and a mini-Miranda looks at me. Mini-Miranda is probably not the best word for her, as she is very close to real-Miranda's height. But this girl definitely gets her magnetic presence from her mother. And her beautiful curly locks.

"Hey, you must be Jessie." I cradle the wine in my left arm and extend my right hand to offer a handshake.

"Um, yes…And *you're* the personal trainer?" Her hazel eyes open a little wider, her right eyebrow shooting up half the distance to her hairline. "Aren't you all supposed to be big and buff? You look a little, um, *little* to be a personal trainer. I kind of think I could take you."

Yup. Definitely Jessie. But before I can answer, a tiny and more feminine version of Jake uses her hip to knock her big sister away from the door before screeching at her fleeing sister, "Jessie! You're so rude!" She locks her deep brown eyes on mine and changes her tone to a soft, delicate, cheerful one. "I'm so sorry for my sister's behavior. I'm Phoebe." She holds out her right hand to gently put her fingers in mine. It's quite a mature gesture from an eleven-year-old, and I can't help but smile a bit.

"Hi, Phoebe. It's a pleasure to meet you." I nod my head slightly in greeting.

"Please come in, George." Phoebe moves back into the house a step to usher me inside.

Once inside, I see the other two kids watching us, or more specifically *me*, from a few feet away, not bothering to hide their curiosity. I'm starting to think they don't have dinner guests very often. This youngest girl looks even more like Miranda than Jessie does, aside from her straight, golden hair. The boy is another clone of Jake, except with Miranda's dark brown, unruly locks.

"And you must be Natalie and Sam." I say it with a strange pride and mentally pat myself on the back for correctly identifying all of the kids. Four kids is a lot of kids. Really, it may as well be twenty. And with all of them standing in front of me, I think I finally understand Miranda's relationship with coffee.

We stand around awkwardly until Miranda's voice calls me from further back inside the house. I remember the kitchen is back through that hallway from my last, and only, visit here.

"Hey George! We're in the kitchen. Come on back!"

I nod at the kids who turn to the right, toward the room flickering with the light and noise of a TV, and make my way to the left.

As I remember, the kitchen is bright and open. To be honest, it wouldn't be on any cooking shows. The table has piles of textbooks and note-books, some still open, and in my mind's eye I can see them all there, Jessie yelling at Phoebe, Phoebe whining at Miranda, Miranda rolling her eyes and snapping at both of them while she leans over Natalie to help her with an equation. I remember back to my mom helping me with my homework, it was never as loud as I suspect this house gets though.

I shake my head to snap myself back to the present and look at Jake and Miranda. Jake is not super pleased to see me, but at least they don't look like they were fighting. He's looking at Miranda, a smile is frozen on his face as if I caught them mid joke. But as his eyes shift to me, the corners of that smile sink a bit and his arms cross over his chest. Miranda doesn't notice because she is bustling around the kitchen, getting the components of an honest to god feast onto large platters that will soon be brough into the dining room. The counters still have crumbs from chopped up vegetables, drops from sauces. Knowing Miranda, I'm surprised she doesn't wipe everything up in her wake as she moves through the preparations. But this imperfection makes me smile.

I clear my throat before awkwardly speaking. "I brought you a bottle of the Nightingale wine you said you like."

Jake reaches for the bottle and when I hand it over to him he studies the label. "Like it? She *loves* this. Where did you even find it? I haven't been able to find it in years."

"Oh, I found a few stores in New Jersey that still had some. It wasn't that hard." I mean, I only had to call three liquor stores and drive forty miles to get it. But I suspect that fact would do little to win Jake over to my side, and Miranda already loves me anyway.

I carry a large platter of roasted carrots into the dining room because Jake beat me to the plate of carved chicken. We all mill about at the table which is set for seven, leaving one place empty. I look around and note that the furniture here, eight chairs surrounding a rectangular table, fills the dining room much more than the table that seats sixteen in my own. This room is smaller yes, but also more intimate–cozy. The one I grew up with always felt so expansive and drafty, more like I was eating in a museum than my own house. I envy the life of these kids, this family.

I wait until the family begins seating themselves, since they probably have usual spots they're most comfortable in. When the rest of the chairs are taken, I take the last, near the opposite end from where Miranda sits at the head of the table, Jake sits to her left, closest to the door to the kitchen. I notice he is jumping up and down to get last minute items and random requests from the kids more than Miranda is. I kind of like that. I'm glad he doesn't just leave it all for her to do so that she can't take a bite of her food until it's too cold to be enjoyed.

Jessie sits down directly across from me, watching me with a pit-bull-like level of distrust. "So...George...why does our parents' *personal trainer* want to have dinner with us?"

Miranda, Jake, and I all freeze, with a wine glass, fork, and napkin halfway to our respective mouths. My eyes meet Miranda's, and we both then look to Jake's. We stay quiet for a few seconds. Miranda clears her throat, takes a sip of her wine, resets her glass, and looks at her oldest daughter.

"Well, Jessie, not that we need to explain everything in our lives to you, but...we're...thinking of setting up a space in the basement to train here. On our own. Between the sessions we're already doing, that is. And George said he would take a look at the space and give us some suggestions of what we can do down there."

Jake and I nod along.

Jessie isn't buying it. Her eyes narrow until I can no longer tell that they are slightly different colors. "Between sessions? Five days a week just isn't cutting it, huh?"

Wow, she's a tough one. I would feel bad for Miranda and Jake except for the fact that she is exactly like her mother, and I have to deal with this attitude all the time. I hide my smirk behind the wine glass I start to drink from when Jessie makes one last jab.

"Are you guys a throuple or something?"

I choke on my wine.

"Jessie Elizabeth Gold!" Not since I first told Miranda she was the Guardian have I seen her so flustered.

Jessie doesn't say anything, but she crosses her arms over her chest and raises one eyebrow, silently challenging her mother's outrage.

Thinking I can lessen the tension, I say, "Sorry, Jessie. The home gym was actually my idea. I just thought it would be helpful and healthy for your parents if they had a few pieces of equipment here so they can do certain exercises we do together every day. At their ages, it's imperative they stay on top of their strength training and core exercises."

In my periphery, I see two heads snap to me when I mention *their ages*. In trying to take the heat off of them, I may have just moved an inferno onto myself. However, they both just smile and nod, too-wide grins plastered on their faces which have taken on a reddish hue.

It's nice not to have to deal with a snappy, sarcastic response, or a violent physical one for that matter. It's a new experience for me when I'm with Miranda and Jake. Maybe I should come over here more often.

I am enjoying getting to know the kids. In direct contrast to Jessie's sullen coolness, Phoebe, who is seated directly to my left, radiates joy and a bright airiness, especially straight across the table, at her older sister. She walks with a bounce in her step that makes her look like she's floating on air. When she laughs with her siblings, sometimes *at* her siblings, her smile takes over her whole little face and I hear the faint tinkling of wind chimes.

Natalie is across from me but down a seat, next to Jessie, and I am sure I catch her looking quickly away from me more than once as I glance her way. Her cheeks are developing a brighter pink glow the longer the meal goes on. Every once in a while, she interjects her own smart-ass remarks into her family's conversation, but she's largely an observer. I see her big blue eyes taking everything in and can almost see the gears in her head turn as she absorbs all of what is being said. Heaven help Miranda when this one decides to really join in the exchange.

And then there's Sammy. I'm not interacting with him much because he's on the far side of Phoebe and I have the least sight of him. But I see Jake's face beam as they converse. He is proud of his son and smiles in a way I'm not used to seeing. Watching him in this moment I get it. I see a glimpse of the Jake Miranda must have fallen in love with.

I wasn't expecting it, but there are even mouthwatering desserts at the end of the already over-the-top-for-a-random-weeknight dinner. Apparently, Phoebe and Natalie are quite the bakers. When Miranda told them I'd be coming to dinner, they set to work. Phoebe made the most ooey gooey fudge brownies I have ever had the pleasure of consuming. Not to be outdone, the smallest of the Gold women prepared a blueberry pie bursting with flavor in every bite I take. Without meaning to, I almost indulge to the point of immobilized sleepiness. But I can't have food render me useless against any trolls we may come across tonight.

Oh, right. Trolls. I choke a little on my water when I remember that Miranda and I still have a mission tonight. I look to my right, out the dining room window, and see the sun has indeed set. It's dark enough now that they will probably be out from wherever they hide during the day by the time we get back. Miranda follows my eyes, then looks at the half-full glass of wine in her hand. Regretfully, she places it back on the table.

"Kids, you all help Dad clean this up. I'm going to show George around the basement." She pushes her chair back and stands, signaling for me to follow her. Jake purses his lips and clears his throat. I follow Miranda, hesitantly at first, because Jake is giving off a vibe like he's going to jump up and bite me. He was so much chiller than I expected this whole meal. I don't know why it surprises me that he's back to his usual attitude now that Miranda and I have work to do.

I also don't know why I'm actually in her basement. "So, um, how far are we taking this lie then?"

"Yeah, I don't know. I didn't think this part through." She's standing awkwardly straight, her hands down at her sides as she looks around the room. The wall at one end has a few stacks of boxes labeled with things like *Girls 5/6 clothes* and *Barbies*. Another wall has a bookshelf full of board games. The far end of the room has the biggest beanbag chair I have ever seen in front of a large TV, which is mounted above a console containing three different video game systems. "I really should do something with this space though... Maybe a craft room or something. Or...do you think I could actually set up a training space here?"

I raise an eyebrow. "And what's wrong with my dojo?"

"Nothing is wrong with it. But this way if one of my kids is sick or something, you can just come here to train me."

I think she's serious, so I indicate the wall with the boxes. "If you were to clean this area, I could see you putting some mats there that we could spar on at least."

"Yeah, that's what I was thinking. It could be interesting. Also, maybe that way I can train with Jake here instead, so my time with you can just be you and me, and then I can pass on some of the techniques to Jake."

My head snaps up faster than I mean for it to. "Does Jake not want to train with me anymore?" I would be lying if I said this wasn't a relief. But I also feel guilt burning in the pit of my stomach. This guy's whole life changed and I'm at least part of the cause, and now I can't even teach him how to protect himself.

And as I'm thinking about all the legitimate reasons Jake has to not like me, a third idea enters the mix: What if he tries to stop *Miranda* from training with me next. I rub a bead of cold sweat from my brow as I try to get my eyes to focus on her.

The face I see is not full of confidence like I'm used to. She bites her bottom lip in a way that makes me fear what is coming next. "Well, no. He doesn't want to. He thinks maybe his time at the official dojo should be...over. It's just been hard for him to be involved in the Guardian stuff. But I really think he needs to keep up with it for his own safety, especially after the fucking muses. Plus, his body now...Oh. My. God. Definitely don't want that going away!"

I can't help but roll my eyes at her off-topic interjection. "That's fine. We should really be focusing more on your training anyway."

She stares at me with raised eyebrows, awaiting further explanation.

"Sorry. I'm just a little protective, I guess. You're already so far behind in your training. I think all my attention needs to focus on you." I take her wrists in my hands, look into her dark eyes, and feel the tension in her arms relaxing. I soften my voice in response, "So, trolls?"

Her brow furrows. "Trolls? OH! Trolls! Right! You head back. I'll say goodnight to the kids and come up with a reason why I need to go out. I won't be more than a few minutes."

I am skeptical of her timing, but what else can I do?

"Yeah. That's fine."

We go back upstairs to her family. I nod good-bye to Jessie, who is still looking at me from a corner with her arms crossed while Phoebe and Natalie run up and hug me, and Sam gives me a fist bump. My eyes squint from the wide smile on my face. I do notice that Jake didn't come to see me off. Against my better judgement, I enjoy spending time with Miranda's family. Seeing her home, meeting her family, eating her cooking, strengthened our bond and made me want to protect her more. Plus, I am leaving her house with a warm cozy feeling in my chest I haven't felt since, well definitely not since my father died, maybe even ever.

"Miranda, please don't forget what we talked about. Our *plans*. Yes?" My eyes are wide, willing her to get my meaning. She had better not leave me hanging about this troll crap. She'd better be shortly behind me.

She nods to me. "I know the *plan*, George. I'll see you soon."

I definitely pissed her off by insinuating anything different.

I just don't know how she does it, balancing both sides of her life. I wonder if her kids have any idea who their mother really is. That she is as powerful as she is. That she's the real deal. Probably not. I don't know many kids who stop to think about such things. They just want their mom. Unfortunately, the world needs her too. Even though the next Guardian has been born, she's still so little, barely a toddler. No matter how any of us feel about this, Miranda is going to be on duty for a long while still.

Chapter 8

MIRANDA

"**W**ell, that was an interesting evening, right?" My voice cracks a little as I look at my kids, all standing around the front door.

"I still don't understand why you had your personal trainer over for dinner. It's really shady, Mom." Jessie's voice is flat, but her suspicion has been noted. She *is* going to be the first to figure this whole Guardian thing out; I just know it. And she can't lie to, or keep a secret from, her siblings. So, when she does figure it out, all the kids will know. Immediately.

"Well, Jessie, believe it or not, moms and dads can make new friends, too." I admit I get a little defensive, but I'm nervous.

Then, in the most predictable-for-a-teenager move she can make, she rolls her eyes while groaning, "Whatever." She pushes herself off the wall she's been leaning against this whole time and stomps up the stairs.

Jake comes in from the kitchen, where he has been cleaning up like the obedient little husband I have him trained to be. More likely, he was all too happy to avoid George.

"Hey Miranda, weren't you going to do some grocery shopping tonight? You should probably head out before it gets too late."

Is he covering for me? I could kiss that man!

In fact, I walk over and do just that. "Thank you for reminding me! I'll go now." Then I walk around, kissing the tops of the three younger kids' heads, who also happen to be the kids still in the room, and say my prayers to them in turn. At the bottom of the stairs, I call up, "I have to run out for a little while, Jessie. I love you." If a troll clubs me to death tonight, I don't want the last interaction with my eldest child to be us rolling our eyes at each other. With the same idea in my mind, I give Jake one more kiss. As I pull away from the kiss, I mouth *thank you* as clearly as I possibly can.

He nods to me and locks his eyes on mine as he says, "I love you. *Drive safe.*"

I have to leave because tears are welling up in my eyes. We're finally connecting again, and I have to go fight trolls. Damnit to hell. I grab my purse and go out the garage door.

As my phone connects to the car's Bluetooth, a notification pops up, telling me I have a text from Jake. I tap the message icon, and my car reads to me:

```
Hey, I just needed to tell you, PLEASE don't
get yourself killed tonight. We all need
you way too much. Can you imagine if I had
to raise the kids by myself??
```

I laugh at the sentiment even though the actual thought makes me want to throw up. Okay, I need to get my head in the game. One quick stop at The Tulip to grab a cinnamon cardamom latte, and I'm really on my way. It is eight o'clock on a weeknight, and I'm about to track down *trolls* to fight. I am going to need a hefty dose of caffeine if I intend to live to tell Jake about this experience.

I've timed my coffee consumption perfectly for the length of the drive because I finish the cup of manna just as I roll my window down at the keypad before George's gate. Of course, this means that by the time I park, I desperately need to pee. I run to his front door and bang on it rapidly with both fists. I'm bouncing from foot to foot when he finally opens the door, trying desperately not to relive the experience of my first training session in his dojo. I immediately push past him to run to the bathroom, not even pausing to say hi or explain. I'm sure he is shaking his head and smiling as he closes the door behind us. Or at least, I hope he is.

When I return from the restroom, he's leaning against the closed door with his ankles crossed and hands in his jean pockets.

"How big a coffee did you have on the way?" His smile is so straight and bright that it catches me off guard. He doesn't often smile so openly. I mentally give myself a pat on the back for the whole dinner idea. I think it made him feel less lonely. Also, my kids can be real charmers.

"It was a normal size, thank you very much. I've just birthed four babies, and that affects a woman, you know?" Although this subject oddly comes up often in our training together, he is just as uncomfortable every time. And I am just as entertained. "You ready to go hunt down some trolls?"

"Yes, please!" He nods and hands me a large flashlight while keeping one for himself and hoists a dark-green, tactical-looking backpack onto his back. "Let's go."

It's a good thing he thought to bring the flashlights because I sure as hell didn't, and once we're outside and away from the circle of light cast by the motion sensor security cameras on the walls of George's mansion we are plunged into a velvety blackness that is beginning to suffocate me, until I turn on that lifesaver flashlight. When the yellow beam illuminates the ground before me the tightness that was constricting my diaphragm lessens. We walk in relative silence, not speaking but grunting breaths and cracking sticks underfoot. When we hear a rustling to the left, we both freeze and swing our flashlights in unison, catching a deer munching on some leaves as a late-night snack. After a few more minutes, the sound of male voices draws our attention ahead. We stop abruptly and look at each other. Our ears are cocked, trying to make out the language, if it even is one.

"Do they sound human to you?" I'm not sure if my Guardian ears are deceiving me or if they really don't sound any different than me and George. But my docent nods, and I am even more confused. "Why do they sound human?"

His brow furrows in response to my own. "You said they are pretty humanoid, right? It makes sense that their voices are too. Can you make out what they're saying?"

I shake my head. "Not quite. Maybe they're just people?"

"But then why would they come out only at night, just as you expected they would if they are trolls?"

Suddenly, a beam of a bright light catches us like unsuspecting flies in a spider's web. After minutes of deep darkness, the light in our faces is blinding.

"You out there, who goes there?" Coming at us like exploding shrapnel, the voice still sounds more human than I would expect from a troll; not that I have had so much experience with trolls. Or any. And, unfortunately, George's library doesn't have an audio section where I can listen to recordings of different creature's noises and voices as if they were bird calls.

George and I look at each other, unsure of what to do now. But since we've been caught in a literal spotlight, I decide to speak up.

"Um, hi. I'm Miranda, and this is George. We live in the house just over that way." I point in the direction I think we came from, although I am even more disoriented in this light than when we were walking in the dark. "Would it be possible to continue this conversation with that crazy bright light *not* aimed at us?"

"Oh, sure. Sorry." With an echoing click, we are plunged into darkness, except for our own small circles of light which may as well be from a Lite Brite in comparison to the pool of light we were just flooded in.

When I raise my flashlight's beam, we are surprised by what we find. Or, I should say, who we find.

Three men, all of whom I'd estimate to be around thirty, stand around a floodlight that had been blinding us a moment ago. All of them look to be human. One is even rather attractive with eyes so blue I see them from here and a strong lumberjack kind of physique going on. George and I look at each other in confusion, then back to the men and smile awkwardly.

George speaks out of the corner of his mouth, "Those do not look like trolls to me, Miranda. I think maybe you were wrong."

I speak back to him through my grinning teeth. "You can think that, but I know what I read. I know what I saw in the daylight, and I definitely know what I smelled and still do. These plants did not rot themselves. If these are not our trolls, there are still trolls out there—somewhere."

One man, the handsome one with long reddish hair pulled back into a low ponytail, speaks to us, the short beard on his chin bobbing up and down. "Hey there, friends. What are you doing out this way so late at night?" His tone is friendly, but his voice gruff.

George takes the lead on our end. "Well, *friend*." His tone is slightly less friendly, but not by much. "This is my property. So, I think if one of us owes the other an explanation, it's you...to me." He stumbles through the end of the sentence, his eyes looking away as he pulls his words together in his flustered state.

The three strangers look back and forth at one another nervously. A mousey blond man, slightly younger looking than Red in the middle, turns his head so quickly that his chin-length greasy hair swings. He mutters something we are not meant to hear. Although, with my super-hearing, I am able to make out some of his words.

"They've seen us. We should spell them."

I grab George's wrist in fear and whisper, "I need to do something. They want to spell us."

"Just wait. Give them a chance. What if they're just lost hikers?"

"Lost hikers?" The question squeaks from my throat much louder than I intended. "On private, fenced-in property? And you think your vegetation just got that way from, what, them peeing there? Come on, George, even you can't be that naïve!"

"Even *I* can't be that naïve? What does that even mean, Miranda?" He turns to me, and beads of sweat are breaking out on his brow. His eyes are wide with annoyance, or anxiety. I can't tell which. Regardless of whether they're trolls or just strange men in the woods in the dark, this is an uncomfortable exchange.

My heart is thumping madly in my chest. All ability to remain calm has gone the way of the dodo, for both of us. Panic blurs the edges of my vision. I try to remember any of the tools Maria gave to me and grab for the bracelet in desperation.

Forcing air into my lungs to prevent myself from hyperventilating, I look back at the men, trying to keep my eye on them as much as I can. Red flashes the evil smile of a cartoon villain, looking self-satisfied when he says, "Well, *friends*, you appear to be having some issues among yourselves. Perhaps you should go back to where you came from and forget all about seeing us here."

The third man, the quietest but also the largest and most troll-looking with his dark hair cropped short, broad shoulders, and flaring nostrils, takes a step forward, effectively blocking the entire floodlight from our view. But the beams of our flashlights illuminate his grotesque smile as it spreads across his soft, round face. Many of his teeth are missing, and the few remaining look too big and circular for his mouth. They also look fuzzy and green, but I convince myself that's a trick of the darkness. The alternative is too disgusting. George's and my hands fly up, as if we're facing officers of the law and not creatures of chaos.

"Hey George?" My voice cracks as I try to keep my volume at a level where he'll hear me, but our three new friends won't.

"Yes, Miranda?" His voice sounds similar to mine.

"I think these are in fact our trolls."

"Yeah, I'm starting to think you were right about this after all." His fast words cause his voice to crack.

The redhead troll is hopping from foot to foot with arms crossed. "Friends, here's what we're going to do. You're going to turn around and forget you saw us." As Red talks, the big guy emits a strange green mist from his mouth. The glowing cloud grows larger and heads right toward us. "We're going to continue living on this land until our clan can come to join us. Then, we'll move on... You'll never even know we were here. We have plans, see. Plans that aren't necessarily pleasant. Plans that don't have to involve you. We're perfectly happy letting you continue on with your night, your land, and your lives."

As the mist gets closer, George's eyes freeze in wide discs. His jaw hangs slack. I know immediately he is hypnotized. Fuck. I'll deal with George later.

I pull the pack off his back and put it on my own, flip the switch on my flashlight to off and cartwheel away from the cloud. Well, kind of. My moves are probably closer to the way cavemen used to jump around while squatting than to anything a gymnast would be caught dead doing. Still, I try to hide myself in the night so I can circle around and surprise them.

"Wait, where'd she go?" cries the mousey troll.

Luckily, these oafs seem to be as smart as I am graceful. At least I have that to my advantage. Now, with no artificial illumination, my Guardian sight kicks in, and I can see clear as day in the dark forest. Big Guy is still breathing what must be the worst smelling spell ever, directly at George. Surely, I can snap him out of whatever they're doing to him once I've eliminated the trolls? Because I'm not sure how to fight foul gas right now.

Hoping to find something useful, I slip off George's backpack and search through the goodies he brought for me. I raise an eyebrow as I pull a big coil of rope that I think is a thick paracord. Oh, I think I can work with this. The conversation I hoped to have, the one in which I would convince them to leave, seems to be out of the question at this point, and even with my training, I can't imagine taking on Big Guy, much less him and his two smaller friends together. They may not seem as scary, but they're still fucking trolls. So I am left with only one way I can think of to defeat them: daylight.

From where I stand, er, crouch and hide in the brush, I realize the three strangers are in front of the huge boulders along the back edge of the plot of rotten vegetation. I look at the semi-stretchy rope in my hands. Maybe I can make some kind of lasso from it. But would I be able to get it around them? I haven't exactly had a lot of practice with a lasso. And by that, I mean I have had zero practice. I have only the one rope so I need to do this fast enough to get it around all three of them before they get a chance to fight back. I am not a fan of the odds that are definitely stacked against me.

On the plus side, the three of them are huddled together before the same boulder, one which is slightly taller than Big Guy. I hold the cord in front of me and unravel a few coils, estimating the total length I have. I don't think I have many options on what to do with it.

"Hey lady, come here," they call for me in a sing-song voice, as if I'm a dog that will trot up to them with my tongue lolling out.

I move behind Boulder Row, staying back so the trolls don't see me between the gaps in the stones., I'm only one boulder away from them when I pause, and I can still see them through the gap. I should be able to fit through it when I need to. Hopefully, they can't. Now, I need something to secure the cord to. Lucky for me, the boulder opposite the trolls is against a tree, large enough to hold strong but not too large in diameter that it eats up my length of rope. Even though I'm a long way out from being a girl scout, I secure one end of the cord around the trunk with a combination of knots and pull hard to make sure the rope will hold. It does for me, though whether or not that will be true for the three beasts I intend to restrain remains to be seen. They may look human, but I remind myself what I read about trolls' incredible strength. They can crush cars with their bare hands! I'll just have to trust my knots.

Holding onto the loose end of the cord, I creep up until I'm at the edge of the boulder nearest them. Big Guy, who's roughly in the same spot where he breathed at George, stands between Red and Mousey but out in front of them and turned slightly away from me. Blindly, he continues belching his rancid, green, dark magic breath into the woods, attempting to spell me when he has no idea where I am. Mousey cowers slightly behind Big Guy. And even though Red seems to be the leader of this shoddy operation, he also hides behind his heavy.

Okay. I got this.

I close my eyes and take a deep breath. I need to move faster than I have ever moved in my life. But this is what I'm meant to do, right? This is what I was born to do. Silently, I squeeze through the gap between the boulders. Then, grasping the rope as tightly as I can, I just run.

Maybe I don't *just* run. Maybe I also yell, "Go Go Guardian Speeeeeeed," as I run the fastest I possibly can, pulling the rope around their waists before sliding back through the gap on the other side of the boulder. I know I need to get this cord as tight as I can, so I repeat the process twice more.

In my second lap, I make sure to pin their arms down so they can't use their hands to work at the binding. The third time around, I get the rope right below their knees so they can't slide out the bottom.

Because they were not expecting it, my plan actually works! The entire chaotic wrap-up takes me only a matter of seconds to complete, and I'm done with the whole exercise before they even know what is happening. I like to think the yelling helped confuse them, if I do say so myself. As I yank and secure the cord around the trunk of the tree, I hear them groan and grumble on the other side of the stone.

Grunts of "How'd she do this?" and "What is Guardian Speed?" hit me as Red's solid voice commands "Stop thinking and help me get this rope off us!"

While I can, I run back to George, who is standing as still as the stone these bastards are going to become once the sun comes up.

"Come on, George. Time to go!" I call to him as I run by, but after two steps, I realize he isn't following me. I run back and look up at him. "What am I going to do with you?"

But the words I hear are not from him.

"You bitch! Come back here and untie us!" As it turns out, trolls are not happy with being tied to a giant boulder to await the stony deaths that will come as soon as the sun's rays hit them.

I don't want to stay here and listen to them screaming at me, so I do the only thing that comes to mind.

"I'm really sorry about this," I say softly. Then I smack him across the face, hard.

He shakes his head and rubs his cheek. "Jesus Christ on a cross, Miranda! What the hell?"

"Sorry, no time to explain right now. We have to get back to your house!" I grab his hand and pull him along as we run the entire way.

Once we are back inside, I look at my watch. "So, George, this has been a real blast, but I have to get back to my family."

I start for the door, but he calls to me. "Um, Miranda, aren't you forgetting something?"

I skid to a stop but don't bother to turn around. My eyelids are heavy and I want to curl up on his marble floor. I have no patience for his docent games. "Did I forget to bow or something?"

"Seriously? No! We need to go find the trolls, remember? Are you feeling okay?"

Now I turn to him. "Am, am *I* feeling okay? Are *you* feeling okay, George? Because *I* just wrapped up three trolls and tied them to a boulder to await their demise."

He furrows his brow. "You, what? What trolls?"

I rub my forehead and sigh. "You were spelled, George. The trolls made you forget about them. They were planning to set up camp in your woods until they had enough of their buddies come join them so they could then take over the town or something, and they didn't want us to ruin their agenda."

His eyes are open and unblinking, but somehow, they look hollow, as if every time he tries to remember what happened, he's spelled all over again.

I walk over and put a maternal hand on his shoulder. "We can talk about this more in the morning. For tonight, just trust me. And stay inside. Got it?"

He nods back to me. "Yeah. I will. I'm just going to go take a shower because I really stink."

I nod along with him as I open his front door. "Yeah, you really do. Night, George!"

Once outside, I jog to my car. I don't want to be out here any longer than I have to, especially alone. As I turn on the engine, I send Jake a text so he knows I'm okay.

```
Mission Accomplished. On my way home.
Love you.
```

Chapter 9

JAKE

George was good with the kids, so I can no longer complain about him coming over. Up until now it's been hard for me to see him as anything but the guy who got Miranda, and, by extension me, into this mess. But seeing him in a different setting, living his life like a regular dude...he's just a kid himself. He didn't make the rules. He wasn't the one that chose Miranda.

Her cover story seems to have worked too, telling the kids he's our personal trainer. Once she left though, I had to cover for her, and that was trickier.

"Where's Mom?" Jessie is the only one who needs Miranda at all times. I'm acceptable only in the direst of circumstances.

"She...had to go get some stuff from the store...?" I know I am not selling it.

"Really? Like what?" She locks her hazel eyes onto me and squints slightly with suspicion. Her arms and ankles are crossed as she leans against the doorframe to her room. In this posture, she looks as if she is twenty-four, not fourteen. She's always seemed older than her age, but this level of maturity catches me off guard.

I'm going to have to sell this a lot more convincingly if I'm to get through this night, or rather, this whole life, without spilling all of

Miranda's secrets. I square my shoulders and look her right in the eye. Teenagers can smell fear, so I need to stay cool and casual.

"She said something about a pop-up bake sale before the long weekend, so she has to bake tomorrow."

"Oh." Luckily, she doesn't keep track of the PTA's schedule at the elementary school anymore. Hopefully, she won't mention it to Natalie and Sam, or they'll expect some cupcakes after school later this week, and Miranda will not be happy with me if she has to bake just because I'm a bad liar.

The rest of the kids are perfectly happy to have me hanging out with them, reading them silly stories, and getting them to bed. I try to stay focused on the silly voices Natalie and Sam still let me use to read to them. Most times they prefer to do their own thing, but once in a while they curl up together on my bed like they did when they were tiny. That was when our biggest worries were when they'd spike their next fever or puke just short of the bathroom.

I look at my watch after tucking in Sammy. It's been about an hour since Miranda dashed out the door. I have no idea how long she will be gone. I have no idea how long it takes to track down, fight, and defeat trolls. I have no idea when I should start to really worry about my wife.

I know she's the one who has to handle all this, but it's hard to reconcile that this woman who can fight monsters and win is the same woman who gave herself tennis elbow folding laundry a year ago. So, I look at my watch and wonder when I need to worry.

I know that it takes fifteen minutes to get to George's compound—that's the only word for it; the place is humongous. So that's thirty minutes round trip. Then they have to track down these trolls, in the dark, and then fight them. All in all, I estimate that Miranda needs about four hours to get this done. Give or take. So when she gets home right after ten pm, only two hours after she left, I am surprised. I'm staring at a cartoon I turned on to pass the time, but I'm so zoned out I don't even know what I'm watching anymore when the alarm chimes that the garage door has opened.

I'm happy she's home and want to hear about what it was like to fight trolls, so I jump up from the couch, forgetting to shut the tv off. I run to see her, desperate to make sure she's okay. But when I meet her in the mudroom, she is caked in literal mud and muck and smells like she fought the trolls in a landfill. My eyes close for a moment as my body automatically does what it can to block as many of my senses from assault as possible.

Despite the stench, Miranda grins from ear to ear as she pulls off her boots, opens the door to our deck, and throws them out into the night air. Then, with zero hesitation, she strips down to her undergarments and tosses all her clothes into the washing machine. She looks at me for one brief moment before shrugging, pulling off her underwear and bra, and throwing them in also. Only after she's filled the detergent drawer with disinfectant and smacked the button to start the wash cycle do I dare speak.

"So, how did it go?" My eyes are wide and bright, like a child waiting to talk to Santa Claus. She may have entered the house only forty-five seconds ago, but I can't believe she didn't immediately begin to divulge the night's events to me.

"I got them, of course, because I'm the motherfucking Guardian! But damn do trolls stink! I need to take a shower!"

She trots her naked self by me, and I can't help but watch her ass as it bounces with each giddy step. Suddenly, I am very grateful the kids are already asleep.

At the kitchen door, she looks at me from over her shoulder with a mischievous sparkle in her eye. "I know I'm a little smelly, but care to join me?"

The look her eyes has something stirring inside me, and inside my pants, but as I move closer, I realize "a little smelly" is an understatement, and all those stirring calm right down. "Um, yes. But I'm going to let you get a head start, if that's not too offensive to admit." I wink so she knows I'm being playful.

She responds with an over the top sultry and campy voice. "Suit yourself." Then, she flips her hair over her shoulder as she walks to the stairs.

I smile at how over the top she's being, but really want to just pull her naked body into my arms. Instead, I catch another whiff of her and hang back, avoiding the cloud of stink I can practically see float toward me, so she has time to de-stink. I smile to myself. This is our new normal now. I'm glad we're finally there. I love how high on self-esteem she gets after she vanquishes a challenger. The new confidence is the sexiest thing I could imagine on her. And now, without regularly seeing the way George sees me, his looks that don't let me forget how I hurt her in Las Vegas, I can start to enjoy it.

A few minutes later, I turn off the kitchen lights and make my way to the bathroom, where I walk into a cloud of raspberry smelling steam. A huge improvement over what my gorgeous, naked wife smelled like just a few moments ago.

I love fucking in the shower and don't want to lose this rare chance, so I strip my clothes as fast as I can and throw them to the floor. I only watch her hands slide over her wet, soapy breasts before I'm too hard to wait and open the glass door to join her.

Chapter 10

MIRANDA

My muscles are tightening up, and I'm wondering how I will even rinse the shampoo from my hair when the flash of cold air tells me that Jake is joining me. My back is to the shower door, and I don't turn around to let on that I know he's there.

My breath hitches when his hands wrap around my waist. He presses into my back as he reaches up to my wet breasts, his fingers slipping over my skin to wrap around my nipples.

I let out a sigh and swing my head back to rest against him while I melt in his hands. "I was worried you'd gone to bed," I admit.

He kisses my shoulder, then along the line to my neck where he nuzzles in. "You know I can't say no to showering with you." More kisses before I feel him inhale against my neck. "Oh, thank God. You don't smell like a skunk threw up out of its anal glands anymore."

I spin around to yell at him but slip on the tile. As I start to fall he steadies me by my forearms. Then he puts a finger to my lips as if trying to keep me quiet, only to replace it with his mouth. The kiss is slow and deep. It is tender and sensual, yet hungry and erotic. It is the most amazing kiss I have ever felt. It is the perfect kiss.

I lean into him as my body chooses this perfectly wrong moment to release the last of my troll-induced adrenaline rush. My legs tremble, and my knees buckle. My lips and tongue cease their active role in the kiss.

He reluctantly moves his mouth away from mine. "Where'd you go, Miranda?"

I slide down his body to the floor and curl up, closing my eyes. "I'm just so tired."

He chuckles sweetly as he shuts off the water. "If I can get you to your feet and guide you, can you get yourself get to the bed?"

I nod, feeling myself being enveloped in a soft, warm towel and lifted gently. I move my feet but can barely open my eyes so I depend on Jake to get me to the bed without crashing me into anything. I haven't felt this tired in ages. Maybe some of that troll spell did get on me when it hit George. Or, maybe this is just how my body recovers after a fight.

Jake manages to get a nightgown on my limp, naked form before laying me down in our bed. He kisses my forehead and whispers, "Sweet dreams, sleep tight, don't let the monsters bite, my beautiful badass bride," before my remaining bit of consciousness drifts out of reach.

I text George when I wake up the next morning, just to make sure he survived his night after being spelled. Thankfully, he replies,

    I'm alive. We'll talk when you get here.

Not terribly encouraging, but I can't worry about it until I get the kids off to school.

Jake and I are back to being a well-oiled, albeit old and a little rusty, machine for our morning routine. I think he needed to see that I could take care of myself in this new role and dealing with the trolls gave him that chance. He kisses me good-bye, a good kiss, as he guides the kids to the mudroom door, and I turn to make myself a to-go cup of coffee. My eyes flick up at the familiar flash of red as the fox kits play in the yard. I wave at Minori, our resident kitsune, as she happily squints her eyes and flicks her tails. We are just two moms tending to our packs in our own ways.

I grab my coffee and my gear bag. I have more than just a gi now; I have full-on equipment: padded gloves, a mouthguard, and a padded helmet thingy. Then I head to my car. George no longer dictates what we'll be doing each day ahead of time. More creatures are waking up and coming out of hiding every day, and he never really knows ahead of time what I need to catch up on anymore. Most days we do a combination of physical training and research in the library. Yesterday's beasts were trolls. Today's could be unicorns. Who knows! Being the Guardian is just a fun and exciting crap shoot of, well, crap.

Before I even knock, George swings the door open. His entire being is buzzing at such a high frequency I can see the air around him glimmering. "What took you so long?" He recedes to the far side of the expansive marble foyer and begins to pace while I lug my bag across the threshold and close the door behind myself.

My eyebrows do a boogie across my face because, unlike his normally reserved self, the energy he exhibits today is downright frenetic. As I watch his frantic steps go left and right and back again across my field of vision, I try to initiate a conversation. "I'm sorry? I'm not even late. What is with you?"

He pauses his gait and looks at his watch. "Oh. You're not late. Huh. Look at that. Sorry. It felt like you were." He locks his eyes on mine as he raises his hands, palms up, pleadingly. "What the hell happened to me last night?"

"What do you mean? What don't you remember?"

He's back to pacing which is making my brain hurt. I'm normally the one pacing. He's normally the calm one. My eyes trace his path back and forth across the room like I'm watching a tennis match. My pulse is speeding up. I wrap my fingers about the metal cuff, forcing my brain to silently recite five things I can see.

He doesn't bother looking at me when he talks. He's too busy trying to recall events just out of his reach. "I remember finding three guys in the woods."

I'm getting dizzy watching him. No wonder he hates when I move like this. "Yeah. The trolls."

He stops. "No, just three guys."

I nod slowly and wish we could fast forward through this redundant conversation. "Yes. They were the trolls."

His head tilts to the left as he plants his hands on his hips. "How could you think they were trolls, Miranda? They were just three men."

The smile I've been trying to maintain slips, and I answer him sharper than I intend. "Trust me George, again. They were the trolls. We went through this all, last night." I walk past him to the door and open it, using my hands to gesture to the not-so-great outdoors. "Shall we take a walk and see?"

He looks at me, then the door, and back to me before running his hands through his hair and nodding. "Yeah. Let's go."

I try to keep my eye on my docent as we walk through his woods, back to where we found the rotted vegetation yesterday afternoon, and then the humanoid (some more human, some more -oid) trolls last night. I have never seen him so frazzled. He is usually composed to a fault. Is this typical George when he's nervous or an after effect of the troll's spell?

Or maybe the spell is still on him? Oh, crap. What if the trolls broke free and weren't turned to stone, meaning the spell is still active? I'll need to track them down and find another way to kill the bastards so I can get my docent back to normal.

I sigh with relief when I see the three stone figures against the boulders. I point so he knows where to look, since they sort of blend in with the giant rock behind them. "See? Like I said—trolls."

George's brow is so low that I don't know how his eyes are still open. He also stares at the boulders slack-jawed. "But, how did you know? That they were trolls, I mean. They look so human. Well, two of them at least. Was it that big guy? Did he give them away?"

"Yeah, especially when he started farting a heavy green spell gas all over us...from his mouth."

In my periphery, I see his head snap around to look at me. I slowly rotate my own, afraid I'll get a kink in my neck if I move as fast as he did. His mouth hangs open, and his eyes blink rapidly. "Why don't I remember that?"

I pat his shoulder. "Oh, Honey..." I sigh. I look back at the trolls and cross my arms smugly. Nodding toward them I announce, "I'm going to be honest here. I wasn't sure that cord was going to hold. I'm pretty fucking proud of myself right now."

George follows my gaze. "How *did* you tie them so securely?" He walks to the boulder with urgency, arms swinging. Then he inspects and maybe even admires my handiwork.

I follow him, and as I get closer, I notice that when they froze (er, stoned? Died? I'm not really sure what to call the action), they were cowering against the boulder, pressing themselves into it. Not only were they not trying to escape, but their faces were twisted in fear, wide, open eyes with eyebrows arched high and mouths twisted in screams destined to be silent for eternity.

"I wonder what they were so afraid of?" I ponder out loud.

"What makes you think they were afraid of something?"

"Look at their faces." All three wore similar expressions when they died:

"I guess," he answers shortly. "Or maybe it was because the sun was coming up and they knew they were about to die."

"I guess." I try to believe that explanation, but I can't help feeling like something is off, something in the angle of their stares. Their eyes are all focused on where I stand, a few feet in front of them, not where the sun would have peeked over the horizon and through the trees to shine on them.

"Wow, trolls sure are stupid." George's voice comes from behind the boulder.

I squeeze through the gap to see what he's talking about. The knots I tied are almost *un*tied. In the very least, they are much looser than I remember leaving them. Either the trolls struggled hard enough that they had almost freed themselves, or I fucked up. No matter which, something other than the way I tied this cord stopped them from slipping the binding and escaping to exhale their horrible breath another day.

"Wow, we got lucky this time. I think maybe we need to incorporate some basic knot tying into my training, yeah?" I turn to George when I say this, but he is focused on that knot. Bewilderment still has his features twisted. "You okay there, George?"

After a few seconds, he shakes his head and looks at me with the glossy eyes of someone who just stirred from a nap. "Yeah. Sorry. Let's go back to the house."

No words pass between us as we walk back to the house. I'm not sure if it is the cool air this deep in the woods or the pollen, but I feel a trickle of snot making its way down toward my mouth. I sniffle loudly to try and suck it back in, a snorting nose coming from my throat. For a moment,

I'm embarrassed, but George is so wrapped up in his own head that he doesn't hear it.

When we walk through the front door, he heads straight for the kitchen. "Coffee?"

I am on my way to the powder room to blow my nose, but I pause so I can answer him. "Have you ever known me to say no to that question?"

While we warm our bodies back up with the hot cups of deliciousness, George is still shaking his head.

I bite the side of my lip, trying to think of something comforting to say to him. "The good news is that the spell seems to have been limited to that time last night with the trolls, right?"

He nods and swallows a gulp of coffee. "Yeah, I think so. Although who knows if any of my other memories were affected, and I just haven't tried to think of them." He drains his mug before continuing. "Okay, I'm going to the dojo to dig up some more rope. You go to the library and find some books on knots. I'll meet you there." He disappears out the doorway closest to the dojo.

I look into the caramel-colored liquid still in my own mug, the glorious nectar I had planned to savor. I guess break time is over, and of course no liquids are allowed in the library because of all the ancient and priceless volumes. I whisper to the mug clutched in my hands, "I'm so sorry for the atrocity I am about to commit." Then I gulp it all down and force myself off my counter stool before I can have the opportunity to pour myself another cup. I walk away, wistfully looking back at the pot sitting on the warming plate, and follow George into the massive, wood-paneled library.

I am grateful that whoever built this shrine to knowledge put in a card catalog and that it is somehow, mysteriously, maintained. I find cards for several books about knots, all in the same area of the Dewey Decimal

System. Hey, there's some random knowledge I should thank my grade school library teacher for.

I look through the stacks until I find the shelf I need, tucked out of the way in a back corner. It makes sense that they're not front and center. I'm a little surprised that we even have them. In this line of work, we're more likely to need *Grimm's Fairy Tales* than something as practical as *The Ashley Book of Knots*.

I bring an arm full of books to one of the tables. I have gotten as far as the differences between knots, hitches, and lashes when George comes in, his arms laden with various lengths and types of ropes. I take two identical segments of rope from the heap he dumps onto the table, about the same thickness as the paracord I used last night, and begin practicing the square knot I remember learning when I was in scouts as a kid. Unfortunately, I acquired any previously held knot tying knowledge so long ago that my Guardian skills are not kicking in to refresh my memory. Every time I tug at the ends to tighten the knot, it all comes loose again.

"Here, try this one." George's blunt fingertip points at a photo labeled "Two Half Hitches: used to secure an animal or item to a bar or pole."

I shrug before diving in to my next attempt. I follow the pictures, and the knot almost looks right. "Oh! I think I got it!" And then it falls apart in my hands. I grunt and smack my thighs in frustration.

George snaps his head to me, his brow furrowed. "What the hell was that?"

I rub my hands down my face as I answer him. "I'm frustrated."

"Okay, I get that. But don't *hit* yourself!" His voice goes so high on the word hit that it cracks.

I can't help but smile. He's so protective of me, even from myself. "I'll try not to, but it's pretty ingrained in me."

"Well, I don't like it. You shouldn't be so hard on yourself." He's quiet and serious.

"Thanks, Doctor. I'm cured!" My voice is full of fake brightness and joy before I go back to my ropes.

The library is quiet the rest of the day, so quiet I could have heard a fairy fart. (I'm assuming. I've never actually heard a fairy fart.) And when I say quiet, I mean aside from my shouts of excitement when I finally master the square knot and two half hitches and my exclamations of irritation with every failed attempt.

Finally, it's time for me to leave. As we approach the door, I blurt out, "If you ever want to come over for dinner again, just let me know. You have a standing invitation. Maybe I really can set up a training space in the basement, and we can get the kids in on it. I think they should know how to defend themselves too."

"That's not a bad idea." He's holding open the door, his forehead resting on his hand. "I would like to know the kids can take care of themselves. Now that I know them, I kind of like them."

I smile, but he seems sad or distracted or something. "You okay?"

"Yeah. I just wish I could remember last night. I think I'm going to take a bath and meditate."

"Just don't drown in the tub or anything, okay?"

He laughs. "I'm not you, Miranda." His eyes are warm and twinkle when he winks, making sure I know he's just teasing.

"Ha ha ha. Very funny." But I *am* smirking as I walk to my car because it was pretty funny.

Chapter 11

GEORGE

I start the bath and sit on my bed to check my phone. There are no new messages, but that doesn't surprise me. The ball's been in my court since Andrew texted me Sunday afternoon. I can't believe I've let a full day and a few hours go by without replying to him!

```
I realize I'm blowing any cover of
pretending I'm cool right now, but I like
you too much to play games. I'm thinking
of you and wanted to tell you.
```

I've read over those words at least a dozen times, even with the excitement of the trolls. I just don't know how to respond.

I can't wrap my head around being able to date someone right now. I need to focus on Miranda's training and keeping her alive. I can't allow myself the kind of distraction a new relationship would be.

And then there's the whole matter of bringing Andrew into this mess of a world. The first big baddie we had to deal with abducted Jake. It would be naive of me to think that anyone I care about will be at any less of a risk. And ignoring that would be selfish of me.

But there's also the simple fact that I really like Andrew, and I don't want to mess this up.

Shaking my head, I check on my bath and bring my phone with me. The tub still needs another minute or two, so I begin to pace in the bathroom, staring at my phone. Finally, I decide to respond.

```
Hey, sry for the slow response. Had some
issues with a client and then had some
property damage I had to deal with. I've
been thinking of you too though. Promise
:)
```

My thumb hovers over "Send" for a few seconds before I breathe, "Fuck it," to myself and tap the screen.

I take and release a deep breath and return to the bath to shut the tap. After lighting a couple of vanilla-scented candles, I throw my clothes into the hamper and lower the lights before easing myself into the hot water.

Closing my eyes, I focus on my breathing with my hands over my diaphragm so I make sure to pull the air in the proper way. In a pattern of four counts, I pull the air in, hold, and exhale through my mouth. I focus on nothing but the air flowing in, through, and then out of my body.

But after a few breaths, I still feel tense. I pull in a deep breath and slip myself under the water.

A throaty laugh, low and feminine, fills my ears or, more specifically, my mind. I open my eyes, but I don't see my bathtub anymore. Instead, water far bluer and more copious than couldn't ever fit in my bathtub surrounds me, all the way to a distant horizon. Even though I see only the wide ocean around me, I still feel the smooth porcelain against my naked back and butt, so what the hell is going on? My heart beat speeds up as I look around for something and see nothing but the surface of the water.

"Oh, sweet docent. How are you?" calls the feminine voice.

I don't know who she is, but her voice is velvet enveloping me. I can't bring myself to respond. I don't know how I even would if I wanted to. I want only to hear her again. "You don't need to answer me. It's okay. I'm sorry I distracted you from your date the other night."

Distracted me from my date? I wasn't distracted from my date.

"You looked so happy looking up at the sky. Are you in love?"

The lady in red. It must be. At least now I can put some amount of a visage to the strange, even if sultry, disembodied voice.

She chuckles. "Yes. That's me. Did you like how I helped you with your troll problem? I told them to stop fighting their bonds. I forced them to wait calmly for their own demise. It was the least I could do after causing that whole dragon turtle mess. I didn't mean to chase him up from the ocean. Who knew those giant creatures had such sensitive ears?"

My mind can't fully grasp what she's saying as her words float away with the water draining from my bath. I'm suddenly shivering as goosebumps pop up all over my wet and exposed skin. I blink and I'm back in my bathtub, though it is now empty. I scrunch my eyes shut to hold onto what she said. Maybe ask for clarification. But she's gone.

If she was ever really here to begin with.

Chapter 12

MIRANDA

When I wake up Wednesday morning, a series of short, half-thought-out texts from George fills my screen. I can't really complain. I too am the type of person that will send six separate texts that could have been one.

You up?

Guess not. Nevermind.

Just, please come right here after you drop the kids off.

I'll have coffee waiting! No need to stop!

I'm not in danger or anything. Just, something super weird happened

I'm ok though. Nothing BAD happened, just WEIRD

I immediately decide Jake has to take the kids to school today. The moment his car reverses out of the driveway, I rush to get to my own vehicle.

Once again, George is pacing frantically when I arrive. Only this time, he is in his driveway instead of hidden in the foyer, so I see him as soon as I pull up. He is walking back and forth so quickly that I'm worried he's going to create a dust devil on the dirty paving stones.

As I approach, he stops and places one hand on his hip. The other, he extends toward me with the palm up as if he is holding something important for me to inspect. Only, his hand looks completely empty.

"Do you see this?" he asks impatiently.

I shake my head. He shakes his own, pinches whatever is supposed to be in his hand between two fingers, and holds it at my eye level. He takes two strides to close the distance between us and continues, "Try again."

I lean in, now seeing a few long auburn strands. My face scrunches up with questions and a little ick factor. "Why are you holding someone's hair?"

He sighs, and his shoulders fall. "It's hers. The lady in red I saw at the restaurant, that I dreamed about. It's her hair! She was *here*."

I furrow my brow and look from the hair to my docent. So many questions that I can neither contain nor control spill from me. "What? Why would you think that? Where did it come from? How did you get it? Why are you holding onto it?"

He lets out a long, slow breath and bows his head in relief that I'm listening. "I found it in the woods. It came from her. It must have gotten tangled in a branch." He resumes pacing and gestures wildly toward the woods while continuing to rant. She was here, Miranda. She was *here*, in the flesh. She's what those trolls were so afraid of when they died. She's why they didn't escape. She somehow made them just wait for their deaths. I think she thinks of it as a favor to me. To us maybe. I don't know."

He sits on the bottom step in front of his door, his face buried in his hands. I try to ignore the fact that random hair is still in his hand, pressing into his face. The thought alone makes me nauseated.

I struggle to form words. My mouth is dry, and my brain hasn't fully woken up yet; it still is wondering how I managed to drive here without any coffee. "I, what? I don't understand."

He pulls his hands down until his cheeks rest on his fingertips. "I'll explain inside." He pops up from the step with a grace and energy I don't think I ever had. I am fairly sure that when I was twenty-five, it would have taken at least a grunt to get up.

When he darts into the house, I force myself to attempt to keep up, although the closest I get is about three steps behind him. We walk straight to the kitchen where he makes me a cup of coffee.

While he fetches mugs from the cupboard and brings them to the counter where the coffee pot lives, he launches into the tale of how he came to be pacing in front of his house, holding a stranger's hair. "Remember how I was going to take a bath last night and try to meditate? Well, I tried, but I couldn't relax, so I slipped under the water for a minute." He pours from the silver pot and then pauses the story to get the half and half. As he lifts the carton to pour it into our cups, he continues, "This voice talked to me, and I just knew it had to be the woman in red. She apologized for distracting me from my date. She said she scared the trolls so they wouldn't fight your ties. Oh! And she even told me that she somehow was responsible for the dragon turtle being in the museum!"

He plops my full mug down in front of me. I look at it briefly and then nod at the hair he abandoned next to me on the counter. "So how'd you find the hair, and why do you think it's hers if she was just a voice?"

He takes a long swig of coffee and holds up a finger so I know he heard me. Then he cradles the cup between his hands when he's done so he can also look at the strands. "I wanted to see if I could find any evidence of her near the trolls so I went out there early this morning. Those were hanging from a branch near the clearing. I think she may have been there the same time we were and watched everything. Maybe I would have noticed her if I hadn't been spelled..."

"Don't beat yourself up too much. I can't think of how that would have been helpful anyway." I drain my cup and help myself to a second. My brain is thanking me as it starts to wake up. I retake my seat at his counter and swallow a few more big gulps. "So, what does this all mean?"

He shakes his head while staring at the hair. "I don't know. She's on land. She's in water. That doesn't tell us what she is. We know she scared the trolls and the dragon turtle. But I've seen her, and she's no larger, or scarier, than a normal woman. She must have some kind of power."

I nod in agreement. "Not to mention showing up as a disembodied voice in your bathtub." We sit in silence, slurping our respective coffees. "Well, I have to go pee." I push myself off my counter stool as George chuckles. When I return to the kitchen, he's leaning against the sink, arms crossed. He appears to be staring at my coffee cup that still sits on the counter, but I can tell he's not really in the room. I recognize his expressions well enough by now to know that he's trying to puzzle out where he knows that woman from and why she seems to be involved in all the things we are doing right now.

I wave my hand in front of his face. "Earth to George."

He blinks rapidly and looks at me. "Hey, sorry. I just, I don't know if I can start a relationship with Andrew after all this. I really like him, but I don't want to put him in danger. I was already on the fence before she talked to me last night, but now..."

I swallow hard. He's hesitant about starting this relationship because of what happened with Jake and the Muses. Another way I'm getting in the way of his love life. Even with the crazy magical stalker lady, I hope he gives his relationship with Andrew an honest try.

I look at my docent, who is usually the one in this relationship who has his shit together, and I see how close he is to coming apart right now. His hair is tangled and sticking up in spots where he's been tugging it. He has bags under his eyes I have never seen before. And his voice is hoarse and thin. The realization turns my stomach. I think about how consistent George has been the last six months, through my training, through everything with Jake. The Guardian keeps the world safe. Her docent keeps her safe. If my docent is off kilter, I don't want to think about what that means for my safety.

I need to get us back on track. "Okay. We obviously need to try to figure this out. Let's go to the library and research."

I grab the giant book of docent notes and look for mythological humans in red dresses, but the only things I can find are about a jilted lover or prostitute killed in a fit of passion.

George has a table full of all the colognes and perfumes he could find tucked away inside the medicine cabinets around his mansion. He found a couple dozen bottles in all. Apparently, guests over the years have left behind a lot of fragrances.

And it's hard to concentrate. Rose is mingling with musk under vanilla, and, I think, pine? The fragrances do not go together well and my lungs are burning, longing for fresh air. I'm getting lightheaded and have read the same sentence seven times and still can't tell what it says. I have to put a stop to this.

"George, you're giving me a headache."

"I just need to figure out what she smelled like. It has to matter."

"Okay, but, Dude, they're all blending together. I think you need to smell coffee beans between sniffs or something. I think it cleanses the palette, or whatever the palette is for noses."

He glares at me over the bottle he's poised to spray. "Miranda, I'm not getting you more coffee."

I roll my eyes. "You just need a little cup of the beans. Not actual coffee. Although...nope, nope, nope. I'm fine. *Fine.* Continue doing it your way then. See if I care."

After five more spritzes, bile is rising in the back of my throat and my eyes feel like they're bleeding. "George, I love you man. I do. But I can't be here anymore. I'm going to puke or pass-out or something."

"You can go then. I'm almost done here anyway. I may head over to the mall and try the fragrance counters. I'll see you tomorrow."

I grab my bag and head for the door, but on the way out, I turn my head to call over my shoulder, "We'll be in the dojo tomorrow so this place can air out. I command it!"

And we are. Well, for the part of Thursday I'm here, we stay in the dojo, working on drills to improve my strength and speed. Then I head home early so I can wash, sort, and fold all of our laundry so we can pack tonight. With most schools in the state having off this Friday as a giveback because we didn't use any snow days this winter, we want to be ready to go when the sun comes up. It's no easy feat to get a family of six ready for vacation, even if it's just a long weekend.

By the time the luggage is stacked by the front door, the kids don't want to fall asleep. Big surprise. They're running back and forth between each other's rooms, comparing their weekend bucket lists, fighting about where we need to go first on the boardwalk, finally agreeing, then running into the next room to start the cycle all over again. Their excitement makes me feel like a shitty parent, honestly. Their friends go to the shore as a regular part of their lives. Their big vacations are to Cabo, Aruba, even Europe. Meanwhile, for us, between timing and our family's innate ability to anxiously talk ourselves out of anything, driving somewhere a couple hours away for a long weekend is all we can seem to manage, such that it becomes the most exciting thing ever to my poor, sheltered children.

Once they're all at least settled into bed and I'm lying in my own, looking up at the blank ceiling and drifting off to sleep, I make a mental note to plan more exciting family vacations, and soon. After all, none of us are getting any younger.

Chapter 13

MIRANDA

"Ugggh. Dad! Can you stop with the Korean lessons? Please! It's been forty-five minutes." Sammy can't tolerate the sensation of any type of headphones. So, while his sisters ignore Jake's language learning app for their own devices, Sammy is left listening to Jake trying to ask for a bus.

"Beoseuneun eodie issnayo?"

I smile to myself but reassure him, "It's only been twenty minutes, Sammy. But I think it's almost over. Afterwards, you'll get to pick whatever you want to listen to."

"Can that whatever be silence? Silence would sound so good right now!"

I laugh. "Yes, silence is allowed. I would make him turn it off, but you know your father signed that K-Pop band this week and will be their US-based manager. He needs to get some basics down."

The man on the app says, "Now try to ask your companion, 'Do you drink a lot of coffee?' Dangsin-eun keopileul manh-i masinda?"

Jake taps my arm excitedly while repeating, "Dangsin-eun keopileul manh-i masinda."

I smile back at him and answer, "Yup. I sure do."

He smiles a goofy grin at me, and I pat his cheek before looking back up at the ceiling in a feeble attempt to stop my motion sickness. It isn't working. I see a familiar blue sign pass my window. The white writing says "Service Center 1 mile. Next Service Center 27 miles."

"Ooh, and speaking of my coffee habit, I need a refill. Also, a restroom."

Jake pauses the audio. "Seriously? We're making such good time!"

I scrunch up my face and look at him with my head tilted to the side. "Are we though?"

We woke up at our usual 6:15 a.m., hoping that if we got on the road early enough, we could avoid the bulk of the traffic. A foolish thought, really. As soon as we get on the aptly named Garden State *Park*way, the sea of cars told us we are not the only shmucks with this idea.

Jake eases the car into the parking lot at the rest stop and finds a spot near the door, which I consider nothing less than miraculous.

"Hey kids, who else needs the bathroom?" When I'm met with nothing but muffled sounds through headphones, I turn around in my seat, look at my progeny all staring down at their respective screens, shake my head, and raise my voice. "Hey kids!" They all jump a bit and at least give me the recognition of pulling their headphones down momentarily. "I'm going to the bathroom. We aren't stopping again for a while. Who else needs to go?"

Three sets of shoulders shrug as the kids replace their headphones.

"I'll come!" Sammy chimes in, looking at his sisters as if they're literal zombies, not just tablet zombies successfully ignoring my reminder to empty their bladders.

Of course, I give them a similar, wilting look when we have been back on the highway for ten full minutes and Jessie throws her headset to the side, screeching, "I need to pee!!!"

Even with our seven-thirty departure, between the morning traffic and the millions of stops we have to make (seriously, why can't everyone in the family just pee at the same time?), we pull into the driveway close to noon.

Eliza's parents cut no corners when they decorated their beach house. The modern farmhouse color palette of grays and whites makes this one of the most relaxing places we frequent. That's not to say I don't add my own splash of anxiety when we come. The living room has an entire wall of full-length windows, a couple of which are doors, that look past the large gray deck and over the beach to the Atlantic. The scene is breathtakingly beautiful, but also completely nerve-wracking for a mother with undiagnosed postpartum anxiety, which I had during our visits when the kids were babies and toddlers. We would be having a wonderful escape from our everyday chaos, and my horrible fears would come knocking on my mind's door.

Jessie can totally open that door. Do you think you can get to the bathroom, pee, and get back here faster than it would take her to wander into the ocean and drown?

You're really going to let Phoebe dance so close to those windows? Wow, okay. Hope she doesn't twirl into the glass and shatter it, scarring herself horrifically in the process.

Oh good! The entire population of Point Pleasant can see your kids as they play here. At least there is easy access for anyone who wants to break in and kidnap them tonight.

Giving a name to those intrusive thoughts, as my doctor finally identified them, was a relief. But even then, anxiety doesn't care about what's rational, and I'm always going to fear for my children's safety. Honestly, I can still visualize my rambunctious kids fighting with each other as we unload and stretch, and can imagine them crashing through that glass less than an hour from now. If any of my kids got horrifically injured, I don't care how much of a badass I am now; my life would still shatter. But I can't let fear hold me back or stop us from enjoying life. So, here we are. Life goes on. Later tonight, I should thank Jake for making this happen. I smile to myself as I unlatch my seatbelt.

Jake catches my expression and playfully asks, "What's that smirk about?"

I look at him with a twinkle in my eye and answer with a raised eyebrow, "I was just thinking how grateful I am that you planned this trip."

His brow shoots up in shock, "Really? That's a switch."

"Hey, I'm already eating crow here. Don't make me feel worse."

He leans across the console and kisses me and a chorus of groans rises up from the back seat in response. We end the kiss smiling against each other. Things really are getting back to normal finally.

As everyone empties from the car onto the driveway behind the house, Eliza opens the door. She has an ear-to-ear grin on her face, reminding me how much she loves to host us here and giving me a pang of guilt for not visiting more often. Through the doorway, I see the clean kitchen with its trendy, poured-concrete countertops and white, shaker-style cabinets. The kids give Eliza hugs on their way in and then proceed to lug their bags down to the two basement bedrooms they always claim as their own when we're here. Jake smiles at me and kisses my cheek before taking my bags and bringing them in and up to the second-floor guest room.

Eliza looks at me with her eyebrows raised and a hopeful smile on her face. When I smile back at her, she does a dramatic but silent clap. She's been privy to all of my emotions these last few months. Now that I've given her the slightest indication that things have turned a corner for me and Jake, she must view this as a reason to celebrate. And while yes, we have made progress, I am not ready to get too carried away with my joy.

I duck my head back into the car to make sure we aren't leaving anything we need, and also to avoid Eliza's watchful gaze, just for a moment. Maybe we should have stayed in a hotel. I don't know how much healing I'm going to be able to accomplish if I feel like we're being observed for a social experiment the entire time we're here.

I straighten back up and almost jump out of my skin when two small red figures suddenly hover on either side of my hand on the car door handle.

"Oh, for fuck's sake, Jerry!" I yell at the imp on my left.

"Um, actually ma'am, I'm Cliff."

"Okay, fine. Whatever. Can you guys please try to not scare the shit out of me?"

Eliza call from the door to the house, "Miranda, is everything ok?" I look up and she is furrowing her brow, balancing on her tip toes, trying to see what made me jump on this side of the car.

I hold my finger up to keep the imps quiet for a moment before responding, "Oh, I'm good. Just have to take a work call."

She knits her brow together even more before releasing them with a nod of recognition. She calls again, "Oh! Got it! Well, take your time," before turning back into the house and closing the door behind her.

The imp on my right speaks, sounding impatient with me. "Oh, okay. Sure. Whatever you command, your highness. We'll be more careful the next time we come bearing the news that *you* commanded us to bring to you."

I look at my toes. I can't believe a tiny, mischievous demon successfully shamed me. "I'm sorry." But I'm also bouncing on my toes at the prospect of gaining some intel. "What do you have for me?"

They exchange a glance, and then Jerry, his little arms folded in front of him, speaks. "I'm not so sure you deserve to hear it right now, to be honest."

"Woah now. I apologized, and I didn't even have to! You guys do work for me now, remember?"

Cliff rolls his eyes "How could we ever forget?"

I squint at him. "Did you just come here to give me a hard time, or do you have something to tell me that could matter?"

Once again, they exchange what I believe to be a knowing look. Then Jerry nods at Cliff, who inhales deeply before beginning to speak. "We have some news. The Muses are moving on. They said they aren't worried about you anymore."

I let out a relieved sigh. "Really? I'm free? I mean, so to speak?"

Cliff tilts his head and furrows his brow. "Huh? So to speak? I guess. Calliope said she's not worried about you because you haven't come after her yet. But she also mentioned a friend of hers. I heard something about her following around and wanting to seduce your friend, I guess."

The memory of George frantically pacing the other morning pops into my head. "Wait, what? George has had a lady in red visiting him. How does she plan to seduce him? George isn't really into the ladies so much. And by so much, I mean not at all."

Cliff shrugs, and Jerry chuckles.

"Well, she's already started and is apparently doing a good job of getting inside your friend's head." Jerry laughs outright now.

Meanwhile, Cliff's eyebrows are going to force his eyes to close if they descend any further in his confused state. Cliff watches his maniacal friend for a moment before saying, "Wait, is that what the 'seeing red' comment was about?"

I don't get what's so hilarious, but Jerry is gasping for breath as he nods.

"Seeing red? What the hell does that mean? What am I supposed to do with that?" I shake my head as the imps, who are proving to be more trouble than they're worth, fly away together. As I slide the van door closed, I find Harmon, Natalie's favorite stuffy since toddlerhood, tucked under the seat. I grab the raggedy koala and lock the minivan. Walking to the house, I send George a text.

I stare at the koala and phone in my hands. George is a better fighter than I am, and he has a head start on trying to figure out who this chick is. Knowing George will be okay, I look at the house. My family needs me present this weekend. My husband needs all of me in it. I take a deep breath, shrug, and slide my phone into do-not-disturb mode before heading in and making lunch for my crew.

Chapter 14

JAKE

I rarely toot my own horn. It's hard to find reasons to brag about yourself when you're married to a mythically supercharged human. But I do have to say that this weekend away was a brilliant idea. Bringing Miranda and the kids down here, back to this place where we have made so many happy memories, is just what our family needed. Even more than that, it's just what our marriage needed. Having to stop every half an hour made the drive down a little tumultuous, but with our kids, I wouldn't have it any other way. And besides, now that we're here, we can relax and enjoy ourselves.

Eliza's parents' place is only steps away from the boardwalk. We can be in tourist central in minutes. Or we can stay here in our own little piece of heaven. The living room has floor-to-ceiling windows looking out at the ocean. A beautiful gray deck separates the house and the boardwalk where we spend as much of our time as possible when we're here.

We are all on the deck now. Miranda told me to relax after driving for the last three and a half hours. So I'm with the kids, camped out on the outdoor sofa, chatting animatedly and enjoying the salty sea air, while Eliza and Miranda set the table next to us with everything for lunch. My stomach growls as I smell the hot dogs and hamburgers on the grill. Miranda sets a plate piled high with various buns on the table and Eliza follows with a large glass bowl full of potato salad in one hand and one full of macaroni salad in the other. I nudge Jessie's foot with my own. She's staring off at the ocean while her siblings are all giggling away around her. She's getting too cool for our family's enjoyment of each other. Or maybe she already is.

Her attention snaps to me. "What?"

I raise my eyebrows and look at Miranda, jutting the top of my head toward the dining set-up before looking back into my eldest's eyes, which she promptly rolls.

But then, to my amazement, she listens to me. "Hey Mom, Aunt Eliza, do you need any help?"

Miranda and Eliza both freeze in their spots and look at each other with a touch of fear in their eyes at this unexpected behavior. Miranda looks at Jessie as she slowly resumes folding paper napkins to set the flatware at each setting onto, then answers, "Um, we're good for now, Jessie. Thank you for offering. But we do still have about nine more meals to eat while we're here, and not all of them can be at Little Mac's, so maybe you guys can take turns helping us out?"

Jessie's eyes flick to me so there is no doubt I'm the one to blame for this turn of events. Then she plasters a sweet smile on her face and nods to Miranda. "It's a deal!"

"Great!" Miranda goes back to chatting with Eliza happily as they finish readying the meal.

I smile to myself, leaning my head against the cushion so I can feel the warmth of the sun on my face. I am going to make this the best weekend ever. I'm even going to take Miranda to dinner tomorrow, a real-life date! I already spoke to Eliza and Rory, who said they'd be happy to keep an eye on the kids. Luckily, watching our kids doesn't take nearly as much energy as watching their own does at this point. In fact, our kids are usually so helpful with Tabitha that the whole thing could end up beneficial to them.

After lunch, Rory and I clear the table. It's the least we can do since the ladies prepared and set out everything. The kids run inside, nearly plowing one another over, to get ready to go to the boardwalk. And on her way in, Miranda smacks my butt when I'm not expecting it.

I smile at her over my shoulder. "Hey, I'm not just a piece of meat, you know."

She smiles back and shrugs before walking through the open sliding door. I follow her in, carrying the stack of melamine plates sticking together with remnants of mayonnaise and ketchup from the meals just consumed. When I get to the kitchen, Miranda is at the island, wrapping up leftovers. Once I deposit the dishes in the sink, I sidle up behind her, wrapping my arms around her waist.

"What was that about?" I murmur into her ear before kissing the corner of her jaw beneath it.

She tilts her head away in response, giving me more access to the curve of her neck where she likes me to kiss most. She moans under my lips. I press my hardening arousal against her ass. She pushes back and rubs against me a few times before she rolls her head back to me and half moans, "We need to stop. We're in a house full of people, and they're all awake."

"If you're sure…" I trace the side of her neck with my lips and tongue.

She uses her butt to tease me once more and then push me back. "I'm sure."

My hands go up, fingers splayed, showing I give up, but still smile at her like a jackal stalking its prey. I shake my head slowly and turn to leave the kitchen, adjusting the bulge I need to hide from the rest of the world.

Walking into the living room, I ask, "Okay, who wants to go to the boardwalk?"

Four little bodies start bouncing around the living room. In the corner, Eliza lets out a huge yawn while handing Tabitha off to Rory with a kiss to each. With Tabby ready for a nap, Rory offers to take one for the team and stay behind to get her settled down. I think he just wants his own chance to nap, not that I blame him. I remember those nights. Phoebe in particular was the worst at sleeping at that age. I spent about three months around her first birthday holding her all night in the recliner we kept in her room so she would sleep. I don't think I'd ever been as exhausted, and likely haven't been since. I wouldn't trade it for anything though, those times I got to hold her tiny body in my arms, the times I had her all to myself. Jessie was always such a mama's girl. I was ecstatic when Phoebe didn't have a strong preference of one of us over the other.

"Have fun, Babe. I'll leave the door unlocked for you." Rory leans in for a kiss, but Eliza erects a wall with her hand as she lifts her palm to cover another yawn.

When she finally closes her mouth again, she turns to her husband with one eyebrow raised. "Um, are you crazy? I have been researching the serial killer Richard Ramirez for the last two days for my next book, and it's left me jumpy. Don't you *dare* leave that door unlocked! That's what keys are for."

Then they kiss deeply. So deeply that I need to look away because I feel like I am intruding on their intimate moment.

I feel an ache inside. That moment in the kitchen with Miranda was so nice, but it was just the start. We're trying to get back there, and we're making progress, but we have a long way to go still. We have had sex exactly one time since Vegas, right after we saw Maria for the first time. It was nice, but it felt more like homework than intimacy. I want to go back to when we set each other's souls on fire. When did we lose that spark? Was it a slow fade since becoming parents, or did it die off after Vegas?

As we walk in the bright sun toward the masses of people, Miranda and Eliza lead the pack, the kids muddle around in the middle, and I take up the rear, observing them all. Sammy eyes the aquarium, wishing he could visit the animals inside.

"Don't even think about it, Sammy," Phoebe chastises him for daring to think about patronizing such an inhumane location.

We don't actually know that it's inhumane, but when Jessie hit age nine, she decided that enough zoos and aquariums were evil that she didn't want to give money to any of them, just in case. Phoebe immediately adopted the same attitude of course. Phoebe used to idolize her big sister.

I make a mental note to sneak back here with Sammy sometime this weekend. I reach out with my hand to get his attention and give him a wink, and he rewards me with a massive smile.

Natalie clasps her hands together and hops forward five times while asking, "Can we please go to the sweet shop?" She would live on salt water taffy and ice cream all weekend if we let her. And when she looks at me with those giant blue eyes, I would totally let her.

I'm about to lose my will to say no when Miranda's voice reaches us from her place at the beginning of our caravan, "Nope. I promise we will at least once this weekend, but not immediately." Luckily, Miranda has the conviction I lack when it comes to denying our children anything.

"Okay, fine. Whatever." She crosses her arms and drags her feet. Poor kid doesn't know her mom well if she thinks pouting is going to get her anywhere.

"Wanna play minigolf?" Jessie, trying to be a good big sister, uses her sweetest voice to cheer Natalie up.

Natalie shrugs. "Maybe later. Maybe we can go on some rides first."

"I hate to be a killjoy, but I think we need to let our lunch settle a little more before we jump on the rides, kiddos." I'm happy to take what is sure to be an unpopular parenting decision off of Miranda for once.

"Okay then. I guess we can do minigolf now!" Natalie tries to fake enthusiasm, but she can't hide her pouting lips and hunched shoulders as she crosses her arms over her chest. Being denied twice is tough. Her siblings at least let her pick which course she wants to take. Ever the adventurer, she chooses the high Crow's Nest path.

The round of minigolf turns out to be relaxing and fun, although Eliza keeps getting distracted. I think she's trying to spy on Rory and Tabby since we can *almost* see the house from the course. Miranda stays behind with her on a few holes, trying to get her to open up a little, as the rest of us move up.

When the ladies are with us, I steal glances to watch Miranda laugh with the kids in a way she hasn't in months. Or maybe she has, but just not around me. Or, maybe she has around me, but I've been so wrapped up in my anger and self-loathing that I couldn't see it.

I almost ruined everything. One could even argue I *did* ruin everything. Not the getting kidnapped part. I know that was out of my control; they were goddesses for fuck's sake. But, I hesitated when it mattered. I almost stayed. They weren't keeping me there beyond not feeling obligated to my responsibilities. As soon as I saw Miranda, as soon as she was there in front of me, I should have known our life together is not just a responsibility. She is not a responsibility. I should have run away with her, without even a moment's hesitation.

And I know she's been blaming herself for this mess as much as I have been blaming myself. I know she feels horrible about what happened with that demon. But, I don't even think of it as cheating. I think of it as sexual assault. I met Lu before Miranda came out to Vegas. I know how convincing he was. Miranda was more of a victim in this than I was.

I shake my head to remove some of this useless pain. We're here together now. We're a team again. I'm going to buy this woman all the cotton candy she can eat and hope she doesn't puke on me on the tilt-a-whirl. I'm going to win her a prize from skee-ball. Maybe I'll even get to make love to her on the beach later.

As I watch, Miranda seems to move in slow motion when she laughs, her smile shining in the sunlight. Her eyes are twinkling, not only when she looks at the kids but when she looks at me too. My heart skips a beat when her eyes lock on mine and she smiles. After we hand our clubs back in at the hut, we join hands as we continue our walk down the boardwalk to the rides.

Chapter 15

Miranda

I had almost forgotten how much we love being here. We love the salty air. We love the rides (even if I'm not wholly convinced they won't fall apart any second). We love the greasy food from carts and stands I'm not sure I would trust anywhere else. I am grateful that we can still be a happy family when we go away together for a weekend. Huh, I guess I do have something I enjoy doing outdoors. I make a mental note to update Maria when we're back.

The only one who doesn't seem to fall back into the old rhythm is Eliza. She's still being her ever gracious, hostess self. But something is not the same with her. She was more anxious that usual when Rory volunteered to put Tabby down for her nap. She stammered and looked back and forth between us and Tabitha as if she were being asked to make Sophie's choice. Even though she relented and seemed to relax as we walked toward the tourist attractions, her emotional state deteriorates once we start playing minigolf.

I hang back with her on the seventh hole so I can talk to her. "You okay, Lize?"

Her lips move in her ridiculously fast way, but no sounds come out. She looks as though she is deep in conversation with herself, but silently. As we stroll to the next hole, I keep looking into her face every few steps, until she eventually notices my attention.

She jumps a little at the recognition. "Um, hi? Miranda, why are you staring at me like that?" She ends with a nervous laugh.

I smile and shake my head. "I was trying to talk to you. Is everything alright?"

"Yeah, of course!" Her tone is overly cheery, either to compensate for her strange behavior or maybe just in comparison to it.

"Eliza, you know I've been dealing with some weird supernatural crap lately, right? Nothing you have to tell me will make me think twice." I tilt my head down and to the side, trying to get her to look at me, but she keeps her eyes focused low in front of her as she rolls her pink golf ball up onto the rubber mat.

"Yeah, I'm okay though. It's just that Tabby's going through a sleep regression, and I'm exhausted." She flashes me a quick smile before she stares back at the ground, swings at her ball, and whiffs so much so that her ball doesn't flinch.

"Okay, but you know you can talk to me about anything right?" I think I see a slight nod in response.

She tilts her head a bit, furrows her brow, and parts her lips. "I just, it's so hard. You know? I thought when I got past the newborn stage maybe I'd be able to breathe again. But then there was teething, and sleep regression, and then starting food with all the digestive changes, then more sleep regression. When does it stop? When do I get back to feeling like myself?" She wipes a tear away before it can drip down her cheek. "I feel like such a horrible mom saying all this!"

I put my hands on her shoulders so we are square with each other. "Listen to me, Eliza. First of all, you are not a horrible mom. Every mom feels this way. Any mom who says otherwise is either in denial or high on something."

Her chest bounces once with a single laugh. I don't know if she doesn't want to let more out, or if she can't.

I smile and continue, "Second, to be perfectly honest, I don't know that I ever got back to feeling like myself. Not the me I was before I had Jessie anyway. I think by the time Sam was four, I had started to reinvent my new self though. And every day, I'm more and more her, er, *me*."

Eliza nods and adds, "Now with added superpowers."

And right then, right when I think we are finally starting to get somewhere, Sammy calls to us, "Mom! Aunt Eliza! Check me out!"

He puts his ball on the starting dot on the green before licking the tip of his finger and holding it up to test the wind. His determination would impress me if I didn't know for a fact that he has no idea what he's doing and is bullshitting us. With both hands on the end of his club, he then wiggles his butt and lines up his shot. He swings the club far too high behind him, nearly hitting Natalie's ear, and then wallops the ball. That red blur pings off the sides and then rolls into the cup, giving Sammy a hole-in-one.

As Eliza, the kids, and I gasp, cheer, and throw our hands into the air, Sammy follows up with the silliest victory dance any of us have ever seen. With his nose and brow scrunched, he pushes his duck-lipped mouth outward and then waggles his knees in and out and his elbows up and down, a la the chicken dance. Even Eliza finally cracks into laughter. It's still not the all-out guffaws the rest of us can't control—even Jessie—but at least it's something.

In this moment, with all of us laughing, my shoulders finally relax for the first time in months. Jake was right: We did need this time away. I needed this time away. We used to simply exist in this mode of joyous laughter. Now, it's the exception to the rule. I want us to get back to that way of living our lives: no Guardian duties, no training sessions or library research, and no monsters (except those I gave birth to). Just us. I watch Jake laughing. He shakes his dark wavy hair out of his eyes. I see him tousle Sammy's curls and scrunch his nose up playfully. He looks at me, and though his laughter quiets a bit, his smile is still wide and brilliant. We're going to be okay. We *are* okay.

After minigolf, the kids are ready for carnival rides, so we decide to continue down the boardwalk, but I make everyone pause to apply another coating of sunblock. With our pasty skin we can't be too careful.

Eliza pulls me to the side while the kids rub in the white goop. "I'm going to head back to the house to check on Rory and Tabby."

A wrinkle forms between my brows. "Really? Are you sure? Do you want me to come with you?"

"No, don't! I mean, you guys need some time as a family. I'm totally fine to get back to my own house." The corners of her mouth momentarily flick up in a wanning smile.

I watch my normally confident-to-a-fault friend glance around nervously before I respond. "Are you sure? Eliza, what is going on? You know you can tell me anything."

Her smile looks painful, too still, like she's forcing herself to wear it. "I'm sure. I'm good. I just want to get back. You know how I worry. I just want to make sure she's napping." My kids' laughter draws our attention for a moment, but she still wants to make her exit, and her voice brings me back to us. "I'm good. You go. Have fun. Reconnect with your husband."

I look from her to my kids and back again. "If you're sure..."

She nods encouragingly. "I am. Go!"

I give her a strong hug, not for my sake but for hers, and she hugs me back in spite of not being big into touching people.

"Call me if you need me, okay?" I whisper in her ear. I feel her chin bobbing up and down on my shoulder when she nods. I take one more look at her before she leaves. Then I jog to catch up with my family, and after a few steps, I look over my shoulder and see Eliza walking toward the house.

Even though the kids have been acting incredibly patient, it just that: an act. Though quiet, they have finished applying their sunblock and are now pacing where I left them, while hopping and buzzing with the excitement that only a walk down the boardwalk can bring. Jake's eyes light up when we pass the arcade. I would love to lose myself in some Skee-Ball at some point this weekend, but we promised the kids they could go on the rides after minigolf, and we have two more full days. I'll have my chance, so I don't interrupt our small herd of children as they hightail it to the amusement park on the southern end of the boardwalk. I'm the grown-up after all. I am supposed to be more patient than my kids.

Finally, we arrive at the Guest Services booth. Knowing these cards are going to need to be reloaded a million times anyway, we start the kids off with enough credits to go on a handful of rides each.

"Phoebe! Come with me to the Pendolo!" Jessie loves thrill rides like this giant pendulum merry-go-round hybrid.

Because Phoebe still has some residual fear of heights from childhood, I'm not surprised to hear an emphatic, "Oh HELL no!"

Jake, who was not yet aware of just how colorful our eleven-year-old's extensive vocabulary has become, shakes his head disapprovingly before joining Jessie on her quest for all the fastest, highest, and spinniest things.

"Mom, can Phoebe, Sammy, and I go around just us?" Natalie's puppy-dog eyes look even brighter blue than normal in the fresh beach air.

I smile and turn to Phoebe. "I'll be tailing you. Do *not* try to lose me. You're in charge of your sister and brother."

"Of course! Thanks, Mom!" Phoebe wraps her arms around my waist briefly before leading her siblings toward the Wave Swinger just as the swings rise into the air and the tower they hang from swings them further and further outward. I'm okay with them running off together because I know how responsible Phoebe is when it comes to her little siblings.

I camp out on a bench. Tilting my head toward the crystal-clear blue sky, I pull in a deep breath of the salty air. I wish those scented candles that are supposed to evoke the essence of the beach could capture all the nuances of the air here. From where I sit between the beach and the rides, the salt from the sea mixes with musk from hot and sweaty bodies, and it is all infused with hints of the vanilla and sugar from the candy makers. I take a moment to breath it all in, trying to hang on to the memory. Then I take my phone out so I can capture some photos.

I am sure I hear Phoebe's, Natalie's, and Sammy's laughter from the swings high above me, so I stand at the metal fence surrounding the ride and video them. Just like I did when they were tiny. And just like when they were tiny, they are still laughing with their mouths split into grins so wide that I begin to wonder if one of them will swallow a bug. But I laugh along with them. Seeing my children so damn happy is renewing something inside me. When the ride starts to slow and the middle column shrinks, bringing the riders closer to the ground below, I pocket my phone so I can find out what they plan next.

The three of them run to me. Natalie brushes her disheveled hair away from her face, and all three kids have cheeks rosy with excitement, and probably some sun burn too.

"Did you guys have fun?" I run my fingers through Natalie's hair, trying to smooth it out before the tangles tighten into knots.

"That was awesome!" Sammy's eyes are as wild as his sister's locks.

I smile. Only my uber tame trio would get off from riding the swings with the same thrill in their eyes as someone who just got off the world's fastest roller coaster.

"What's next?" Natalie's normally calm, honey-sweet voice is rushed and scratchy as she looks to her big sister for guidance.

"Well, that depends." Phoebe relishes being the oldest when Jessie is off on her own and not able to undermine Phoebe's wisdom. "If you want to stick to slower, calmer rides, we can go to the kiddie ride section. Which I'm fine with. But I may be too tall for some of them. Or, if you want to try something a little more exciting, we could go to the Fun Slide or the Crazy Cabs over there."

After a brief deliberation, they run away from me and get in line at the Crazy Cabs. I watch them climb onto the platform and climb into two of the bright yellow cars. I walk back to my bench to watch them from where I can sit. You'd think after the training I've been doing for the last six months that I could stand around without my legs starting to cramp and my hips get tight, but you'd be wrong. Apparently standing requires a completely different set of muscles from the ones use in martial arts, because I am not feeling like I'm in shape at all right now.

As I sit, I take out a map guest services gave me and make a simple fan out of it. Jake and Jessie check in on me and then continue their circuit while I watch the other three make their own rounds of the rides they prefer. The sun has noticeably shifted its position in the sky before everyone meets up and decides to head over to the Fun Slide. I take my place by the metal fence once again, waiting for the perfect shots of my family coming down the slides together. While I wait, I watch Jake joking with Jessie, tickling Phoebe and Natalie, mussing Sam's hair. I smile to myself as I remember the time in college when our friend told him he's more maternal than most of the girls she knew. He has always been the best dad. Even Jessie looks to be enjoying herself. When we have disagreements or I get frustrated because of how often he has to travel, I always know that he is an amazing dad. I love this man with all my heart.

They pop up at the top of the slide waving to me. Jessie, Phoebe, and Sammy all get situated on their burlap sacks and push off in sync. I take a few live photos so I don't miss a moment. Next Jake carefully puts down Natalie's sack and helps her to sit on it. But before he is fully on his she pushes off, starting down with a laugh. I watch on my phone screen as Jake throws his head back in a deep guffaw and calls to her.

"You're such a cheater!" But he can barely catch his breath for his laughing before he pushes off as well.

While I wait for them to dust off and hand back in their sacks, I kill some time by looking through the pictures I took.

As I unlock my phone, I see the small moon icon. My phone is still in do-not-disturb mode from when I texted George, hours ago. My stomach drops. How could I be so irresponsible? I have too many people depending on me to allow myself to become unreachable, even if just for a few hours. My hands shake as I go through the taps necessary to reawaken my alerts.

I start breathing again when I check my text messages and see that I have none from Eliza or George. But I do have missed texts from Rory, which makes me furrow my brows and scratch my cheek. We don't talk much. I saved his number only for emergencies. I read the string of texts he sent over the last hour or so.

> Hey Miranda. It's Rory. Is Eliza still with you? I tried calling her to ask her a diaper question and she didn't answer.

> Hi again. If you're with Eliza, can you have her give me a call?

> I'm officially nervous. Her phone goes straight to vm. Do you have any idea where she is???

I tap over to my voicemail and see six messages from him. I don't bother listening to them before I call him back.

He answers immediately. "Miranda? Is she with you?" His spits his words out faster than a lotto machine. In the background, I can hear his footsteps echoing on the hardwood floors as he paces back and forth.

"No, Sweetie she's not. She left us to head back to the house at about two thirty. She didn't come home yet?" It is now five o'clock. She was only ten minutes away from the house when she left us. My heart feels like it's stuck between the bumper cars. Even Jessie hates the jostling on the bumper cars. I look up to find my family and everything is a blur. I can't see anything. All I hear is the roaring of the rides. No, that's my blood rushing to my head. The screams no longer sound fun. They are screams of terror. But I need to breathe. I need to be there for Rory.

Rory's voice shakes on the other end of the phone as he replies, "No. She's not here. I'm really freaking out, Miranda. Can you come back? I'm going to call the police, but with Tabby here..."

"Of course. Let me just talk to Jake, and then I'll be right there." I swallow hard.

My family is almost to me by the time I hang up, and Jake and I lock eyes. He must see the tears in my eyes or way I keep running my hands through my hair because he tells Jessie something and then leaves her with our other three kids as he comes running over to me. Not wanting to draw attention to us, I drop the volume of my voice. "Eliza's missing. I need to go back to the house to help Rory with Tabby so he can talk to the police."

The smile on Jake's face shuts off as if I just flicked the dimmer switch. "What do you mean Eliza's missing?"

I try to stay calm and business-like; otherwise, I'm going to collapse in a heap right here. "She never made it home when she left after minigolf.

I need to go, okay? Just tell the kids Rory and Eliza needed help with something at the house. Can you take them to dinner?"

He nods along with everything I ask. I stand on my tiptoes and give him a hug and a peck on the cheek. "Thank you."

"She'll be okay, Miranda." He breathes his words into my ear. "She'll be okay. How many women have an honest-to-God superhero for a best friend?"

A small, nervous laugh makes its way out of me, and I wipe my eyes quickly as I pull away from our hug. After one last scared smile, I turn and run back to the house. As I approach the walkway to the deck, I see red and blue blinking lights pull into the driveway on the opposite side of the house.

Chapter 16

George

"Sir, are you planning to buy anything?" The saleswoman's bored voice distracts me from my quest.

I open my eyes and glance at the clerk over the glass rim of the candle jar. "Yes, I'm sorry. I just have to find the perfect scent."

She rolls her eyes and turns, walking back to the cart of colorful glass containers she's putting away. I feel a little bad. It's not her fault I haven't been able to find anything close to the right combination of smells. After my second fragrance department search proved fruitless, I came to the candle store. At this point, I've smelled so many different perfumes and candles that someone could hand me a bag of dog shit, and I would detect notes of freesia and musk.

I have smelled almost every candle in this store. I have two shelves left to work across, and then I'm giving up. The store arranged the candles by color, and I'm moving into the neutral section, all beiges, browns, and creams. I love these shades, but Andrew would probably find them boring. He seems more a vibrant hue kind of guy. I like that about him.

While my mind is elsewhere, I take a deep inhale of a coffee scented candle, which reminds me of Miranda. I hope the kids are having a good time at the shore, and I hope she and Jake are able to find the peace they deserve. I may not love the guy, but she sure does. And she's the one whose happiness I am worried about. As her docent, I get reports from their counselor—nothing super detailed, but notes she thinks I should know about for our training. And Miranda and Jake know about the reports. Getting those reports was one of the conditions of the League providing a counselor. The only condition in fact. So, we had to go along with it.

I take a whiff of the next beige candle.

An ice-cold chill works its way up from my tailbone to the base of my skull, and I almost drop the candle. Jackpot. This is the one. I scan the label and murmur to myself, "Sand and sun."

"Did you say something, sir?" The bored employee is at my side immediately. "Do you need any help?"

"Uh, yeah. Actually, I do. How do I know what smells are in this?"

She points to the placard on the shelf and paraphrases what's printed. "Orange, lemon, lavender, and musk."

I'm impressed with my ability to have pegged so many of those in my guess. I'm sure she thinks I'm a total douchebag for my behavior today, but I also don't care. "I'll take a dozen."

She raises one eyebrow at me and questions, "A, dozen, sir?" But when I nod in confirmation, she starts to carry the large jars to the cash stand to ring me up. I look back at the shelf, grab one of the coffee scented candles for Miranda, and make my way to the register as well.

As I walk to the car with two bags of wax filled glass, I wonder why I felt the need to buy so many. One of each probably would have sufficed. I load the bags behind my seat so they don't crash around and break. When I settle into the driver's seat, I get a text from Miranda.

> Hey, we're in Point Pleasant. Our imp buddies came by. BE CAREFUL. Some mythical something or other is trying to seduce you.

The only clue I have is seeing red? Ok,
going on vacation now. TTYL

"Seeing red." Huh? So, I was right after all. The lady in red *is* trying to seduce me. I reach behind and grab one of the candles. When I close my eyes and take in a deep breath of the scent, I can picture her so clearly. The long, dark auburn hair. The red satin dress. Yes, Miranda, I am well aware. I can't help but wonder why she's trying to seduce me though. I don't seem like the best target. Also, if she gives off such a strong beach scent, and Miranda is currently at the beach, why is she all the way up here?

Got it. Sounds like the dream lady you
thought I was crazy to worry about. I'll
be careful. Found the smell. Orange, lemon,
lavender, and musk: a beach-scented candle.
Since you're the ones at the beach, you
should watch out also. Hate to have to rescue Jake's ass from another seductress.

Only, by the time I go to send that message, I see that her notifications are silenced. I don't want to ruin her vacation on a hunch, so I delete the text. I could call her twice to break through the do-not-disturb mode and make sure she knows to keep an eye out, but she always has at least one eye open for weird things. Especially since Las Vegas.

As for me, I should at least pretend to be responsible and attempt to research whatever is following me around. But the last few days have been long and tiring, what with me trying to track down this scent in any place I could think I might smell it. Before I tried this place I'd been to cosmetics stores, perfume counters, and soap stores. Now that I've solved this mystery, my brain needs a break before I'm ready to move onto the next.

Once I step foot in the library, my eyes drift to the plush armchairs by the window. I shake my head and stroll up and down the bookshelves, but all the titles sound the same in my head. Not even a specific topic calls to me. So, I collapse in the armchairs by the windows and try to collect myself.

I massage my temples, but the room, no, the whole world still slants sideways as I stare outside at the trees. The afternoon light grows brighter and brighter until it whites out all of my surroundings. I see the woman in red before me, only she's replaced the tight satin dress with a summery halter dress that flares out below her waist. She faces away from me, her dark auburn hair flowing down, around her shoulders. She is still so close I think I might be able touch her, if only I could move my arms.

I can't see anything beyond her but the blinding light. But I can smell. Chocolate and vanilla and an overbearing sweet smell so strong that my stomach turns. But something salty, earthy cuts into those scents. I hear children's laughter all around me. Then, ahead of the lady in red, Miranda and Eliza come into focus. They are deep in conversation. Well, Miranda is deep in it. Eliza looks like she is somewhere else entirely. They hug and Eliza turns toward me, toward the lady. She passes us, and I can hear the lady's breathing quicken. She's excited for something. She starts to sing, but I don't hear the lyrics so much as feel them reverberating through my soul.

Oh come to me,
Sweet angel, now
And let me take

Good care of you.
You have been strong
For far too long.
It's time to come rest your head.

I blink.

When my eyes open, I'm back in the library, sweating. I'm not the one she wants to seduce. Miranda is in trouble. Eliza is in danger.

My phone starts ringing. When I look at the screen, I see Miranda's name pop up on the caller ID. So maybe it's not too late.

I answer quickly, and before I can speak, I hear sobs.

My heart drop in my chest, and I ask frantically, "Hello? Who is this? Is Miranda okay? Hello?"

Between sobs and sniffs, I hear the only voice I want to hear right now: Miranda's. "George, it's me. I'm okay. It's Eliza. Eliza, is, missing."

I stand up and start to pace. Miranda is okay, so my blood can pump again and make my brain work. "Okay. It's okay. I think it's the lady in red, Miranda. She's not after me. I don't know why I am the one who has been seeing her, but it's not me she wants. It's Eliza she was after. She seduced her, with a song..." I stop in my tracks and practically scream into the phone. I can't believe the answer wasn't more apparent to me before this moment.

"Miranda, she's a siren!"

Chapter 17

MIRANDA

"**M**iranda, she's a siren!"

George's words echo in my head. My head that is empty, aside from the snot pouring from my face because my best friend is missing. No. Not missing. Kidnapped. By a motherfucking siren.

"George, you need to explain what the actual fuck you are talking about. I can't think straight right now. Who's a fucking siren?" I pace around the deck, staring through the panes of glass at Tabitha, securely snuggled between Natalia and Sam on the couch while Phoebe reads to them, but I don't really see them. All I can think about is what's taking place on the other side of the house, out of sight of all the kids. Rory is talking to the police, again. And he must be a mess. Thank goodness Jake was home when they came back. He insisted on going outside to be with Rory through whatever news the officers have to report.

George's voice cuts through my brain fog. "The lady in red. The one in my dream. I don't know why I saw her at the restaurant the other night or why I'm dreaming about her, but I just had another vision or whatever they are. She was watching you on the boardwalk with Eliza. She saw you hug, and then Eliza walked one way and you walked the other, and the lady started to sing."

I think back over the day. "We did hug on the boardwalk before she headed back to the house a few hours ago. That was the last any of us saw her before she went missing. But I didn't notice anyone in red near us. I mean, fuck. I don't know. This place is fucking packed this weekend. Maybe there was, and I didn't notice? I didn't hear anyone singing though. But who the fuck knows? It's so loud here!"

"Okay, I don't have much to tell you right now. I'm going to hang up so I can look through the library for information."

"I'll call you if I get anything. You just stay with your family and keep everyone else safe." He takes a breath, and when he speaks again, his voice is slower and softer, with less urgency and more care. "I hate that I'm not there to help you through all this."

I nod, not that he can see me. "Yeah, but if you were, neither of us would be able to search through your handy dandy books. Maybe you should think about digitizing your collection. Then it could be portable, ya know?"

After a beat of silence, George says, "Yes, if only there were some virtual well of knowledge we could have at the tips of our fingers whenever we need. Maybe we could name it the internet."

I roll my eyes. "Okay, my best friend is missing. Shut the fuck up."

"Just trying to lighten the mood, boss."

"Don't lighten the mood, docent. Do your fucking job." But right before I hang up, I realize I should have said more to Eliza before she walked away from me on the boardwalk, so I blurt into the phone, "I love you and thank you and please stay safe yourself."

I stare through the windows into the living room again, but this time I'm able to appreciate the scene. The sight of all my big kids with Eliza's tiny one causes a fresh batch of sobs to rack through me, bringing me to my knees. I can't comprehend the idea of Tabby not having her mother. Eliza is such a good mom. She is fiercely protective of that little ball of pudge and that little girl deserves to have someone who would do anything for her. My heart pounds away in my chest and it gets harder to pull air into my lungs. I grab for my wrist but I don't have my bracelet. Shit. What was it again? Five things I can see...this little angel's life crumbling around her, myself and my own children trying to fill in the holes, Rory dissolving into a shell of who he is with Eliza... no, this isn't right.

Okay, let's try this again. In, two, three, four, five, six, seven. As I hold for four counts my heart is struggling to keep its tempo against my attempts to slow the racing beat. But after the complete breath cycle it loses the fight and I feel the beats space out.

Then a voice pops into my head, clearer than any thought: This is my fault. I've heard this voice before. I try to turn it off, but the voice is too engrained in me. For years, for what feels like my entire life, it has popped into my head whenever I feel I am failing, whenever I am not perfect. Because not being perfect was failing when I was growing up. I pick up my phone and, with shaking hands, I text Jake.

`I need to tell Rory about me.`

Because he's with Rory at this very moment, Jake knows better than I do what state the man is in.

`How is that going to help? This isn't about you...Wait, is it?`

I want to throw up as I reply to him, my husband who knows first-hand the dangers that come with being associated with the Guardian.

    I think it is. I just talked to George. He
    thinks a siren seduced Eliza.

Almost immediately he responds.

    Why does he think that?

I hesitate to write back, but I know I need to.

    Well, the imps I caught outside of the
    diner may have stopped by this morning… I
    got some intel that someone was trying to
    seduce George, so I sent that info on to
    him and put it out of my head so it wouldn't
    ruin our vacation.

I can almost hear him shaking his head from here, but his reply makes
my heart stop.

    I appreciate that. But you and I are a team
    too. I need you to tell me these things.

I sigh because, he's right. I nod to myself as I reply.

    I will from now on. I promise. I love you.

Three dots pulse for long enough that I think something big is coming.

I love you too. Let's tell Rory when he's
done with the police. Can you summon your
little red friends back here? Maybe we can
get more info from them.

I exhale quickly in relief.

Deal… I'll text George and see if he knows
how I can do that.

I am finding my text chain with George when Jake's reply comes
through.

See if he can get his ass over here too.
I want you to have everything you need to
get Eliza back.

My skin is clammy from the salty night air, and now that the sun has
gone down and I'm standing still instead of pacing, a chill blows through
me, making me feel hollow inside. I send a quick text to George.

Any idea how I can get my imp friends to
come back here?

When I don't see any signs of a response, I brace myself to go back inside the house. Eliza's house. So that I can tell my best friend's distraught
husband that I am likely the reason the mother of his young daughter is
missing. But also, so I can tell him that I am going to get her back.

The house is cooler than the night air was against my skin, and I shiver as I slide the glass door closed behind me. Since Rory is still with the police, I skirt around the room and the kids playing to go upstairs and find a sweater. I finally locate the lone one I brought and tug the soft-brushed hacci mock turtleneck down past my face when Jake walks in.

His hair is disheveled, I imagine him running his hands through it while standing, useless, while Rory talked to the police. Frowning, he stops in his tracks and crosses his arms over his chest as if to shield himself. Then he releases a long exhale, and his shoulders sag.

We look at each other for long enough that I think the silence will crush me if I don't break it. "How is he?"

Jake's shoulders curl in with exhaustion. "He's completely beside himself. The police have nothing, no new information, no leads. He's so scared for Eliza, and for Tabby and him if she..." He looks away from me.

"Jake, I'm going to get her back."

His eyes meet mine as he chews the inside of his cheek. I know he doesn't want me to see that he has his doubts, but I do see it.

"I know it's still hard for you to believe, but this is the kind of bullshit that I was born to do. I rescued your ass, didn't I?" I try to joke but there is no heart behind it.

Not even the hint of a smile. He whispers, "You had George with you then."

Ouch. I flinch as his word stab me in the heart. "George didn't climb that mountain with me. George didn't fight a fucking incubus to the death. George didn't snap you out of your goddess orgy trance so you would come home. George is not the Guardian, Jake. I am."

"I wish it were him," he admits.

Even though he's glued his eyes to his shoes, I stare at him for a long moment before I am able to collect myself enough to speak again. This has all been about his fear. All of the attitude toward George, not wanting to train with me, all the anger he's been showing me, it's all been because he's so afraid to lose me. He was kidnapped by muses, I was fucked by an incubus, we have a kitsune family living in our backyard, and now my best friend is missing, presumably with a siren. Literally anything could disrupt our lives forever at any time, and he knows it. But none of that matters right now. When I finally speak, I first take a deep breath so I don't lose control. "Please, trust that I can do this."

After what feels like an eternity, he nods. "So, how do you want to tell Rory?"

I sink to the edge of the bed, my knee bobbing up and down so fast that the mattress could compete with some coin-operated ones. "I, I'll think of something. Can you bring him up here? Away from the kids?"

He nods. "Yeah, I'll go get him. I love you." He grabs my hand and looks me in the eyes.

"I love you, too." I reply.

I've barely had the chance to pace the room, much less figure out what I'm going to say, when they come back. Jake closes the door behind him, but leaves it open an inch.

When I look from the gap to him, he says, "So we can keep an ear out for the kids."

I nod my head in agreement, even though I can't stomach the idea of something happening to one of them. No wonder Jake's been on edge since finding out about me. "Good call." I close my eyes, regroup my thoughts with a head shake, and turn to Rory. "Rory, you need to know something. It's about me, but, it, it relates to Eliza. I think...I'm pretty sure."

Rory's red-rimmed eyes look into mine. His brow furrows but just barely. He's too tired to give me more than that. "What are you talking about, Miranda?"

My entire body turns tense, and I intertwine my fingers before me, my subconscious attempt at a shield. "I think you should probably sit down."

He sits at the edge of the bed, a heap of meat and anguish. I want to look at him when I tell him this. That had been my plan. But seeing him there, so lost, my heart starts to race, and beads of sweat break out on my brow. My limbs are restless. I have to struggle to keep myself here because my legs want to run the rest of me as far away as they can. I clench my fists so tightly, needing to hit something, that even my bitten-to-the-quick nails dig little crescent moons into my palms.

"Okay, so, there's something about me you need to know." As I speak, I feel Jake move close behind me, feel his breath on my shoulder. I finally feel like he is supporting me, like we're on the same team. Now I know I can do anything.

But before I continue, Rory speaks. "I know you're some kind of super-hero, Miranda. Eliza doesn't keep secrets from me. I know you protect the world from mythical creatures and goddesses and shit." His voice is dull, monotone, like he's reading off movie times or the weather report. He doesn't make eye contact with me, just stares ahead.

I stop look to Jake, whose eyebrows have shot upward. Then I look back to Rory, my jaw slack, my eyes squinted. "You...know?"

"Yup. You can't be that surprised. She had to tell me when she went to watch the kids so you could go to Vegas to save him from that pop band of muses that had kidnapped him and replaced him with the sex demon guy."

"I'm sorry, WHAT?" The door slams open, revealing Jessie with her mouth agape and eyes bugging out of her head. "What happened in

Vegas? And don't you dare say anything about it staying in Vegas!" She withers me with the stare she throws my way.

I drop my finger and close my mouth after Jessie called out for the crack I was about to make. "Okay, here's the thing. I will explain it all to you. I promise."

She crosses her arms and wags her head around, ever the Jersey girl. "Oh, okay. So glad you're willing to tell me the truth *now*, after I overheard it all and left you no choice."

I draw in a deep breath and literally bite my tongue before I level her with my own glare. I use my fingers to enumerate my points in my own Jersey girl way. "First of all, there is a difference between overhearing and eavesdropping. Second, I know you don't want to hear this, but this is not the time for this conversation. Eliza has been seduced by a siren, and we need to get her back before it's too late."

Rory seems to wake up at these words. He stands and takes a step toward me, his shoulders hunched forward. "I'm sorry, what? My wife was *seduced* by a siren? How? How do you know? And how do you know it's not too late already?"

I widen my stance, and my nostrils flare as I brace myself for impact. "I don't know that it's not too late."

Rory's shoulders straighten, making him five inches taller than me. We stare at each other while Jessie's and Jake's eyes ping pong between us. I take in his dilated pupils, the sweat on his forehead, the blush in his cheeks. In my periphery, I see Jake's body tense as he gets ready to defend me incase Rory attacks. At the same time, my own jaw clenches, and although I'm trying to stand tall, it is taking everything in me not to curl into the fetal position right at Rory's feet.

Part of me wants him to hit me, the part that doesn't care how much it would hurt, because it will help dissolve some of this guilt. Because in my mind, I hear that voice I have been trying to shut out for years, the one telling me I deserve it. Telling me everything is always my fault. That everyone's pain is my fault. And I know he's right, this time at least. A siren captured my best friend because of me, and I don't know anything about how to help her. I don't know where she is. I don't know how to get her back.

But I also know this voice doesn't have the same power over me that it used to. What I do know is that I will figure this out. I have to, and fast.

Chapter 18

JAKE

The whole room seems frozen in time. Rory, standing over a foot taller than Miranda, could probably crush her in a second if he wanted to, or so it would appear. I naturally fear for Miranda, but I should be more worried about Rory if they were to fight. Rory hasn't sparred with Miranda at the dojo. He hasn't seen how quickly she can dodge a punch and return with a counterattack that leaves a bruise for weeks. I rub my side from the memory of one such blow.

Despite Rory's puffed out chest, Miranda holds her ground. She's stands as tall and strong as she can. But I know her too well to believe what I see at first glance. When I really look at her, I see her lips pressed together so tightly that they are tucked in on themselves, and the corners of her mouth are pulled down and quiver almost imperceptibly. I know that mouth. She is trying not to crack into a puddle of a thousand tears. Her eyes get glossier, and if the tears filling them leak out, she may never stop crying, or at least not in any sort of time to save Eliza.

I open my mouth, not sure what I'm about to say, but Jessie is the one to break the silence. "Um, this is stupid."

Fuck. I can't believe Jessie decided to eavesdrop on this of all conversations. I had momentarily pushed it from my mind to focus on the tableau of a confrontation in front of me, but now the truth hits me: One of our kids knows. Fuck.

"Mom, Uncle Rory, I need to ask: What the fuck is wrong with you guys?" Her language surprises Rory enough that he breaks his stare to look at her. Rory's face hasn't changed though. His brow, red now like the rest of his face, still has tiny beads of sweat. His nostrils are still flared. At least his eyes soften a bit when they light on Jessie.

I, on the other hand, am not so pleased with the interruption, afterall.

"Excuse me, young lady?" I say to my oldest child.

Jessie rolls her eyes. "Oh, get over it, Dad. That was nothing next to the vocabulary Mom uses! Also, in this moment, with Aunt Eliza who-knows-where with a siren, is this what you want to be focusing on?"

Miranda looks down and away from Jessie. Her entire face relaxes, and I worry she's going to break. She closes her eyes and bites on her lips. Then she looks at Rory again, but without any façade of strength. "Rory, we need to figure out how to get her back. You can be mad at me later."

"Did you call George?" I'm still not sure why I was the one to suggest that. My wife needs backup, and I don't care who that is, so long as they can kick ass. I sigh and close my eyes for a moment. Damnit, I don't think I can stop training. I may hate everything about this entire Guardian thing, but we need that kid. We need what he has to give Miranda. And if we can't go longer than six months without a new crisis popping up, then I need to stop hiding behind my emotions and avoiding him. I cannot let my wife and kids down again. "Is he on his way here?"

"How is your personal trainer going to help?" Jessie looks between us with her arms out, waiting for an explanation like she's the parent. Miranda raises one eyebrow and bunches her mouth to the side. Jessie closes her eyes and runs her fingers through her hair, grabbing it like she needs to pull it out or she'll lose her mind. "Oh for fuck's sake! He's a part of this too? Of fucking course!"

"Hey, watch your language, young lady!" I hate hearing my kids curse, and I have heard it a lot more than I want to today.

She turns on me, nostrils flaring, finger pointed at me, almost jabbing me in the chest. "*You* don't get to tell me that. *You* didn't bother to tell me that you had been kidnapped." Then she takes a deep breath, probably remembering why we're all here in the first place. Shakily, she lowers the hand she's still pointing at me and says with way too cheery a demeanor, "Hey, let's call George!" Then she stomps to the bed and collapses on the edge, burying her head in her hands and rubbing her temples.

I turn to Miranda who is maneuvering her phone to George's number. I want to remind her how much faster it would be to use voice commands, but at least I know this isn't the time for me to bring up that marital pet peeve.

"Hey George. Have you learned anything about the siren?" Miranda digs through her huge weekender bag until she finds a notebook and pen. Then she sits on the edge of the bed and rests her notes on the nightstand so she can lean on it as she writes.

Sitting on the opposite corner of the bed, Jessie places her elbows on her knees and presses her mouth into her steepled fingers. She stares ahead, forcing herself to keep taking deep breaths while trying to piece together the last few months with the information she gleaned from the last few minutes.

As much as I would prefer to hover over Miranda's shoulder and read her notes, I give her space to do her thing and sit next to Jessie, rubbing her back and letting her know I'm there for her without saying a word. Her eyes close, and a tear rolls down her cheek. Her body start to pulse with choked sobs. She is so overwhelmed right now, but like the good rule follower she's always been, she won't dare to take too much of our attention. Not right now. Not when Eliza needs everything we have to give.

I wrap my arm around her shoulders. Leaning in, I whisper, "We will all get through this. We will get her back. Your mom is amazing at this. She defeated a bunch of goddesses when she was brand new at this. You'll see."

The look she shoots me when she whips her head around takes my breath away. Her eyes are ice cold, her jaw set like stone. None of this amuses her. She may be too old to believe in the fairytale monsters Miranda has had to fight in real life these last few months, but she's still too young to be able to fully process the truth that they actually exist and her mom has to fight them. When I think her glare is thawing, I try again. "I promise we will have a proper discussion about all of this. I can only imagine what is going through your head right now."

The edges of her begin to soften. "I'm sure it's not as bad as being kidnapped by muses." She gives me a brief, completely insincere smile. The smile you give a stranger you pass in the grocery store, the one you want to be kind to just because you are walking down a particular aisle at the same time.

"Well, I wasn't just kidnapped. I was under, let's just call it some kind of goddess magic when I was kidnapped, so I wasn't even really thinking about what was going on. It wasn't until your mom—" Her raised eyebrow tells me to shut up. "You know what, not important right now. But I promise when we are through this, we will all sit down, you, Mom, and me—"

"Don't forget Phoebe, Natalie, and Sam."

I stare at her with my mouth hanging open. "Wait, what? We can't tell your sisters and brother about this."

She shrugs. "Well, I can't keep it from them. So, one of us will have to tell them."

I stare at her in silence, trying to decide an appropriate way to tell my eldest child absofuckinglutely not when I hear Miranda.

"Okay, George. Thank you. Call me if you learn anything else. Thanks."

We all turn to her expectantly as she hangs up. There's a moment of silence as she looks at each of us in turn. A moment of silence that I am beginning to think will kill us all until Rory busts through it.

"So? Anything?"

Miranda shakes her head and then nods. "Yes and no. George doesn't know how I can summon the imps, but he did find info about sirens. They usually live on rocky islands in the sea or rocky alcoves along the shore, but, really, they could be anywhere touching the water. They likely called to her with a song that promised her what her heart desires most. So, I don't know if they made her think they had Rory or Tabby or what they said."

"Okay. So how do we find her?" I ask, glad we're making progress.

"I think I need to bring someone with me as bait." She looks between all three of us as we give her blank stares. I don't feel like being used by a mythical being again, but I instinctively move to stand between Miranda and Jessie, until my wife looks down at her feet and says, "Rory. It has to be Rory."

I begin to breathe again, but when I look at Rory, his eyes are as big as saucers, and his mouth looks like he's trying to catch flies. Maybe airplanes would be more accurate for the size of the opening.

His bottom jaw half closes and drops back down a few times before he finally begins to annunciate words and refer to himself in the third person. "Wh-why does it have to be Rory?"

Miranda's shoulders hunch with the weight of having to explain it all, but she looks Rory in the eye and speaks with measured patience. "You're the one who is missing what you desire most. Also, I'll probably need you to help get Eliza out of whatever the fuck spell they have her under."

Rory nods. "I mean, of course, I will do anything to get her back. I'm just so nervous about Tabitha. Her mom is already missing. What if something happens to me?"

Jessie puts her hand on his forearm. "Nothing will happen to you. You'll be with my mom. We've got Tabby, Uncle Rory. Please, go get Aunt Eliza back."

Rory looks into Jessie's eyes and tears fill his. He knows Eliza was our kids' aunt long before she was his wife. He nods.

I clear my throat to keep from crying myself and ask the question I assume is on everyone's mind. "So, what's the plan?" But three faces snap to me in surprise, so I guess I was wrong. "Are you just going wander around, hoping Rory gets spelled?"

Miranda shrugs. "Yeah, basically."

I give a nervous laugh. I run my hands through my hair, imagining Miranda and Rory, walking up and down the boardwalk, just waiting for this siren to attack. The idea nauseates me, but we don't have many options here. "Okay, and what then?"

She looks me straight in the eye and, with no mirth, replies, "I follow him, and hope I'm not too late." The room is beyond silent. She looks down with a hint of shame and tries to backtrack on what she just implied. "For whatever reason, this siren wants me. She seduced Eliza to get my attention, to draw me in. I have to believe she's keeping her alive, at least until I get there."

I look at my wife, disbelieving the question I'm about to ask her. "How do you kill her?"

Miranda shakes her head. "I don't know. George is still on that." She looks at the cell phone in her hand. "We have a good plan, right? You think I'll have a signal underwater?"

I can't tell if she's serious, but if it's a joke, her timing has never been worse. I'm too worried about her to find anything funny right now. "Well, does the plan depend on you having a signal underwater?"

"George said he's going to call you on his way down to help once he gets more information." She finally looks away from her phone and back to me. "I guess, try to call me when you know more?"

I move to her so we are a breath apart. I wrap my fingers around her wrist, where she would wear the bracelet from Maria if she had thought to bring it on our trip. "Remember to breathe. You've got this. You're my wife and you're a motherfucking superhero."

She collapses against me as we embrace. I kiss the top of her head.

We all walk downstairs to the living room where the kids are still snuggled on the sofa reading to Tabby, who is starting to doze off since it is passed her bedtime. Rory picks her up and gives her the kind of big bear hug only a dad can give.

Miranda wraps her arms around Jessie who stands stubbornly still, until her shoulders round and she wraps her hands around Miranda's waist. When they separate, she tries to hide the fact she has a tear running down her cheek.

Miranda tells the other kids, "Uncle Rory and I are going to go take a walk to see if we can find Aunt Eliza."

"Oh, okay." Phoebe shrugs, looking at her feet with red-rimmed eyes.

"Hey," Miranda hugs Phoebe tightly, "Sweet dreams, sleep tight, don't let the bed bugs bite." She kisses the top of her head and looks up. I'm sure she's praying.

She hugs, kisses, and says prayers over Natalie and Sammy, then tells our children collectively, "We'll be back before you know. Listen to Daddy while I'm gone, please."

They all nod slowly. They are worried for their mom. I silently thank God that they don't know how worried they should be.

I walk Miranda and Rory to the door. Before they leave Miranda and I hug. Then she looks into my eyes and I kiss her. I need her to know now, before she leaves this house, how much I love her, how much I will always love her. The kids don't even groan, which is kind of scary.

When the kiss is over, I hold her a few more moments and whisper, "Be safe. Come home to us." We lock eyes as we separate.

Rory hands Tabby off to me and wipes his eyes as he nods to Miranda. Jessie and I stand close together, watching them through the large windows as they turn left to go up the boardwalk, away from the ever-busy tourist attractions, toward the more secluded stretches of beach.

Jessie shakes her head to clear the cobwebs and figure out what she needs to do next. She takes Tabby from me. "Let's get you to bed, little girl. It is way past your bedtime!"

Tabby giggles. She's past the stage of only cooing. She is growing so fast, and my heart aches a bit for the days long gone when our kids were that tiny. Looking out at the ocean beyond the glass, I hope Miranda can bring Eliza back. I have to have faith that she can.

Chapter 19

MIRANDA

The cool breeze blows right through my sweater and chills me as if my arms are bare when Rory slowly slides the glass door closed, separating us from our collective children. Thankfully, the temperature is not top-of-a-snowy mountain-outside-of-Vegas-level cold, but I still have goose bumps. At least I wore a sweater this time. Even so, my teeth chatter involuntarily. We walk in silence until we reach the end of the footbridge that spans from the deck to the boardwalk. Then we stop with a mutual understanding that we have no idea where to go now.

"Which way?" Rory's voice is gravelly and quiet. He has to force his words to reach my ears.

I look to the right, past Rory, to the touristy part of the boardwalk, the spot where I last saw Eliza. It's so close. And so busy. It's busy with people enjoying their vacations, their lives, unaware of the dangers lurking so close, maybe even among them. They'll stay out here, like we used to do, into the late hours of night or even early morning, just living a life I no longer have the luxury of living.

I wonder if the intoxicated sounds emanating from the boardwalk irritate sirens. I don't know a hell of a lot about their kind, but I know they prefer seclusion. I wonder if one would have dared to try to captivate someone in such a populated area?

I look left. Could Eliza have decided to not go straight home? I scrunch my eyes shut and try to imagine the scene. She was so dazed, so overtired. Could she have walked right past her own family's house, the one she's spent every summer at since she was six, without even realizing it?

I open my eyes and look at Rory. "I think it has to be left. Something is telling me, even if she caught Eliza's attention over there," I jut my chin toward the weather-worn planks lit up by so many lights that one would think it's day and then twist my neck to face the darker stretch on our left, where the planks fade into oblivion with only small patches of light every few feet to guide the way, "she had to have led her somewhere down this way."

A breeze from the water hits us, a breeze that's somehow warmer than the night air and smells of pineapple, as if some benevolent sea sprite is confirming my gut instinct. Or maybe it's a coincidence, but it's getting harder for me to believe in those.

I look at Rory. His bottom lip sticks out from the intense frown his face is stuck in, but his blue eyes meet mine as he nods. "You're the boss." His hands are stuffed into the pockets of his hoodie. I take a moment to commend his foresight in wearing it (and on his first time out as a superhero), but then push that thought out of my mind. I need to focus.

We continue in silence, both because we have literally nothing to say to each other, and we need to listen for the siren singing. I hope the distant sounds of beeps and boings from arcade games, of laughter and music, or loved ones calling to each other, aren't so loud that they will drown out what we need to hear. But the waves lapping gently against the shore encourage us along, and the loud sounds of happiness recede into the background.

I debate asking Rory for his sweatshirt since the wind is blowing right threw my sweater, when he stops in his tracks. I stop half a step ahead of him and look back at him, but his face is frozen and empty, like when they test one of the rides my kids went on earlier with no riders in it. His eyes are still angled downward, at the ground, to keep his footing in the poor light. But they are now wide open, so too much of the whites show around his irises. His bottom lip is no longer jutting out because his whole being has gone rigid. Even his chest and shoulders are still, making me wonder if he's breathing at all.

My breath, on the other hand, comes in short bursts. I force myself to slow down, to do the Nogare breathing George taught me but without perceptibly moving my body. I don't want to disturb whatever is happening right now. Even with my super hearing, I can't make out any siren call over the blood rushing in my ears and the pounding thump of my heart as if I am running a city marathon, not taking a leisurely paced walk down a quiet boardwalk.

A curtain of cloudy gel seems to cover his eyes. The general effect reminds me of when the trolls spelled George. Rory's neck uncurls, and his gaze levels ahead of him. Then he begins walking forward without hesitation. I follow.

At the next access point to the beach, he turns right, casually contorting his six-foot-three body to bend under the chain hanging across the gap in the railing due to the hour. I follow, impressed at my relative grace and the fact that I didn't get any of my hair caught in the chain that's long rusted from exposure to the sea air.

The pat on my back, however, was premature as I stumble to keep up with Rory's confident strides down the sandy slope toward the beach. I kick off the tennis shoes I mistakenly expected to be practical for this adventure. I don't bother taking the time to pick them up. If they're gone when we come back here, oh well. Shoes can be replaced. Best friends, not so much.

As our feet kick up sand, it occurs to me that Rory shows no signs of slowing down. He marches toward the water's edge. Thankfully, before he marches himself to a watery death, he hangs a sharp left and continues his journey mere feet from where the white-tipped waves kiss the smooth, dark sand that glitters wet in the moonlight.

My heart kicked up another notch when I thought I was going to lose him too. Visions of Eliza drowning herself while on a hypnotized quest make my stomach twist into a hard knot.

This is all your fault.

My inner voice hisses at me. Only it isn't my voice at all. In the back of my mind a movie is playing out. No, not a movie, a memory... My father drunk, stumbling around a campsite, cursing at my mother and me.

This is all your fault.

It must have been all my fault if he said so, but what was *it*?

A crisp voice snaps me back to the beach, to this night, to this moment. "Hey you, Guardian!" I hear to my right.

My right. Where the waves are. Where the sea is. Where this voice calls to me in a way that I suspect is different than the one that is illusively beckoning to Rory.

I hesitate, but the risk of losing Rory in this straight stretch of sand is low. So, I chance a look at the ocean beside me as I continue following in his footsteps.

Out a bit, farther than I would feel comfortable trying to swim if I ever *wanted* to swim in the ocean, which I really don't, I see a head bobbing and arms waving to get my attention. I stop, and my shoulders collapse at the sight.

Oh, you have got to be kidding me. Do I have to save someone else now?

I hear a soft silky giggle, and she stops waiving her arms. I see her black hair in an intricate up-do. "No, Guardian, you do not need to save me."

While that's good to know, at the word *Guardian*, my spine tingles and straightens, putting me on high alert.

What the fuck? I'm not talking out loud, am I?

I continue behind Rory, having fallen only a few feet further behind him.

"That is correct, Guardian, you are not talking out loud. I am Mazu. I am protector of the humans on the sea." She jumps up and dives down into the water, looking like a whale breaching, and shows me her fin. Tail? Fin. Fin tail. Tail fin? Whatever I should call it.

Are you a mermaid?

"That is one word for my kind, Guardian. We have been called mermaids. We have been called sirens. We have been imagined in many forms. And, as all things humans have created in their minds, most of those forms have existed in your world, at one time or another."

I start to get a headache. Trying to follow this conversation and Rory may make my brain eat itself.

Mermaids and sirens are the same things? Are mermaids the good ones?

"Are all humans good?"

I chortle. *Oh hell no. But we're not all bad. I'd even say any one human is neither all good nor all bad.*

"And that is where we overlap. Mermaids are sirens; sirens are mermaids. But we are neither good nor bad. Though some of us are more good, and some of us are much, much more bad."

I don't understand how I can hear her so clearly when she is so far out at sea. She doesn't sound like she's yelling. But I also am not hearing her in my head. I remember what that feels like, unfortunately, from back when I first found out about all this Guardian shit.

"The waves are carrying my voice to you. And as for how I can hear your thoughts, well, humans give off subtle sound waves with your minds that no other human can pick up on. All mermaids are more sensitive to these sounds, but I must admit, yours are...less subtle than most."

Gee, thanks. What do you want m—

"We will talk again. Right now, I have to swim ahead to catch your friend."

What do you mean catch my friend?

But she is already gone. She disappeared under the water as soon as she said "friend." And I soon see why.

The distance between Rory and me has grown while I'd been mentally conversing with my new mermaid friend. (At least I think she's a friend. Only time will tell for sure.) I've been stumbling in the sand while he's been as sure-footed as if he's walking on a paved road.

Even though he is farther from me than I would like, I can still see when he abruptly stops moving forward and hangs a right. Right into the ocean.

Somehow, his feet aren't sinking in the wet sand. Now I am the one frozen where I stand. I can't tear my eyes away. I'm so shocked at what is playing out before me that it takes me a few seconds for it to all register. I swallow hard, dragging my feet through the sand. It may as well be cement for how cooperative my limbs are being. Not because I've been spelled, but because I am using all my energy to will time to reverse itself.

As the waves reach Rory's calves, I realize that he is walking into the sea. I open my mouth to push sounds out. At first, they are just a whimper of denial, but then a scream of protest.

"Rory!" I shout his name as my limbs finally cooperate, but not even my Guardian speed is fast enough for me to reach him, to pull him back. I wave my arms in a great circle over my head and around me, as if making a spectacle of myself from fifty feet away will miraculously break the spell he's under.

Within seconds, he crashes deeper into the waves as I run and ponder how I can ever explain to little Tabby that I was responsible for both of her parents' deaths. Time seems to slow down as the waves reach his thighs. Once again, the air is cold, and the goosebumps on my arms return. The wet sand fights to hold onto me, to hold me back. I blink, and the water hits his belt buckle. The waves lapping at the shoreline beside me are the only sound I hear. By the time the water reaches his shoulders, my throat burns from screaming his name over and over. I choke on my snot and tears, watching his chin disappear into the dark water.

In my mind something snaps and life is back at full speed, as a black-haired head with a jade green tail breaches the water, grabs Rory, and disappears again beneath the glassine surface.

Now that time is moving again, I hear my heart pounding loudly in my ears. My lungs burn from the suffocating, rapid breaths that are all I can force into them.

Please. Please, let Mazu be a friend.

Chapter 20

GEORGE

I press the pads of my fingers against my closed eyelids, rubbing along the tops of my cheek bones and out to my temples where I heavily trace small circles, willing my mind to relax.

I wish this library had more information on sirens. I've leafed through seventeen books, including *The Odyssey*, and cannot find any records, myths, or guesses on how to defeat them.

My phone chimes and I grab it frantically. I just hung up with Miranda and suspect she thought of more questions, but I'm wrong. It's Andrew.

```
Hey there. Just got to the bar. Should I
order you a drink?
```

Shit. Is it eight already? Damnit, it is. I need to shit or get off the pot, so to speak. I need to make a choice about Andrew right now. I stare at the phone, my leg is bouncing rapidly. I let out a breath so forcefully my lips puff out. I shake my head as I bite my lip and start typing.

```
Please don't hate me… I can't meet you
tonight. I know I seem shady. I do want to
see you. I need to take care of a friend
```

who is in trouble. I promise to explain
everything when I can.

I get up and pace so I don't stare at the phone while I wait for a response I am dreading. I want to see him again. I do want another chance. I want to kiss him again; his lips are so distractingly perfect. I want to tell him everything and have him know all of me and, hopefully, still want to be with me.

The urge to pace the room is strong, but giving in to that urge will only give the panic credence. Instead, I force my head high so my spine aligns straight. My hands form a circle around my belly button, and I call out, "Mokuso!" I call it out even though I am alone in this room, this house. I call it out even though I'm not in the dojo. I call it out because that is how the meditation begins, and I need to do something right.

Although I sometimes use the meditative breathing exercise to begin and end training sessions, I do it now to calm my pounding heart and clear my frantic mind. I finish the three deep exhales. With my next inhalation, I immediately recognize the smell. Musky and floral, the scent of the candle. The lady in red. The siren.

"My name, docent, is Beatrice." Her voice is deep and velvety. But it's not in my mind. It's in my ears, in the room with me.

I open my eyes slowly. She sits across from me in the library, perfectly straight, perfectly still. Only a table separates us. She intertwines her fingers, resting her hands on the tabletop. Her long, dark auburn hair cascades around her shoulders. She slightly purses her deep burgundy lips. She's trying to entice me with their lusciousness. Contrary to my expectations, it's working. I can't look away.

The moment she knows she has me, the corner of her mouth quirks up, giving a serpentine quality to her appearance. When her lips part, the tip of her tongue darts out to wet them. My dry mouth longs to partake in that moisture.

She leans forward. Her breasts press into her hands, pushing them so that a bit of cleavage appears in the open space where her crisp, dark-red blouse is unbuttoned lower than probably necessary. I don't know for sure though. I've never paid much attention to how women dress.

But my eyes are drawn to that line in her otherwise smooth and milky skin, and it is my turn to lick my lips. A deep, breathy laugh tells me she noticed this action also.

"It's okay, docent. No human is impervious to my seductions. Well, none but the one I really want…" Either she trails off, or my attention to her words does.

"Miranda." It's not a question. I know who she wants. But I still can't tear my eyes away from that crease beneath the material. I start to loathe that material.

"Yes. Miranda. Do you have any idea what I could promise her to get her to pay me a visit?"

My brow furrows at the question, and I look into her face. "You already have Eliza, don't you? So you already know. It's her people. Safe. That's what Miranda cares about most."

Her mouth widens into a bright smile. Her teeth are brilliant white, and her canines look too pointy. She cocks one eyebrow. "You've been very good, docent. Is there anything I can give to you in return?"

My jaw drops. I stammer. "I, I, um." I don't know what to say. I know what I want, but I don't know how to tell her.

She throws her head back with a laugh, and I trace the skin of her throat with my gaze. When she looks at me, her eyes are dark blue, the sea at night. "You'll have to come to visit me at my home to get what you want, docent. I'd love to add you to my ever-growing collection." Again, that wicked, crooked smile.

My phone begins to buzz in my pocket before I can ask a collection of what. I pull out my phone and see Benjamin's name pop up on the caller ID. I don't have time to wonder why my predecessor is calling because Beatrice is fading away, her hand up and giving me a cute little finger wave. A cheery smile on her flawless face.

I give myself a shake and answer the phone. "Benjamin? What can I do for you?"

A panicked voice answers. "Oh, George! Thank the gods you answered! Is Miranda okay? I need to talk to her. I need to talk to you both. How soon can you get out here?"

"Benjamin, I'm sorry, but we can't. Miranda is on vacation. And trying to find her best friend who is apparently missing." Then, almost as an afterthought, I ask, "What's going on? Maybe I can help you."

After a moment of silence, Benjamin's strained voice cracks. "It's Joanna. She's missing."

The stacks of books swirl around me. Beads of cold sweat break out on my brow.

Ever-growing collection. Could Beatrice have Joanna, too? How could the siren have drawn her down there? What could she have promised her?

While my mind is racing, Benjamin's voice pulls me from my spiral. "George there's more." He takes my silence to mean he should continue. "Are you sure Miranda is okay? Because Joanna left a note. All it says is *Be back soon. Miranda needs my help.*"

I pinch my eyes shut, trying to focus, trying to keep my thoughts straight. Everything I've been researching, everything Miranda has told me, everything going on has become a mass of knotted yarn in my head, and I'm having trouble finding an end so I can begin to untangle it. I need help.

I ask for it, "Benjamin, how soon can you get here? I think you should pack a bag. We need to go to the shore. Oh, if you have any information about how to track, fight, and maybe even kill a siren, can you bring that along too?"

After a moment of silence, Benjamin sucks on his teeth. "Sirens, huh? They can be the worst. Real assholes. But don't worry. I have something even better than information. I'll be there as soon as I can."

I'm curious what my predecessor has for me, for us. I am nervous about what this sea witch is up to, particularly what she has planned for Miranda. But I am also super psyched to see how my Guardian is going to take her down.

Chapter 21

MIRANDA

I'm treading water, and my lungs expand larger than my chest can comfortably handle as I take a deep breath and fight to stay afloat. With every second that passes, I lose more hope that Rory might be okay. I've already dipped beneath the surface many times, searching for some sign of him. Now I'm searching the surface for ripples, bubbles, anything. But the black water and the waves rolling in rhythmically are trying to push me back to shore, trying to exhaust me, trying to make me forget why I'm here.

I look at my watch, but it died as soon as I crashed in after Rory, so I have no idea how much time has gone by. I close my eyes and inhale the salty air. It stings the back of my throat that's scratchy from screaming. I concentrate on the water as it rushes toward me, feel it pushing me back toward land. A moment later, the waves push me again, but gentler, this time back out to sea. Keeping my eyes closed, so I can focus my senses on the sensation of the water moving all around me, I count the space between waves.

Five seconds.

How many waves have crashed into me while I've been floating here, doing nothing useful. In four more waves I'm going to dive in after him for real. I open my eyes and stare into the depths before me.

One.

Come on, Rory. Tabby needs you.

Two.

I must be the worst Guardian ever. How could I let him get lost right in front of me?

Three.

Oh god oh god oh god. If Rory is gone this fast, is there any hope that Eliza is okay?

Four.

Fuuccccckkkkkk!

I take a deep breath, and a head pops up in front of me, likely saving me from my watery death.

"What are you doing, Guardian?" Mazu's voice is a lot less sweet, and a lot more annoyed than when she was off the coast earlier. Now that she's so close, I can see how beautiful the mermaid is. Her dark hair is piled in fancy twists on top of her head and somehow dry even though I just watched her emerge from the water. Her plump lips are a brilliant red that doesn't look like lipstick; I think it's just the color they are. Eyes so dark they are black, at least in the dark night, flash as they await my answer.

I realize I've been gawking at her beauty instead of explaining myself to the obviously frustrated, possibly angry, mermaid. "I, I–"

"You thought you could hold your breath long enough to dive down to Beatrice's lair and save Rory? I thought you were smarter than that, Guardian."

I cast my eyes down to the water, wishing I could see straight through it to where my friends are being held. "I hoped maybe I had some kind of underwater breathing superpower or something." Then I look back at Mazu, one eyebrow raised, and ask, "Wait, who is Beatrice?"

"Beatrice is my sister. She is the siren who has your friends. We don't have time right now for more of an explanation. And as for this underwater breathing you hoped you have," Her brows relax and a devious smile spreads across her porcelain face, "You don't, Guardian. But I do."

She swims closer to me, close enough that if I were to reach my arm out, I could touch her. And still, she moves closer. She rises from the water until her face is almost even with mine. I can smell her, salty and musky. I would have expected her to smell fishy, but her scent more closely resembles a soap or a lotion, I can't place my finger on it.

She leans in until we share the same breath. "You need to trust me, Guardian."

I instinctively close my eyes as her red lips meet mine. They are not as soft as they look. Dry and scaly, they make me feel like I'm kissing a snake's back. But then her lips part, and her tongue gently taps my own lips, asking to be let in. My mouth opens of its own volition, wanting this new experience. I've kissed girls before, but not since college. And if you count my experiences with Lu, then I've kissed a mythological creature too. But I have never kissed a mermaid.

Her tongue enters my mouth slowly but not timidly. The tip tickles my own as Mazu uses it to explore my very essence. As our tongues slide against each other, I note how smooth hers is. I don't feel the bumpy friction that I feel when Jake kisses me, that I've felt with every other kiss I've ever had. Hers is also the wettest mouth I have ever kissed, but I guess I should expect that from a mermaid.

The kiss makes my entire body tingle with anticipation. I also quickly forget why I came here in the first place. I press my body into hers. She is what I want right now, even as I feel myself fading. I don't care about anything but her, this, us.

Suddenly, she pulls away. My eyes snap open, and all I see is murky blue. We are underwater. I gasp, but no water enters my lungs. My eyes snap to Mazu.

"What was *that* about?" My voice comes out, not quite as I'm used to, but still recognizable to me.

Mazu giggles and shyly covers her mouth. I think her cheeks flush as she casts her eyes away from me. Down here, she appears to be a young lady in her early twenties and is the epitome of sexy to men.

Why Mazu, what a youthful glow you have. *All the better to lure men to a watery death with...*

I shake myself to get back to the matter at hand.

"I'm sorry if I frightened you, Guardian. That was what I had to do so you could breathe under water. Most believe sirens and mermaids lure people to their deaths. While that has happened, generally speaking if we like someone enough to pay them attention, we want to keep them around. Don't worry though. Once you surface, the spell will break, and you'll be back to breathing air."

"Oh, sure. Okiedokie then." I feel myself blush, knowing I enjoyed that kiss more than I was supposed to.

I look around, noting seaweed floating by us and lots of sand below while trying to focus on something that isn't the sensual mermaid before me. At last, I give in and look at her smooth face again. "So, where to now?" I force the corners of my mouth upward momentarily, trying to imitate a smile. Fake it 'til you make it.

"Follow me, Guardian," she commands before turning away from me and diving further into the ocean where the sand falls away and the view gets even darker.

We swim in silence, Mazu leading the way. I'm still replaying that kiss in my mind and therefore afraid that if I say anything, it's going to sound like I'm hitting on her. The blue that surrounds us grows darker the longer we swim and lower we dive.

This is a strange sensation. Due to my body's natural buoyancy, I have never been able to swim below the surface of the water. But now, my arms and legs move as if I am an experienced deep-sea diver. And one that doesn't need any equipment to boot!

We've been swimming lower, into darker waters, for so long that I think I'm beginning to hallucinate when I see a glow ahead. It's like approaching a city after driving through farmland in the middle of the night.

The glow gets brighter the closer we get. Beyond a large reef, rays of light shine up into the ocean like searchlights announcing the opening of a new, hip club, only not swirling around in a dizzying dance.

Even though I have been silent this whole time, Mazu turns to me with a finger pressed to her lips. She beckons me to come closer and lie belly-down on the reef beside her and to look ahead from our hidden position. I am grateful for the protection my clothes provide as my hands and feet, my only exposed flesh, brush the rough coral. We lay on our stomachs beside one another and army crawl through the thick atmosphere to look down at the source of the light.

Beyond the reef, the ocean floor falls away. The cavernous space below us is lit like a modern home on land, but it takes me some time to find the source of the light. I expecting some kind of lamp or bioluminescent creatures hung from the rock walls and coral partitioning the cavern from the ocean behind it, making this undersea home its own three-walled room, like the set of the sit-coms I watched growing up. But the light doesn't come from something as simple as a lamp lit with stolen power or electric eels. Instead, balls of energy floating in the water here and there cause the illumination.

A breathtaking mermaid sits on a stool made of sea urchins. Staring into a piece of dark, polished glass that reflects her beauty, she brushes her long, dark auburn hair. Unlike Mazu, this other mermaid's skin is dark bronze with a metallic luster. Her eyes are such a bright blue that I can see them reflected in the mirror from here. And she's long. Longer and taller and bigger than Mazu. I look at Mazu with my brow lowered, asking without asking, and she nods.

Beatrice is also singing. Her voice doesn't have the same effect on me it must have had on Eliza and Rory, but it is hauntingly beautiful and enticing nonetheless. My muscles unclench, my shoulders relax, and my eyelids feel heavier with every note.

But I quickly snap back awake. Oh. Eliza and Rory. Where the hell are they? My eyes scan frantically as I finally remember my reason for being in this glamorous and terrifying place.

Mazu rests her hand on mine to get my attention. When I look her way, her eyes are on mine. Then she deliberately moves them away, drawing my attention to a large cage on the floor of the lair. The size of a small room, the cage is so rusted that it blends in with the coral around its base. But when I strain my eyes to focus on the coral, I see people lying on the cage floor. Something magenta floats gently in the water, creating a halo around the coral from my perspective.

I blink hard. Mazu feels the shift in me as I find my best friend's wafting hair and grabs my hand hard to bring my attention back to her so I don't rush off stupidly. I take one last long gaze into the cage. If that magenta haze is Eliza, then the other figure next to her must be Rory. I look back at Mazu.

We stare into each other's eyes, trying to telepathically connect the dots and make some kind of rescue plan. I can't focus on her well enough though, not with the incessant singing from Beatrice. I didn't realize before, but her voice is familiar. It also has a husky quality I didn't notice until now, scratchier and deeper than I would have expected. I look back at her, sitting at the vanity. The melody I hear has changed, and I don't think the music is coming from her anymore. At least not right now. It's hard to trace through the water, but I think it's coming from the cage. But that voice doesn't sound anything like Eliza, or Rory for that matter.

On the far side of the cage and in the shadow of the stone ledge hanging overhead, I can almost make out one more form, one more prisoner. This third person sits on the ground and leans against the bars. Wild curls tangle as their hair floats above their head.

So familiar, but the answer is just out of reach of my overloaded brain waves.

"Oh my gods, Guardian! You really must stop!" Beatrice's voice is as smooth and rich as my favorite hot fudge, but I still jump when she addresses me. Was I thinking too loudly again? Did I really give myself away already?

But then she swims off her stool and hovers just above the ocean floor, toward the cage. Her body slams against the bars, creating such a clatter that when Eliza and Rory don't even stir, I know they must be under a spell. The third figure, however, jumps away from the bars while turning to face Beatrice.

The siren's hands grasp the bars so tightly I can see flakes of rust floating away in the water. She contorts her beautiful face with rage but keeps her voice eerily calm and controlled. "You need to stop, dear Guardian. I need to be able to listen for when your friend approaches, you know."

The water around me turns to ice as Joanna's voice drips with sarcasm. "Oh, I'm so sorry. Was I distracting you?"

Chapter 22

Jake

I'm snuggled on the couch between a half-asleep Natalie, her eyelids drooping heavily, and a sound asleep Sammy. On the far side of Natalie, Phoebe sits with her knees pulled up to her chest, and she's completely engrossed in a movie I can't remember the name of, much less follow, when Jessie comes back from putting Tabitha down for the night.

I was worried that if I left her alone with her siblings, she would spill the beans about Miranda. Thank goodness she took Tabby's responsibilities upon herself when Rory and Miranda left.

Our eyes meet as she walks over and collapses next to her sister, snuggling into her like she hasn't in years. They used to be inseparable, two peas in a pod. The entire couch would be empty except for the two of them huddled under a blanket together, taking up half a cushion between the two of them. Miranda credited that to the fact that they had to spend the COVID year with only their siblings for friends.

But I credit Miranda. She's the glue of this family. I meant what I said back in Vegas, when I told her it makes sense that she's the Guardian. She's the perfect balance of protective Mama Bear, guidance counselor, and Russian Olympic Gymnastics coach. She knows when to push the kids and when to hold them close. She knows what to say to move them forward in everything they do. She's the one they've always gone to when they skinned their knees or needed advice or had a problem at school.

I silently wipe away the tears that have begun dripping down my cheeks and turn to Jessie. She's staring at the movie, a movie made for tweens that she's seen a hundred times, and her eyes also fill with tears. I reach around her sisters to pat her shoulder, but as soon as I make contact, she shrugs out from under my hand.

"Hey, Jessie?" It's a little louder than a whisper, but not by much.

Her only response to me is the glare I get from the corner of her eyes.

"Can we go talk?" I know at her age she is going through life on the edge of a coin, not sure which way she'll land on her opinions of us. I don't want to lose her over this.

"Nope. I'm watching the movie."

I want to yell at her to come talk to me, but I close my eyes, take a deep breath, and try to channel Miranda. What would she do in this moment. "Okay, well, *I'm* going to the kitchen for some snacks. If *you* want to talk about anything, you know where to find me."

After twisting, wiggling, and extricating myself from my little ones and making sure they stay upright on their cushions, I feel Jessie's eyes burning holes in my back as I walk to the kitchen and force myself not to look back. I grip the edge of the kitchen island and close my eyes. The cold marble counter top bites into my fingertips while my thumbs glide along the warm grain of the wooden cabinets below.

For a few minutes, I just breathe and focus on the way the oxygen fills my lungs. My heart beats stronger as I exhale. I remember my lie to get snacks and realize I need to deliver on that now, so I turn to the pantry to find a bag of microwave popcorn. As the kernels hit their mad popping stride and I'm nursing a tall glass of orange soda, the doorbell rings.

"What the fuck," I murmur to myself while stealing a glance at the clock to see that it is ten thirty at night. I look toward the front door and consider if I really need to answer it. Then it rings again. Twice this time. I jump a little when I hear Jessie clear her throat.

"Dad, whoever that asshole is, they're going to wake up Tabby." She's standing by the door to the family room, arms crossed, jaw jutted out, one eyebrow raised. She's trying to be tough, but she widens her eyes and is bouncing one leg on her toes rapidly. I know that she is nervous that we have such a late-night visitor, especially given all that's happened today.

I nod and walk to the door to prevent a third ring. I open it a crack, expecting some lost tourist—or some horrible beast. My eyes widen when I see our guest is a bit of both.

My tired voice cracks. "George, what are you doing here?"

Okay, it's not fair to say that George is a horrible beast. But I still hate that he introduced our entire family to constant danger and haven't completely shifted my gut reaction to his presence yet. I know, like Maria told me, George isn't to blame. This kid is just as much a victim as we are. And we do need him. Hell, the fact that he drove all the way down here to help Miranda is pretty fucking decent of him. Damnit. I might start to like this kid. Maybe.

A second man shifts behind George, making his presence known. He is a couple inches shorter than George, and they appear to be opposites in every way. The new stranger is stocky instead of slight, and his hair and eyes are dark whereas George is so fair that he could easily play Rolf in a community production of *The Sound of Music*.

George holds up a book bound in cracked brown leather. The outer corners are plated in rusty metal, and the front has a metal coat of arms with a 3-D emblem of a sword running down the center. The blade is so realistic that I almost want to take it in my hand King-Arthur style, only pulling the sword from a book instead of a stone.

George clears his throat to make sure he has my attention before he speaks. "We need to come in and talk. We have to find Miranda and get some information to her."

I back up to open the door wide, silently inviting them inside. They cross the threshold, and I shut the door, not sure what I should say. I lead them a few steps further into the kitchen where the odor hanging in the air indicates my popcorn has burned.

"Shit!" I grab the bag from the microwave and throw it in the sink. I can't deal with that issue right now.

"Ew, what's that smell?" Phoebe hates everything about popcorn, especially the smell of it burnt. I watch in what feels like slow motion as my second born walks into the kitchen. Her oversized lavender sweatshirt with bunnies on it makes her look years younger than eleven. She still so tiny and innocent. And her entire world is about to change.

I wasn't prepared when Jessie overheard the truth about Miranda, but this time I know in advance that Phoebe's walking into a confusing scene.

"Um, hi." Phoebe's eyes drift to the younger, more familiar, though not by much, new person in the room. "George, right?"

He smiles tightly and nods. "Hey Phoebe." His eyes flick to Jessie, who is still leaning against the doorframe with her eyes closed as if she's wishing this entire day is just a dream.

Phoebe turns her face a fraction of an inch toward me but doesn't move her eyes from George until she is mid-sentence. "Hey, Dad? Why is your personal trainer in Eliza's beach house?"

Jessie moves directly behind her little sister and settles her hands protectively settling on Phoebe's shoulders. "Yeah, Dad. Care to explain what's going on?"

My chest curls inward. I do not want to be dealing with this. Not now. Not when my wife is out hunting a siren with her best friend's husband on a crazy rescue mission. Oh, and I have a stranger and a kid standing in the room with us while I have to deal with it. Fan-freaking-tastic!

I take in a deep breath and let my words out in a fast sigh. "Phoebs, is there *any* chance whatsoever we can discuss this in a little while? Or maybe tomorrow?"

She glances over her shoulder and looks at Jessie, whose single raised brow and pinched mouth tell Phoebe this is something big. My younger daughter looks back at me and shakes her head. "Nope. 'Fraid not."

I brace myself on the counter and look at George. I still don't know who this other guy is. "Fellas? Can you field this one maybe? George at least? You're the expert."

They look at each other, trying to figure out how to begin. I almost expect them to play rock, paper, scissors to decide who will speak next. Maybe they are, only mentally. Maybe it's a skill they've mastered.

Finally, George takes a step toward us. His eyes are soft and squinted, like he's in pain at having to explain things to the girls. His voice is soft and gentle, trying to lessen the blow. "Phoebe, Jessie, I'm not your parents' personal trainer."

"Oh, I know," Jessie snaps. "I found out earlier today. I just want to hear *your* explanation for this. And let *you* explain it to my sister." Jessie crosses her arms, self-satisfied with her attitude.

Phoebe furrows her brows and looks down, puzzling out what she just heard.

George squeaks out, "You know, Jessie?"

Phoebe's stance hasn't changed, but her brows are pulled down and her jaw is clenched tight. This creates even more tension in the room which I didn't think was possible. She glares at Jessie and then George. "What exactly do you know?"

To his credit, George doesn't waiver in his decision to explain. "I, I did not know you knew, Jessie. But that won't change what I have to say." He straightens his spine so he looks strong and reassuring. "Your mother is someone called The Guardian. Back when she was born, she was chosen to become a great protector of humanity."

Phoebe's brow is still furrowed, and it is her turn to cross her arms. She bites her bottom lip while staring into George's face, deciding if she believes him. "Our mother. A great protector. From what? Like vampires and werewolves?" She shakes her head on the last words.

"Among other things. In the simplest explanation, mythological creatures are real, but your mom has to make sure our world doesn't find out about them. Or fall victim to them? I guess is the best way to say it?" George no longer looks so strong or confident. He chews on the inside of his cheek as he waits for a response.

Phoebe's eyes are wide, and she nods as she looks all around the room, trying to picture any of this being possibly true about the woman she knows, the woman she has known forever, the woman who has raised her and loved her and been there for her always.

Jessie takes deep breaths, trying to control the diatribe I know is floating just under her surface.

When no one speaks for few minutes, I look back at George's companion. "And you are?"

He shakes himself out of the trance we've all been in and takes a step toward me, reaching his hand out in the process. "I am so sorry! I'm Benjamin. I'm Joanna's docent."

I stare at his hand, sigh loudly, and shake his hand. "And Joanna is?"

Benjamin stuffs his hands in his pockets and then blurts out, "Joanna was The Guardian before Miranda. And she's my wife. And she's missing."

My eyes close as I breathe out loftily. My shoulders slouch under the weight of everything going on. "I thought Miranda was the first married Guardian."

Benjamin clears his throat. "Joanna was 18 when she became Guardian. We weren't married until many years later, after things had calmed down and The League had moved us out to the farm—not that this matters right now. That's a story for another time." He clears his throat and shrinks back down to take up as little space as he can in the kitchen that has grown thick with both people and truth.

I nod at the book in George's hand. The knife on the cover glints in the light like a real blade. "So, what's this information we have to get to Miranda?"

Chapter 23

MIRANDA

"Oh, I'm so sorry. Was I distracting you? Confusing you maybe? Messing with your melody? Messing with your head?"

How, why, how is Joanna here? I don't know what to do now. Not that I knew what to before I saw my predecessor had been captured, but now...now I'm sure I'm screwed.

How was Beatrice able to get her to come down here anyway? Her voice doesn't affect me enough to get me here. I didn't even hear it until I was already in her lair.

Joanna begins to whistle a bright, cheery, familiar tune. Something about enjoying life even though it sucks. I smile to myself. I really like Joanna. I wish we could have worked together instead of the League waiting until she retired to call me up.

Mazu squeezes my arm, shaking me from my thoughts. She bends her neck to the side to show me she wants me to follow her, so I do. We swim away from the siren's den, away from my friends, and when she decides we've swam far enough, she stops and turns to me. "I need to go, Guardian. I will be back soon, but someone needs me at the surface." She looks toward where we entered the sea, where we kissed, and I think I see a tear in her eye. "I cannot ask you to promise me you will only watch Beatrice and your friends. I do hope you will wait for me to return before you take any action, but you are The Guardian. You must trust yourself to know what to do."

To reiterate that she is not abandoning me, she takes my hands and looks deep into my eyes before finishing, "I will be back." She turns quickly and swims toward the surface, much faster than we swam here together. I wonder for half a second why she's in such a rush. But then I know I have to get back to the task at hand.

I rotate back to where Beatrice is holding my friends captive. Rotate is definitely the best word given how thick the water is when you're under the sea. Combine that with my own thickness and, well, you have rotation.

I bite my lip while considering Mazu's words. Trust myself to know what to do. HA. Can I trust myself to stay hidden and watch while I wait for my mermaid guide to return?

Not. Fucking. Likely.

I swim back alone to the perch we had just been laying on together, steeling myself for what I am going to see.

Beatrice is close to the cage, arguing with Joanna. They're too quiet, or I'm too far way to make out what they're saying, but their exchange looks pretty heated. Every so often a word makes it way to me.

"Too late."

"Ludo."

"Revenge."

And then, loudest of all when Beatrice screams, "Shut up!"

The siren closes her eyes and opens her mouth, her haunting melody filling the space between us, filling the entire ocean, maybe even filling the world. Joanna stops arguing. She sits still. She's not asleep like Eliza and Rory (I hope they are just asleep). Instead, Joanna stares at the seabed while Beatrice sings.

I cannot force my eyes away from her. I think I am crying but my cheeks are already wet from the sea so I can't feel the tears. Her melody mesmerizes me, so much so that she's almost finished with her song before I realize she's singing about me.

Shit.

That can't be good.

When Beatrice opens her eyes, they are no longer only bright blue; they are glowing. With her voice still in song mode, she looks right at me and asks, "Are you going to join us, Miranda? I'm sure your friends wouldn't mind if I woke them up to welcome you."

Before I know what I'm doing, my legs push through the water, bringing me toward the siren. Mazu is going to be so disappointed in me.

"Hello, Beatrice. I am glad you brought that up because why are my friends asleep anyway?" If I'm walking to her, I may as well talk.

She laughs, but the sound that reverberates through the water is not the girlish giggle of Mazu. Beatrice's is deep and haughty. A Woman's laugh. And yes, that capital W is on purpose. "Oh, Miranda. I am sure if you stopped and thought about it, you'd know the answer to your own question. What else do you think I could promise two toddler parents that they would want more than anything else?"

I think on this for a moment, all the while my feet swim me closer. "Oh. I hate to admit it, but that's actually smart."

She looks surprised by the compliment. "Thank you, dear! So kind of you to notice."

I nod, "Of course. And Joanna? What did you promise her?"

She smiles a wide, deep, red-lipped smile and runs her tongue along the bottom edge of her top teeth seductively. "Since you so kindly complimented me, I'll tell you. I didn't promise her anything. I just told her I had you, and she came running. Once a Guardian always a Guardian I suppose."

I look around to see if Mazu has yet. I could really use her help here.

Beatrice rolls her eyes. "My sister will be back soon. She's just collecting my last surprise for you. One more who loves you."

I swallow hard. It has to be someone from my family then, but who? Jessie knows about me now, but she should be taking care of Tabitha. This bitch wouldn't call to one of my kids, would she?

Again, Beatrice rolls her eyes. "No, Guardian. I wouldn't entice your children. What kind of monster do you think I am?"

Damn my loud thoughts.

Okay, not one of my kids. I know Jake wouldn't put himself in this kind of position. Not after last time.

It has to be George with more information. He learned something I need to know, and my phone doesn't work under the sea, so he had to bring me the information himself. Which means he knows what he's getting himself into. And as a bonus, because he trains, once I wake him up, he'll be an asset to the team. But he's not here yet, so I need to stay in this moment and not jump ahead.

I look at the cage. Maybe I can get my friends out of here and not have to worry about what George has to say.

"You are trying to figure out how to break them out." There is no question there. I need to stop thinking so loudly. Shit.

"Not at all. I was trying to remember when I last had a tetanus shot. Do you think you could have found a rustier cage, Beatrice?"

She throws her head back, and I watch her throat bob with the laughter. Why do I want to kiss it? Why do I want to kiss *her*? I'm not supposed to be affected by this shit, but I want her so badly. The desire to hold her sickens me. But I can't help it.

Her head returns to its normal position, and she locks those blue eyes on me. Eyes that emit sparks of starlight as I stare at them. Those sparks ignite a fire deep inside me that I need to clamp my legs shut to keep under control. I want to run to her, wrap my arms around her lithe waist, and bury my face in that wild, dark red hair floating around her like the petals of a ranunculus.

I shake myself out of this trance. I'm The Guardian, goddamnit. I need to be better than this. Being only ten feet from the cage now, I resume looking for a weakness or latch from where I float while I inquire, "So, Beatrice. I was listening to your song before. Am I correct to guess that I killed your lover?"

She's not smiling now. Her jaw is set, eyes narrow, brow furrowed with a deep line running up her forehead. "Yes. Ludo. You killed Ludo."

I stop thinking of the cage and instead think back to who and what I've killed. "I'm afraid I don't make a habit of asking for names before I get in a fight. I've never killed a mermaid or merman though. Are you sure I killed him? Is it even really me you're mad at?"

Her eyes are colder now, shooting blue fire in my direction. "Oh, I am sure, Guardian." The last word is dripping with vitriol. "And he was not a merman. Mermen are so common, so boring. I am better than that. I needed someone strong. Someone rare."

My toes touch the bedrock, and I begin to pace in front of the cage as if I wasn't wading through water at the bottom of the sea. I'm only three feet away now. "Was he a troll by any chance?"

Her face screws up at the very idea that I could think she would be with a troll. "No, Guardian, he was NOT a troll. He was a minotaur."

I stop pacing. Oh. Shit.

I swallow hard before I find my voice. "Let me get this straight: Your lover, was the minotaur, the first creature I killed?"

She begins to sob. Or at least, her torso curls in on itself, shuddering as if sobs are racking her body. Any actual tears mix into the salt water all around us. She takes a deep, shaking breath and screams at me, "Yes! Guardian, *protector*, ha! You think you are protecting humanity from murderous monsters, but you don't protect anyone. You're League is the real monster, and your kind are the real murderers."

The League. Joanna told me once that the League used to keep creatures for Guardians to train with. To murder? I feel bile rising in my throat. But I can't give in to this guilt. I need to save my friends.

So I clear my throat, make sure my face is neutral, and hold my hands up in defense. "I'm sorry! I just...I just, I can't picture this coupling. I mean, a bird may love a fish, but where would they live, ya know? Only, if the bird were a giant half-bull, half-man creature, and the living was fucking..."

Her head snaps up with a glare that would shoot daggers at me, leaving me grateful she doesn't have that power. "He didn't even do anything to you! He was brought there with the sole intent for you to put on a little show for your docent!" Her voice is no longer seductive or smooth. It is whiny and hoarse when she screams at me. "He was innocent! And you *murdered* him!" She dissolves into her sobs once again.

I feel bad for her. I can't imagine how I would feel if the muses had killed Jake instead of just using him like a toy. Then I look at my abducted friends, and my pity dissolves, mostly. No. Even if they had killed him, I'd have hunted down every last muse, but I wouldn't have involved innocents. "Look, I am really, really sorry. I can't even tell you how sorry. I had no idea what was going on. I didn't know he had a girlfriend. All I knew was that I was trapped in this maze with this monster an–"

"Monster? Monster! You're the monster, Guardian. You are the monster who killed the love of my life. And now I will have my revenge!"

What the hell does she mean by her revenge? What is this psycho bitch planning to do? A gentle hand on my shoulder coaxes me to turn.

Mazu floats before me, as beautiful as ever, but with a frown on her face and a deep sadness about her. "Miranda, I am so sorry. I could not break her hold on him. But I was able to get to him in time so he will be safe here under the water, like I did for you and your other friends."

"What are you talking about?" But in my gut, I know the answer already. She was kissing George so he could breathe down here. My heart beats a little fast at the prospect because in my mind, I'm already winning the impending fight with him by my side.

I turn back from where she came, looking for my docent, I am sure he will come marching through the heavy water any moment. I see him far in the distance, but the water is so thick that I can barely make out his dark figure.

Why does everyone Beatrice spells move so damn slowly? My heart is beating rapidly in my chest as his figure looms ever closer.

I glance around for a possible weapon. No statues of Zeus down here. I look back to see how much time I have before George enters the encampment. Not very long. That's a problem but not the biggest problem that makes my mind go blank.

Because as I watch the figure get closer, the water becomes less obtrusive and reveals that's not George marching along the ocean floor. It's Jake.

Chapter 24

GEORGE

We hear the reverberations of Phoebe's screams and Jessie's pleading through the floor while they argue in the basement, and Jake, Benjamin, and I debate who should go after Miranda. After Jake, reluctant to part from the little ones, carried Natalie and Sammy up to his guest room forty-five minutes ago, he sent the big two downstairs to work things out so they don't wake up Tabitha or their siblings with their fighting. He's hoping Phoebe forgives Jessie soon for not immediately telling her about Miranda being the Guardian.

Jake can barely stay upright. His clothes are disheveled and one side of his bright yellow beach shirt is untucked. "Okay, so let me go over this one more time so I know I have it all: Someone has to bring this book to Miranda, because only the Guardian can take out the dagger. Then she has to somehow get blood on the dagger from one of the people this siren, Beatrice, has kidnapped. As of now we think that list is Eliza, Rory, and Joanna. Then Miranda has to stab the siren."

I nod along as he spells out every step. "Yes. And I should be the one who brings it to her. You don't exactly have a great record when it comes to mythological women who like to spell and seduce men." I know that this is a low blow but I'm protective of my role in all of this. It should be me down there with her.

He can't look at me when he answers, "I haven't forgotten, thanks."

Something in my chest tugs when I see him staring off into space, likely remembering that lowest moment he had in Las Vegas.

My cheeks get hot.

"Gentlemen, we need to focus on Miranda." Benjamin's matter of fact, no-nonsense, boom of a voice snaps us back to the present. He looks back and forth between Jake and myself, waiting for a sign that we hear him. When both of us nod in agreement to move on, Benjamin continues in a quieter but still commanding voice. "Now, it is obvious you both care for Miranda and want to save her. The question becomes: How does this hostility help anyone?"

I can't tell if the question is rhetorical, but I'm not going to take the chance on answering and pissing him off.

Benjamin's eyebrows raise as he continues, "Good. Now, I'm the most impartial, having never met Miranda. I've also been a docent and a spouse to a Guardian. I know how you both feel, and I know the most about the enemy we're up against. So, I'm the one calling the shots right now. Capiche?"

Jake and I lock eyes for a few heartbeats before we both nod again and look at the floor. At least we have enough common sense to show some shame.

"So, here is how this is going to work." Benjamin hesitates for a moment with his eyes closed. They flutter while he puzzles out some details before making his declaration. "Jake is going to find Miranda. George, you're staying with the kids, and think up a cover story. You'll have a hard time explaining where everyone is if they wake up before Jake gets back, but hopefully that won't happen."

The room is silent as Jake and I stare at each other, Jake looking a lot like he's going to throw up. I wish he'd trained more. When this is all over, I'm going to encourage him to come to the dojo more. He needs to know what to do in these situations and right now he is completely unprepared.

My heart is thumping a million beats a minute. I want to be the one to go after her. Jake isn't ready to go into the sea, find Miranda somewhere in the fucking ocean, and help her fight a siren that will hypnotize him long before he gets there. He doesn't have as much combat training as I have. He doesn't have as much mythological intelligence as I have. And then there's the question of how Miranda will get the blood of someone she cares about on the knife—without that blood washing away. I grind my teeth the more my mind runs rampant. I don't doubt whether any of them will return. But the situation includes too many variables, too many chances where this could go wrong, and even more where it could go wrong for Miranda, specifically.

Benjamin turns his almost black eyes to Jake, but his words help both of us to breath a bit more easily. "I know you don't think you can do this, Jake. But you can. You're Miranda's mate. You're the one who will be pulled the strongest. You're the one she'll fight for at any expense. It has to be you."

"Where will you be, Benjamin?" I didn't even know I wanted to ask the question until the words tumbled out of me.

He juts out his bottom jaw the way it did when he was tired and didn't know what to say. "I'm too old for heroics, George. I'll be here, helping you to stay out of it and think up a story to explain to the little ones, stepping in if the big two get too close to killing one another, and waiting to see my wife again."

Jake nods. "Okay then. I don't want to waste any more time. I'm going to go find Miranda." He picks up the book and starts for the door we entered the house via earlier, but stops and turns back to us, flustered. "It might help if I go the way she and Rory did though, out the living room to the boardwalk."

I give a curt nod, a wordless good luck. He maneuvers around throw blankets and pillows discarded on the floor in a sloppy game of the Floor is Lava and reaches the glass doors.

Before he opens the door, he stares at the blankets he just traversed and his face wilts. Without lifting his eyes from the floor, he says, "Promise me you'll look after them, train them." Jake locks me in a desperate gaze. "Promise me you'll train them, George. They'll be better students than me. I can't leave them if I don't know they'll be safe."

I stand there, frowning, eyebrows pulled together, shoulders rounded. Finally, I blink. I say, "Jake, you'll be back in a few hours, tops. You'll see. You and Miranda, you're the team. You've got this. But I do like the idea of training the kids. Let's hash that out more when you're all back safe." I end with a wink in a feeble attempt to lighten the mood.

He gives me a half-hearted smile, takes a deep breath and opens the door. The blast of cool sea air reaches Benjamin and I where we stand in the doorway by the kitchen. I have no choice but to trust him now.

Jake takes one last look at us, gives one last nod, and steps outside, sliding the door shut behind him.

In five strides, I quickly lock the glass door tightly behind him. I watch Jake walk from the deck to the boardwalk where he takes a left and heads north. After a few steps, he stops dead in his tracks and stares ahead. I can make out only a sliver of his face from here. It's too dark to see any details, but I'm sure if I could, I would see his eyes glazed over.

He's just been spelled.

Chapter 25

MIRANDA

No. It's not supposed to be Jake down here. It's supposed to be George. I don't want my husband to be the victim of a siren. I don't want him to be a victim ever again. My heart is racing and the edges of my vision begin to blur. I instinctively grab for the bracelet, but it wouldn't help even if I had brought it with me because all of my senses are dulled in the water anyway. I try to do the breathing but whatever it is I'm able to do down here thanks to Mazu's kiss, it isn't breathing as I know it on land. There is no air to pull into my lungs, to force my body into calm. There is no calm to be found. Jake is here, spelled by Beatrice, in danger once again, because of me.

That's when I start to hear that fucking voice again.

"This is all *your* fault!" The seething tone distorts the voice so much that I can't make out who it belongs to. "This is all your fault. All of this. Everything happening to us right now. *You* should be nicer. *You* should know your place. *You* should keep your mouth shut."

I clench my eyes closed against the voice, but I can't shut out something that is inside my head. I see the old pop-up camper from my childhood. I'm standing beside a campfire long burned out and cold. Muffled angry voices reach me from inside: his yells and a slam as something hits a wall. I don't know if it was part of him, part of her, something thrown... Her sobs get louder when he rips the door open and stumbles down the front step. He barely looks at me as he raises his hands and pushes the air between us away; he can't be bothered to interact with such an inconvenience as me right now. Kicking the dry dirt up into a dusty cloud, he storms off into the night.

I walk toward the door and look into the camper, but I don't see her. The voice speaks again, angry, spiteful, from somewhere deeper inside. Her hatred cuts through the darkness, repeating once more, "This is all your fault."

Then my mother's wails float out the door and punch me in the gut. I want to run to her, to comfort her, like I always have. But she blames *me*. So instead, I stand there frozen, until the anger has melted into sadness. Her words eek out between sobs, "Why can't you just be nicer to him? He wouldn't want to leave if you were nicer to him."

That voice inside my head has been my mother all this time. They made me hate the woods. They made me hate a lot of things about my childhood. They made me hate a lot of things about myself. But I've been working too long at loving myself, and surrounding myself with people like Jake and Eliza helped me to get there.

A new memory fills the field of vision in my mind's eye. Jake and the kids waiting in line for the fun slide. Our family, enjoying each other, happy together. I am a good mom, a good wife, and a good Guardian. At this point in my life, I am surrounded by love—which is why I don't have time for this shit. My friends need me, now.

At least I know I can rescue him, seeing as how I already have once, but George is a better fighter than I am. He was supposed to be an asset in this fight.

While I was lost in my own head, Mazu had somehow dragged me back to where we had been hiding out before. Beatrice already knows we're here, but at least this nook affords us some privacy to talk. And a chance for Mazu to show me what she has in her hands.

"Jake was holding this, Guardian." Mazu gets half my attention by pressing a cold book into my hands.

My eyes are unfocused, barely seeing. "Ouch!" The pain in my palms wakes me the rest of the way. The book I am holding has metal corners long since oxidized. The rusty points prick at my skin, which has softened from all the time submerged down here. The embossed front features a coat of arms, and an old-fashioned miniature sword is somehow fastened to the center. The blade is shiny and looks sharp, in direct contrast with the rusty, haggard book cover. I study the book for a few seconds before I speak, turning it over and over again in my hands. "I don't understand. What good can a book be under water?"

Mazu puts her hands over mine and when I look into her face she is focused on the book. "This is the book of Nimue, The Lady of the Lake, a British myth. She is thought to be the one to have given Excalibur to King Arthur. She was a Lake Fairy, similar to Beatrice and I as a siren and mermaid of the sea." Her eyes flash up to mine. "This book is so old that you have very little chance to read what is written inside, even if we were reading the book on land."

My shoulders slump. "So what good is it to me? Why would Jake bring this?" I run my finger along the blade of what I now assume is a model of Excalibur. Although it looks dulled with age, to me it feels sharp, like it could actually cut me if my flesh was on the edge instead of the flat. So, not just for decoration, I guess.

Mazu smiles. "If you could read it, you would learn that the way to kill a siren is to stab her with a specific blade. This blade." Her perfectly manicured finger taps the hilt of the tiny sword. "You see, Nimue had a bit of a siren problem herself once. Some of my sisters thought if they could move inland, to the lake, they could have better access to mankind. The Lady of the Lake wouldn't hear of it."

"So where is this blade now? A crest on a book isn't going to help me much." I look into her face and gasp as she raises her brow. "Wait, *this* is the actual blade we need? But if I need to use this, how? The blade is part of the book. Also, it's really small. How much damage can it do?"

Mazu smiles and nods. "Guardian, you of all people should understand that the power in an item is not always reflected in its appearance. And as for your other question, how familiar are you with the myths of King Arthur?"

I press the heels of my hands against my cheeks to keep me in the moment, instead of running off screaming into the oceanic oblivion. "I don't know. Not very? I watched that cartoon movie a lot as a kid. But I mainly remember a heartbroken squirrel."

She chuckles. "Before he would bring Arthur to the Nimue, Merlin the Magician tested the young king with a sword he himself set into a stone. As Arthur was the one true king, only he could pull the sword from the stone." She adds with a smile, "Nimue always loved that bit."

With my brain scrambled, I wonder if I'm looking at her with a cross-eyed expression.

She smiles at me expectantly, her eyes wide and brow halfway to her hairline. "As Arthur was the one true King, you are the one true Guardian. Only you can remove the blade."

I furrow my brow and bring the book closer to my face so I can examine the cover more closely. The entire book is about a foot tall, and thick, probably three inches when including the leather cover. The sword is about ten inches long from top to bottom. I run my fingers along the flat once more, down to the handle, where the metal has been formed into an intricate basketweave pattern. Feeling foolish, I grasp the hilt between my thumb and forefinger as best I can, and I feel an almost imperceptible click as the weapon pops free from the cover. I hold it in front of me, feeling the bumpy hilt in my hand and noticing how much heavier it is than I expected. I see in my periphery that Mazu is as enthralled as I am.

"So, I just have to go stab Beatrice with this now?"

"Well, it's not quite that simple." For the first time since we have been together, she can't look me in the eye, which means I most likely won't like what she's about to tell me. "There is one other small detail. It needs to be coated in the blood of one of the siren's victims."

I forget what I am holding and drop my arms to my sides, the knife almost slipping from my grip. "I'm sorry, what now?"

At this moment, as if on cue, Jake trudges past us on his way to Beatrice, still under her spell.

Mazu swallows hard, but to her credit, she doesn't avoid the question. "You need to coat the blade with the blood from one of your friends before you stab her."

I shake myself back to Mazu. "How much blood?" I close my eyes and swallow hard while I await Mazu's answer.

"The blade needs to be well-coated. So, you will need to do some damage, unfortunately. And remember, we're in the ocean. Blood expands, travels, and... attracts things. So, this is going to be tricky."

"Fanfuckingtastic." How am I supposed to just walk over and cut one of my friends? And how am I going to do this without kicking off a shark feeding frenzy?

With my thoughts a violent whirlpool in my brain, I also watch helplessly as Beatrice waves her hand and unlocks a small but ornate lock on end of the cage closest to where she earlier sat in front of that mirror. The door swings open to let Jake in.

"Welcome, Jake, mate of Miranda! There is plenty of room for you with her other friends." She looks right at me as she closes the door softly behind him and re-locks it with a wave of her hand. Then she returns to her stool. Maybe it's because looks have never been a big asset to me, but I wonder how much time one being can spend staring at herself.

I also can't help but wonder why she's playing with me like this. Did she really just bring me down here to play at some sick twisted cat and mouse game? But then something else pops into my mind and distracts me. I turn and look with squinted eyes at Mazu and ask, "Why are you helping me? Why save my friends? If Beatrice is your sister, why help us at all?"

She looks past me, to the psychotic siren she's helping me to defeat, and speaks softly, "Mermaids and sirens are both sea spirits. We are two sides of the same coin. Sirens are mermaids, but dark mermaids. Beatrice and I are sisters, but we are not the same. She seduces men to their deaths; I give them the gift of breath under the sea. You are the Guardian of this world, but I am Protector in the sea."

I look back at the knife in my hand. "I'm, I'm going to go try something, Mazu." Without looking at the mermaid directly, I pass the Book of Nimue back to her and half walk, half float down the sandy hill, toward my friends.

Beatrice won't allow me to get to the door of her prison. But I have to try. Joanna makes eye contact with me. She's lucid. I guess you can't really retire from being The Guardian after all. She glances at my wrist, where I'm pressing the knife against my skin and hoping it remains unnoticed by our captor. She flicks her eyebrows up, almost imperceptibly, then looks to the door. I think I understand her meaning and lower my head in one brief nod.

I have to do this if I'm doing it. I pull my shoulders high and bounce on the balls of my feet, which only has me sink into the wet sand a bit. Showtime, I guess.

I rush to the side of the cage closest to me and begin shaking it. "Jake! Snap out of it. I'm here, but I'm okay. I need to know that you are too."

Sitting against the bars far opposite the door, he stares ahead with no emotion or animation. He doesn't show a single sign that he can hear me. "Eliza, Rory, wake up! You can't stay sleeping here forever."

I feel Beatrice's cold eyes on me, not sure what I'm trying to accomplish by my obviously fruitless gesture.

Joanna rushes to me, making a show of calming my actions with her hands on top of mine. "Stop it, Miranda! You're going to damage the coral! Don't you know how sensitive the ecosystems are down here? Damnit, woman, you're a Guardian, not an eco-terrorist!"

I release the bars with my empty hands up, displaying my innocence. While Joanna tucks one arm behind her back, I swim a foot back from the cage and focus on distracting Beatrice. I walk over to where she sits. She is still watching at me with a raised eyebrow, not sure what the fuck I'm doing. Not that I am sure of that myself.

"Okay, Beatrice. How'd you get Jake down here?" As I talk, I pass her so that she pivots on her stool in order to keep her eyes plastered on me. Her fins swish in front of her like a dog wagging its tail, only slower.

"You realize it doesn't matter what I promise in my songs. I don't have to promise anything at all. I just have to sing, and they come to me."

"Okay, so you didn't promise him anything? What did you sing about then?" I need to think fast and keep her facing my direction if we are to have any luck whatsoever here. "Was it the song about me and Ludo?"

Her mouth tightens as she shudders. When she speaks, she grunts through a clenched jaw. "Yes."

I nod. Come on Miranda, say something else. I'm afraid to look behind her to see how Joanna is doing because I don't want her to notice, so I have to keep her talking. I ask, "What is your end game here?"

She shakes her head, and her shiny hair shimmies behind her. "What do you mean, end game?"

"Your final goal. By getting my friends here, what are you hoping to accomplish?"

She laughs, but the forced sound is mirthless. "The end goal was to get you here, Guardian. So that I can exact my revenge."

"Okay. Did you want them here alive like this? Because I thought sir—"

"No, I didn't want them here alive like this!" She screeches as anger flashes across her face. "I wanted them to drown, like my victims of old, back when I could do what I wanted. But my sister ruins all my fun! She saved them like the perfect goodie two shoes she is. I would have been perfectly happy if everyone who loves you drowned in the sea."

Ouch. That kind of hurts to hear.

"Sorry to disappoint you, Sweetheart." Joanna's dry, cracked voice cuts through our conversation from much closer than the cage.

When Beatrice rotates on her seat to face Joanna, I pounce. I am in mid-air, er, mid-water, and everything seems to slow down. (Not just seems, I'm floating through the water instead of flying through the air, so I really am moving slower.) Joanna's eyes go wide as I attempt this tackle. Thankfully, Beatrice notices the change in my predecessor's expression. The siren snaps her head back to look at me over her shoulder and glare at me. Perfect. Joanna almost has her back.

As I swim toward her, the water pushing against me slows me down. Beatrice raises both of her eyebrows, revealing the whites of her eyes. Her irises glow dark blue as she pulls up the corner of her burgundy mouth. I suppress my own smirk.

The closer I approach to her, the water reduces my speed until I'm floating toward her like a ginormous bubble that she intends to pop. Oh, just wait until I burst her fucking bubble.

She rises from her perch, her fin pushing her upward so that her eyes are level with mine, and chuckles. She actually laughs in my face. I bite my tongue and focus on the fact that Beatrice isn't paying attention to

Joanna. The moment I remember I'm under water, not flying through the air and at gravity's mercy, I kick my legs to dive left. But Beatrice is a part of the sea. This is her home. This is her turf, or surf. Before I move half an inch away from her, she turns her whole body away from Joanna (yes!) and flicks her tail fin (oh, shit!).

Her long tail must be solid muscle because, as it slaps me, I feel like I'm being body slammed by a rhinoceros. Or Ludo. No wonder they were such a good pair. They're both so muscular and athletic. The sex must have been spectacular.

Luckily, the density of the water prevents me from torpedoing all the way across the ocean, although I still go pretty far, belly up, from the force of that tail knocking me backward. I throw my arms out like a deranged starfish to stop my displacement and get my feet back under myself.

As I swim back toward the fight, Beatrice locks her eyes on me and licks her lips as she waits for a second chance to hurt me. Joanna, however, slides slightly to the right, just behind Beatrice's back. The shinning orbs overhead reflect off the sword hidden behind her back. With me only twenty feet away, Joanna lunges for Beatrice, with the blade still clean and shining. But that's okay. This is only phase one: Distract and wound Beatrice. Phase two: Get blood. Phase three: Finish the job.

Unfortunately, we're not off to a good start. Beatrice deftly swishes to the side, causing Joanna to slam into the door of the cage, which swings closed but is not locked. With a clatter so loud I can see the sound waves move through the water, Joanna drops the sword. Red swirls dissipate into the water from a scrape on her head. Didn't Mazu say something about sharks? Double shit.

Joanna teeters on her feet, looking like she may pass out. I hold my breath, praying Joanna rights herself, because the last thing I need is the only person fighting on my team down here to suddenly not be conscious.

I inch my way forward, holding my breath because I am not close enough to be a part of this fight. If I hadn't been knocked so far away we could be tag teaming her right now. Beatrice grabs Joanna in a rear bearhug and pulls her away from the cage. Joanna must still be very disoriented because instead of grabbing Beatrice's hands and spinning to knock her attacker off her, she kicks off the ground and loses any leverage she even had. Then again, even though this technique was one of the first self-defense moves I learned, I've never had to do the techniques in the ocean. The physics are probably off.

Beatrice drags Joanna away from the cage, and I have to make a fast decision: Do I go to help Joanna, or do I take the opportunity to grab the sword? Not a difficult choice to make really. I take one last look at my predecessor tangled up with our foe. I know what she would do, what she would want me to do.

I focus my attention like a laser on that blade and kick my legs as fast as a motorboat's engine whirrs. Nothing else matters right now but getting that sword in my hands. I will worry about the next step when I get to it. I use my arms to pull myself through the thick water. With only a few feet left, I dive forward, like I'm going for home plate, my arms scrape along the grimy seabed, kicking up a cloud of sand that clouds my vision and stings my throat. Even in the gritty haze, the hilt of the little sword slides under my fingers. I wrap it in my palm and push myself to my feet.

I glance back and see that Joanna and Beatrice are still distracted, locked in hand-to-hand combat with spurts of waves whooshing around them, Joanna, on her feet again, moves as quickly as if she was on land, but Beatrice still moves faster than I'm comfortable with.

Quickly, I crack the door of the cage open just enough to shimmy inside and pull it shut behind me. I look at them, my husband, best friend, and best friend's husband. Who can I bring myself to stab for this?

I would expect Rory to be the easiest to me in the moment. I have the least connection to him. But that also makes him the hardest choice. Eliza would be pissed at me. He's supposed to be the furthest removed from this whole Guardian business, but he's also the one Beatrice has tormented the most from the moment Eliza went missing.

Eliza...I can't hurt her. She's like a little sister to me. And as for Jake, he's Jake. He's my husband, the father of my children the love of my—

"It has to be Jake," Mazu says as she swims into the cage. "It will work best if you use your mate's blood."

The answer is always Jake. Poor Jake. I can't believe I have to stab my one-and-only. Even in the ocean of salt water my tears start flowing. "Is there no other way?"

She shakes her head. "This is it. But you only have to coat the blade. You do not have to kill him."

Grateful for that tiny bit of good new, I glide to where my husband sits.

Sitting cross-legged on the ocean floor, he stares straight ahead. I position myself so I am kneeling in front of him, my hands on his knees. I look into his blank face. Again. I know I have to do this soon, that it's only a matter of time before Beatrice sees where I am, what I'm up to.

I lean forward and kiss his lips, then his nose, then his forehead. I whisper, "I am so, so sorry about this." I pull my hand back. The hilt of the knife is at my belly as I plan to plunge it into my husband's.

But right when I'm about to strike, Mazu grabs my wrist. "What are you doing? I told you, you don't have to kill him!"

She moves my hand so that the sword slices his bicep. Once one side of the blade is coated in thick red blood, which the sword seems to hold onto as if it too knows its mission, its purpose, she helps me turn it over so that the other side is as well.

"Now go," she breathes into my ear.

Standing up, I look down at my bleeding husband. My eyes burn with tears I can't feel in the water. "Please, watch over him." I see her nod in my periphery. Then I close my eyes and turn around, opening them only when I know he won't be in my field of vision any longer.

With Joanna and Beatrice still fighting, they have spun and stumbled much closer to the cage, making this a little easier. Still, I need to move quickly. I quietly push the cage door open and step outside. Even though they are only steps away from me, they rotate in their wrestling match at such a speed that I don't know how I'll focus on Beatrice to stab her and not Joanna.

I slam the rusty metal door shut with a clang loud enough to reverberate through the water. The fighting stops. Joanna and Beatrice separate and look at me, but I don't hesitate. I push my feet against the rusty cage to propel myself, plunging the blade deep into Beatrice's abdomen. The corners of Beatrice's smug smile drop. Her face crumples and her bottom lip sticks out as she lowers her gaze to her belly. When I pull away, keeping the sword with me, a plume of red rises into the water while Beatrice falls to the ocean floor.

Under my breath I utter, "Good riddance." I don't feel the slightest bit of guilt about this fight, this death on my hands.

To my right, Eliza and Rory stir. Slowly they rise to their hands and knees and shake their heads. They look at each other as if both are waking from the same horrible nightmare, give each a quick once over, and embrace before kissing all over each other's face. Jake, still sitting against the bars, blinks rapidly as he comes out of his trance. The moment he stands up, he winces and grabs his arm. More blood swirls around him. Mazu wraps her hand on either side of the slice in his arm and talks quietly to keep him calm.

"Oh thank god." I breathe a sigh of relief, or whatever it is I'm doing down here without air since Mazu kissed me.

I hold the cage door open and usher my friends outside to their freedom with big hugs and smiles. Rory and Eliza are still in each other's arms; Eliza's eyes twinkle as she nods thanks to me. They leave the cage and Joanna is there to start walking them back in the direction we all came from.

Jake stays behind for a moment. Looking into my eyes he says, "I'm glad the plan worked."

My brow wrinkles, "What plan?"

One corner of his mouth rises in an awkward crooked smile, "Getting you the little sword dagger thing, you cutting me, that siren bitch getting killed... You know, everyday kind of shit."

"You knew I was going to cut you?"

He arches his back, making himself look taller before coyly responding, "Of course I did! George prepared me for this mission well. He's not so bad you know."

My eyebrows shoot up. "Not so bad? How much blood did you lose?" I look over his arm to make sure it's not worse than I thought.

He laughs and takes a hold of my shoulders, holding me in front of him so he can lean in for a kiss.

But the happiness doesn't last long. Mazu stares into the distance in the opposite direction from which we arrived. "Guardian, we need to get you all to shore. Now."

I swim to stand next to her and follow her line of sight. Five, now eight, distant silhouettes slowly grow larger. But these don't look anything like Jake did as he approached us. These aren't walking on the ground. These are ovals with a thin triangle on top. "Oh, fuck me. Are those sharks?"

Mazu nods before she gestures toward Jake's wound. "The blood."

"The blood?" Jake looks at his arm and back up. "You mean *my* blood? There are sharks coming for my blood?"

Shit shit shit shit shit shit shit. I turn back to my friends, who are still rightfully celebrating our win over Beatrice. "Guys, we gotta jet. FAST."

Eliza, who's closest, looks over my shoulder. Her eyes widen and jaw drops. The three of them are standing frozen, not sure how we are going to out swim eight sharks.

Before everyone can panic, Mazu commands us all. "I'll carry Jake. You all just get yourselves. Follow me."

I take up the rear, even though it's not like I've been learning to fight sharks in the dojo or researching their weaknesses in the library. But I'm still the Guardian, and I did not just go through all this bullshit with Beatrice to lose my friends to some great white shark mother-fuckers.

We swim, well, like our lives depend on it. At one point, the water behind me feels bubbly to me, like it's being churned by something bigger than my feet. I make the mistake of turning around, which only slows me down. He is only a few feet behind me, and he catches up quickly. From somewhere in the deep recesses of my mind, I remember something about punching them in the snout. Since I can't think of anything else to do right now, I ball up my first and push my elbow forward, cracking him right under the triangular tip, between his black nostrils, with my first two knuckles in a perfect jab, just like George has taught me to do. He turns away quickly. Thank goodness I learned to punch in the dojo.

The rest of the sharks are further back. I guess the first was the alpha or something. I don't stick around to fight the others though. I take my speed up a notch and head for that shoreline where the water starts to feel thinner and less oppressive. Everyone ahead of me breaks through the surface in turn. Then they each disappear as they make their way to the coastal shelf. I'm not too far behind them and can't wait to breathe oxygen again. As my head rises above the plain of water, my face feels as if someone is stabbing it with a thousand icicle, my soaking sweater is stuck to me, trapping the cold against my skin, making me shiver down to my bones. And if that's not uncomfortable enough, my skin prickles and sizzles from Mazu's magic wearing off.

Speaking of that beautiful mermaid, Mazu disappeared after handing Jake off to Rory. Once we've all crawled forward and collapsed on the shore, catching our breath and filling our lungs fresh air, I sink to sit cross-legged, the sand sticking to my sopping wet legs, staring out and search the waves for any signs of her.

Her head pops up where the sand drops away and the waters open up. "You did well, Guardian. I knew you could trust yourself, believe in yourself. Remember that you can. Take the memory of succeeding forward with you."

Where are you off to now? Do you live close by?

That sweet giggle tickles my ears. "No, I live off the coast of China. But I must be on my way to check in on a colony off of Denmark and then, who knows. I am the Protector of the Seas and must go where those need protecting, particularly from my own kin."

I nod. *Well, we make a good team, you as Protector and me as Guardian. Maybe we will work together one day.*

"I would like that very much, Miranda."

I smile and wave as she dives away from me, toward her next adventure. Then I turn back to my friends, my chosen family. Together, we walk back toward Eliza's house.

Jake cradles his arm against his chest gingerly, wrapping the good arm around my waist, as much to support himself as to keep me close. Rory and Eliza are holding hands and chatting with Joanna who is buzzing. She may be the oldest of us but in this moment, she is the most energetic.

"That was just such a rush! Just like the good ol' days. I can't wait to tell Benjamin all about it. Oh! Benjamin." She pulls a cellphone from her the back pocket of her soaking wet jeans. "Rats. I don't suppose any of you have a phone that's still working? I should probably let that husband of mine know where I am." She looks around at us with her eyes wide open and brow high.

Jake smiles at her before reassuring her, "He came down with George. You'll see him in a few minutes, when we're back at the house."

"Oh, that's even better!" She claps, looking like a kid who just met Mickey Mouse and is rushing back to her parents to tell them all about the experience, rather than someone who just fought a fucking siren and out swam a school of sharks.

Once everyone is quiet, I have the rest of the trudge back to think about the further implications of what just happened. I am the reason a pair of lovers is dead. To be more specific, *the League* is the reason. I need to look at my training differently, now. I need to look at this entire situation differently, now. Protecting humanity from these creatures is one thing. But indiscriminately killing beings... I don't think I've been doing this right. There has to be another way to be the Guardian. There have to be other options. And my family is going to be the group to break this system and rebuild it.

Chapter 26

JAKE

We reach the beach house at one in the morning. Eliza unlocks the glass door with the key she didn't lose in all of the commotion. Thank god for moms and their belt bags. She turns to us as she backs into the house.

"Shhhhhhhhhh. Hopefully the kids are all asleep. Let's not wake anyone up." She whispers so sharply to the rest of us that if any of us are going to wake any of the kids up, it will be her.

As soon as we walk in, I see Jessie and Phoebe asleep under a blanket on the couch.

"They wouldn't go to bed. They finally stopped pacing because I promised I'd start training them. Per your orders, Sir." George keeps his voice low and it cracks a little with relief. He and Benjamin appear from the doorway to the kitchen. Bouncing slightly on his toes, George has his hand on Benjamin's shoulder. Benjamin's mouth hangs open while he crosses and uncrosses his arms, wrings his hands, and then shoves them into his pockets.

But when Joanna walks in, that stops. He cries. He walks, not runs, forcefully across the room until he takes his wife in his arms. After a long embrace, he moves his hands to her cheeks and looks into her eyes. He inspects her face before asking, "Are you okay?"

She nods and collapses into him in exhausted but relieved sobs.

"She was phenomenal," Miranda assures him.

Rory is the last one in. As soon as he crosses the threshold, he locks and relocks all three deadbolts and then pulls the cords to slide all of the wooden blinds shut. He turns around to six sets of eyes staring at him. He shrugs, momentarily widening his eyes as he does so. "I'm sorry, do you want to take any chances leaving those open tonight? Because I sure as shit don't."

A clumsy chorus of "Nope, nope, not at all. Good call!" is the general consensus.

I shrug. I get it, I know we're all shaken up. But I tell myself that we are all probably safer than we've been in a long time. Miranda took care of the threat. Any other creatures that might be in the vicinity would have heard about Beatrice's demise and the fact the Guardian is here and not to fuck around with her.

"Let's get you the first aid kit," Eliza chirps as she takes my elbow and leads me toward the kitchen. Rory explained everything that happened after she left on the way home. Now she appears to be back to her normal every day self, even more so than she's been out entire time here.

George nods his head at my wound. "What made you pick Jake?"

I'm sure that's only the first question on a list George has been writing while he sat here wondering what was happening with us.

Miranda cocks an eyebrow at him. "George, you should know. It's always Jake."

I smile at my wife's response as I sit down, leaving Miranda to answer George's questions and trying not to pass out from the antiseptic Eliza wipes over my wound. I grit my teeth to keep from screaming out in pain. I wonder if I should go to the hospital, but it seems to have stopped bleeding and I'm not sure how I'd explain the injury. So, I just deal with it.

While Eliza patches me up I think about where we stand. Two Guardian battles, two times Miranda had to rescue me. I better train even harder for the next one so I can kick ass right alongside her. Whether this League likes it or not, when they chose Miranda, they also chose me. We're the Chosen Two, whether they like it or not. And honestly, I wouldn't let Miranda face this any other way.

"You had to go off on one last adventure, huh?" Benjamin rolls his eyes as he gently chides his wife, smiling and beaming at her through eyes he's having trouble keeping open now that she's home and safe.

She shakes her head slightly with narrowed eyes and reproaches, "Don't be an idiot," before allowing him to guide her to the kitchen stool while he tends to the cut on her forehead.

After he's pleased with the position of the band-aid he adheres to her, he then smiles and gets her a glass of water. "I may be an idiot, but I'm your idiot. Now, drink." He points to the water he just placed in front of her, and she listens.

"Okay, all done." Eliza pats the bandage she just expertly applied to my arm. I cock an eyebrow. "What? My mom's a nurse. I picked up a few things."

"Well, I thank you, and her, but mainly you." I smile and stand up, heading for the living room where George is still interrogating Miranda. I walk toward my wife, my Guardian, the woman I choose every day and will choose every day for the rest of my life. I only have eyes for Miranda.

When I reach her, I step between her and her docent, who steps back to give me space. I guess the kid recognizes that it's my turn with my wife. I put my hands under her jaw and gently move her head back and forth, examining her for any damage. She is soaking wet and shivering, just like me, but, aside from that, I see no harm has come to her.

"Are you alright?" My eyes are laser beams looking into hers, awaiting her response.

She nods, and a small "yes" creeks out from between her lips as tears begin to run down her cheeks.

"Are you sure?"

She nods again.

I wrap my arms around and feel her shake within my embrace. I whisper in her ear, "I'm glad we're back."

I feel her nod against my chest this time. I look over her shoulder, taking in the world around us for the first time since touching her. George is watching us, a lonely smile on his face. Rory has wrapped himself in a throw blanket, but he's still shivering a bit.

George seizes the opportunity to take charge. "You all need to get changed into dry clothes."

"Aye aye, Captain." I give George a mock salute.

He chuckles and shakes his head as he disappears into the kitchen and comes back a moment later carrying his duffel bag. "Rory, when I went down to check on Jessie and Phoebe, I noticed a couple extra rooms. Can Benjamin, Joanna, and I please crash in those for the night?"

Rory nods, "Yeah for sure."

Joanna and Benjamin don't waste a moment to wave goodnight and pick a guest room.

On his way to the stairs, George stops and turns to us. "I almost forgot! I carefully moved Natalie and Sam back to the basement. I thought you should have your room to yourselves, so you can sleep comfortably after such a long ordeal." He flashes a knowing smile with a wink and continues down to bed.

I bend my head toward Miranda's ear and murmur, "I have something else in mind for you." She's already shivering, but something different shudders in her when I lower my mouth and kiss her right below her ear.

I lead her up the stairs and into our room, making sure to fully close and lock the door this time. When we're inside, I look at her. She is standing there shivering. I start to unbutton my jeans and nod at her soaking clothes. "Get undressed."

"What? I'm freezing."

"So am I. And we're freezing because we're still sopping wet. We need to get out of these clothes so we can get warm. We're going to get into bed and share our body heat. I'm not going to try anything. I just want to warm each other up."

Her eyes get wide, and she looks shyly to the side. "Umm, okay."

I don't want this to be so clinical though, so I try to joke with her. "I mean, I'm not going to turn you away if you want to try something on me...but I won't start anything." I raise the corner of my mouth to give her what I hope is a sexy smile, and my cock perks up when she returns the look.

We each strip down to nothing, depositing our clothes into the hamper, and then stare at each other goofily until her body starts to quake. Her eyes close, and she leans into the bed a little.

"Shit, Babe, we need to get you warm. Into the bed now. That's an order." I'm starting to worry about how cold she is.

She begins to peel back the covers but stops, sniffing herself. "Uh, Jake. I kind of smell like a three-day old sushi platter."

I smell myself. "Wowser! Yeah, me too!" I look around and see our towels hanging on the warming rack in the attached bathroom. "Ok, new plan. How about a redo on that shower we wanted after the trolls.

She smiles and we head into the bathroom, kissing and stumbling on the way. The hot water is perking us both up. We're careful to keep me against the wall so my arm is out of the spray of the shower. She soaps both of us up so I don't risk getting the bandage wet. It's hard not to wrap my arms around her though. It's hard not to spin us around, bend her against the wall, and take her right here. Something else is getting hard, too. There's a twinge in my chest when she shuts the water off too soon for my thoughts to turn into anything more.

Warmed up but still exhausted, we climb into the bed under the fluffy comforter. I am still a little high on adrenaline from getting to be a part of the solution this time. Once we're wrapped around each other she realizes how excited I really am and shifts her head back just a bit and tilts her chin so she can see what is going on below my waist.

I bite my bottom lip, embarrassed by this part of me I can't control. "Pay him no mind. He doesn't know he's not needed here."

My wife's breath warms my neck as she chuckles.

He twitches. "Shit, maybe I should put on some boxers."

As I try to roll away, she grabs me around the waist and pulls me close to her, somehow closer than we already were. She wraps a leg around my hips and pushes herself up so we are face to face. In the same motion, she leans in and presses her lips to mine. Then she pulls away, looks straight into my eyes, and breathes, "Don't you dare."

I widen my eyes and open my mouth to make a smart-ass remark, but before I can think of one, she brushes her tongue against mine. When I moan, she slips her tongue inside my mouth. Instinctively, I pull her in to me, deepening the kiss and making sure she knows with each flick of my tongue that I crave her today even more than the first time she let me have her. It is getting increasingly difficult to keep from just flipping her onto her back and sliding inside her. She pulls herself higher and grinds against me, letting me know how wet she is now. I wrap my arms around her waist, groaning into our kiss, and she smiles against my mouth. She knows how badly I want her, and she is enjoying every second of it.

But two can play at this game.

I move my lips off of hers and kiss a trail along her jawline until I get to the hollow behind her ear. She gasps sharply as my tongue traces a spiral on that favorite spot of hers and her breasts press into me. My hands grab her ass, I kiss down her throat, but I haven't gotten very far when her hand wraps around my cock. I groan against her delicate skin.

She then brings her lips to my ear, and I hear her voice, strained from trying not to be too loud. "Jake," she moans my name, my cock is aching for her. I shudder in her hand. "I need to feel you inside me. I need it!"

Never one to deny my lady her needs, I push her shoulder until she is on her back, one knee bent and falling down to the side a bit, showing me just enough of her hidden treasure that I bite my bottom lip and hold my breath as I move into place above her.

I slide between her legs and press myself to her warm opening, but before I have the chance to advance, she wraps her legs around my waist and buries me inside her to the hilt. We move together smoothly, rhythmically. We are back on the same team, ready to move forward through this crazy world together.

Our bodies rock against each other easily, and we both form a sheen of sweat. When I try to lift myself up to try a different angle, Miranda's finger tips burrow into the hair on the back of my head and pull me down so she can keep kissing me deeply. Stretching her throat upward, she pushes her chin into mine as she gasps and squeals, trying desperately not to scream out and wake the houseful. She tightens around me in waves, and that's all I need.

With a few more thrusts, I feel a clenching in my belly. I push into her as far as I can, trying to make us into one. I release deep inside, and then we roll onto our sides. Spent, we lie together, wrapped in each other's arms for a few minutes, before she gets up, throws on a shirt, and goes to the bathroom.

When she returns, she is still smiling but also crashing into furniture from her half-closed eyes. She is beaming as she climbs back into bed.

"I really need to sleep, Jake." Miranda's audible happiness tells me I did my job right. "Especially if we're going to drive home tomorrow morning, which I think we should. We've all had enough of this place for one trip."

"Agreed. By the way, Phoebe found out about the whole Guardian thing." I cringe waiting for her response.

"I'm sorry, what?" She props herself on one elbow so she can properly glare at me.

"It wasn't my fault! I didn't expect a docent parade to come through."

She rolls her eyes, which makes me smile because now I know she's back to herself.

I need her to know something else. "Oh, and, one more thing, I told George I want to train more. And I asked him to train the kids."

My wife's eyebrows shoot up.

I laugh, "I mean it was when I was on my way to certain death, but I stand by what I said at the time. I want them to be as prepared as they can be. For anything."

"I can definitely get behind that," she barely whispers the words as she nuzzles into my neck, starting to drift off to sleep.

Just as I hoped, coming here brought our family together again. Well, maybe not just as I hoped. But despite the whole monster-fighting situation, I can't wait to come back here. Next time, I'll make sure to take Sammy to that aquarium. Hell, I'll even get the kids all the sweets and ice cream they want.

"Ooh, you know what? I'm going to run over to that twenty-four-hour sweet shop. The kids didn't get to indulge in nearly enough junk food while we were here, and I think it will soften the blow of us cutting the weekend short if we have candy to bribe them with for the rest of the weekend." I push myself out of bed and yank some fresh clothes out of my bag.

"Now? You're going now? It's two o'clock. Can't you just go in the morning? The actual morning, I mean. When the sun is out and all?" She's collapses onto her back in complete exhaustion.

"I'm not even tired. I got such a rush from getting to help you. Plus, I don't want to forget tomorrow. You know how stressed we'll be, trying to get all the bags and kids and everything packed up." I button up my favorite yellow Hawaiian shirt and search for my wallet.

"Well, at least you won't need a flashlight with that shirt. But please, be careful." I know she's nervous, but she's also already fading into unconsciousness.

"I will. But I want you to know that I feel perfectly safe because my badass superhero wife and her friends have control over the situation." I lean in and kiss her, deep, long, with passion.

"Okay, well, I'm going to go to sleep then." She rolls onto her side, facing away from me, and I smile at the sight of her as I hear a gentle snore starting. This whole Guardian thing took some getting used to, but we're going to be okay. I know we are. I love this woman more than I ever have anyone else in this world.

I move silently as I push my wallet and keys into my back pockets, descend the stairs, and exit the house. I whistle softly as I walk the boardwalk, which is still relatively active, even at this late hour. I smile at the college kids who make up the majority of the people, besides me, crazy enough to be out here right now. A saxophone player stands next to the rail that overlooks the beach. Even in the dark, he wears sunglasses. I nod to him as I enter the sweet shop, leaning against the door frame for a second to wait for the déjà vu to pass.

Humming along to the soft music, I peruse the aisles, filling a hand-basket with boxes of salt-water taffy, wax soda bottles, and tubs of cotton candy. Outside, the shift in the musician's melody is almost imperceptible. I barely notice when the saxophone stops, and his voice begins. Such a beautiful song...

Chapter 27

MIRANDA

The rays of sun shining through the window are my natural alarm clock this morning. I'm not ready to wake up though. The night was long; my body doesn't want to move because it's so worn out from moving through water for hours and hours, not to mention getting bitch-slapped halfway across the ocean by a fishtail. Plus, the sex with Jake...at least that part was enjoyable.

I stretch my arms over my head and then out and around in a big circle. When my hand doesn't smack into Jake, I flip my hair away from my face so I can see better. His side of the bed looks like he hasn't touched it since we made love last night. I furrow my brows but shrug. He probably woke up early to start getting everyone mobilized to leave. He's always antsy to hit the road early.

I hope he waited to pack the treats he got last night. Otherwise, we'll have disappointed kids when it's all a melted sticky mess. I throw the covers back and stand up, stretching again. At least I won't have to do much but nap in the passenger seat for the next few hours. I tap the screen of my phone to check the time. I fell asleep only five hours ago. Jake didn't even fall asleep when I did. How could he have woken up before me? Is he *that* anxious to go?

I take my time getting dressed and packing up our toiletries, mainly because I can't move any faster than turtles-fucking-miles-per-hour.

About an hour later, I head down to have breakfast and check on the rest of the family's progress. I expect to walk into a full and bustling kitchen, even with the events of last night keeping most of us up passed our bedtimes. But I am very wrong. Rory is feeding Tabitha in the kitchen, but they're the only ones I see.

I yawn. "Good morning! Is Jake loading the car?" I open the fridge to look for some iced coffee.

Rory raises an eyebrow and shakes his head. "I don't know. I haven't seen him today. But we just got down here about five minutes ago. I wanted to let Eliza sleep in a little, so I figured we could have some Daddy-Tabby time." He coos the end of his sentence to his daughter, who eats it up with a giggle. Then he resumes cutting up a peach into bite size cubes and placing a few at a time on Tabby's highchair tray.

I stare at their motions for a few moments, my mind trying to turn off and go back to sleep. But a nagging voice at the back of my brain won't stop screaming to pay attention. I'm missing something. Something important.

Again, I furrow my brow and look around at my surroundings. "Have any of my kids come up?"

Again, he shakes his head. "Not that I've seen. Sorry." He nods toward the living room. "I think everyone needed to sleep in this morning."

I rub my eyes, trying to bring some sanity back to my semi-awake brain. "I'm sure you're right. I'm going to check the basement. Maybe he's getting the other ones up and moving."

But the air in the basement is as still as in the living room. Gentle breathing comes from Sammy and Natalie's room. I peak my head in. Each of the four kids are snuggled into a bunk bed. No Jake.

The not so gentle snoring coming from another guest room tells me where Benjamin and Joanna are sleeping. Their room and the one next to it, where George is, have the doors shut.

I stand in the hallway with my hands on my hips. Where the hell is my husband?

I climb the stairs and hear Eliza's voice in the kitchen. She sounds groggy, but much more her than yesterday afternoon. "No, I'm fine, Rory. Really. I just want to be with you and Tabitha."

I smile as I pour myself a cup of coffee. I'm happy my friend found someone who takes such good care of her.

"Good morning, girls!" Eliza greets Jessie and Phoebe with an extra cheery tone. The girls must have been steps behind me.

"Aunt Eliza! It's so good to have you home. Are you okay?" Jessie's voice is full of concern and relief.

"Are you some kind of superhero too?" Phoebe's voice is full of vitriol. She doesn't sound anything like her normal happy self. She sounds jaded, like she aged fifty years in the last twenty-four hours. I turn around so I can be in the conversation that is about to happen.

"Good morning, girls." I echo, smiling weakly, when I look at my two eldest daughters. Phoebe's face scrunches up in disgust, looking at me like she's never seen me before, like I'm a stranger that she doesn't even know. Her arms cross protectively in front of her body.

I try to keep the smile plastered on my face, but my heart is cracking in my chest. I can't remember a time Phoebe was angry with me. Jessie, yes, all the time. But Phoebe? Never.

To break the intolerable silence, Eliza asks, "Is Jake still sleeping?"

My inner being collapses at the question. "No, you haven't seen him either?" I go to the kitchen door and open it a few inches to look at the car in the driveway. My face falls into a frown as I start to worry, but I also don't want to scare my kids, so I try to stay calm on the outside while my heart beats like a hummingbird's wings in my chest.

At this moment, George comes upstairs. His hair is mussed, but other than that he looks well-rested and raring to go. Ah, youth...

"Good morning, every—Miranda, what's wrong?" He expression shifts when he catches my eye.

"Nothing's wrong. I'm sure everything is fine. Can you come for a walk with me on the boardwalk, please?" I'm talking too fast for any of my assurances to be convincing.

Phoebe rolls her eyes. As I turn and enter the living room, I hear her quip, "Must be some big superhero business. Too important for us lay-folk."

She is really hurting. I want to hug her and talk to her and answer all her questions, but right now I need to find my husband.

George follows me onto the deck and closes the glass door behind me. "What's going on?"

I look out at the ocean and cross the deck to the walkway. "Come with me?"

He looks skeptically at the water, but follows. As soon as we walk away from the house, I speak but make sure I keep my eyes ahead instead of looking at him. If I look at George, I'm going to collapse into a puddle of tears. "Jake is missing."

He stumbles at the words. "What? What do you mean? Since when?"

The salty air stings my face as we walk toward the sea. A brilliant blue butterfly flits across our path. Normally I would admire it, but not today. I don't want to be here. I don't know what we're going to find, but my gut tells me it can't be good. We reach the end of the walkway and turn right toward the sweet shop Jake headed to. "He went out late last night, well, early this morning. At 2 a.m.—"

"Wait, he insisted on going out in the middle of the night, after everything you all just went through?"

"He went out for the kids, to get them candy, to soften the blow of us leaving early," I say through gritted teeth.

George cocks an eyebrow and opens his mouth, but when I clench my fist and tears blur my eyes, he bites his tongue. He doesn't have to tell me what he's thinking, how foolish Jake was, how foolish I was.

"We killed her, George. *I* killed her," I say, more to convince myself than him. "She's not a threat to us anymore."

George nods, but he starts walking faster while trying to not run ahead of me.

We enter the populated part of the boardwalk. I take a deep breath and consciously force myself to put one foot in front of the other, over and over again. The sweet shop is on my right, just past the aquarium. I start to angle my course so I can get to the shop without pushing through the lines already forming at the entrance to the beach, even at this early hour. Most of the people who lined up talk animatedly, looking over one another toward the ocean.

I shake my head as I open the door to the candy store and murmur, "Tourists...," under my breath.

"Jake?" I call his name before I even think about it. He's not in the aisle ahead of me, so I head toward the back of the store. I yell his name at every aisle I pass. As I pass the second to last, my foot kicks an abandoned shopping basket. I stumble backward as the basket tumble away from me. "Jesus! Who is so care—"

My sight zooms in. Salt water taffy. Cotton candy. Those big swirly spiral lollipops...each our kids' favorites. This was Jake's basket.

"George!" I scream. My voice is high pitched and yet scratchy, a combination of a fire alarm and a broken clock.

I don't know if George was behind me the whole time, but he's there to catch me as I collapse. He guides me to the ground and then let's me go. While I stare at the pile of candy, at the basket I know my husband once held, I hear George's voice from a few feet away.

More accurately, I hear people chatting, but all of their words sound like muted trombones. Then he's back, his hands press hard into my underarms as he heaves me to my feet, letting me lean on him as he guides me out the door again.

Across the boardwalk, people still crowd around and watch the beach while more of those blue butterflies hover around them, glowing in the morning sunlight. Everything I see appears hazy, and everything I hear sounds like I have cotton stuffed in my ears.

I force my lungs to breathe, but every breath feels full of glass shards instead of oxygen. I fall more than walk over to join the crowd of would-be beachgoers waiting at the dead end created by some cops standing guard. I start to call again.

"Jake? Jake? Jake?" The crowd quiets and splits to let me through to the railing. The beach is closed with police tape. Out near the water's edge stands a group of people in navy blue with shiny brass badges pinned to their chests. Something, someone, lies on the ground at their feet. A tussled mess of brown hair. Sunlight bouncing off a wedding band. That stupid shirt with pineapples and palm trees.

Time stops. My hands are shaking as they reach up and grab at the roots of my hair. Tourists are stepping back and looking away, no longer gawking at the commotion keeping them from their beach vacations. Visions bombard me, the kids singing Jake happy birthday, Jake tousling Sammy's hair in line for the fun slide, our wedding day.

"Jake!" The scream is blood-curdling as it tears through my body. I will never stop screaming.

The sounds of the people around me flood back into my consciousness as time resumes its normal pace. I push under the tape, leaving George behind. I run past the ramp, past the cops who try to stop me but know they can't, that they shouldn't. I stumble in the sand and fall to my knees, still screaming Jake's name. No. No. No. No. No.

The faces above the navy-blue clothes turn toward me, but I can't make out any of their features. I focus only on the person at their feet. The body at their feet. That stupid yellow Hawaiian shirt at their feet.

I crawl through the sand until I climb on top of him. His beautiful face is pale and bloated and caked in sand. That face that I looked into as I gave birth to our children. That face that looks at me like I'm the only woman in the world. That face that is always so animated as he reads the children funny stories. Now it is so still. His hair is plastered across his forehead. I use my finger tips to swipe it out of his face and gently call to him as I straighten his crooked collar, "Baby, wake up. Wake up, Jake. Wake up. How did this happen? She's gone. She's gone! We are all supposed to be safe now."

I press my eyes closed. When I open them, he'll be full of life again. I twist my fingers in the fabric of his shirt, pulling him to me and me to him. I collapse on top on him and sob and scream. Something scratches my cheek through the wet fabric. A voice calls to me, but I know that only I can hear it.

"Guardian. I am sorry I wasn't here. I tried but I was too far away when I realized he was in danger. I couldn't make it back in time."

Mazu. Mazu what happened to him? How? We killed Beatrice!

"Beatrice is not the only of her kind, I told you that. That thing that you felt through his pocket...Don't leave it there. You'll never see it again and you *need* to see it. Trust me."

I did trust you.

"Trust me one more time."

I place my hand over his breast pocket and feel a piece of paper inside, something meant for me. I know it. As I wail again, I move my face over Jake's chest and palm the note. My heart feels cold inside my chest, maybe that's my fate as the Guardian. No matter, I can't let my Jake's death be in vain.

An hour later, I'm still on the beach, wrapped in the blankets the cops use for victims of major catastrophes like shootings, bombings, and finding the love of your life washed up dead on the beach. The victims that have to stick around and stare at their greatest traumas so they can give their statements.

I stare out at the sea. George is by my side, his arm around me, not letting me fall again. He called Eliza, told her he couldn't tell her much but that we'll be back as soon as we can. I can't imagine she thinks anything good is coming. I don't know what she's telling the kids.

Thoughts like these pass through my mind, but only fleetingly. They float away on the blue wings of the butterflies that keep flying past, there one moment and gone the next. But as they flit away, they are replaced by something darker, heavier. How am I going to do this alone. All of it. Any of it. How am I going to tell the kids. Fresh tears sting my eyes. I scrunch them closed against reality. A fresh scream lodges itself in my throat. I choke it down into a sob that racks my entire body.

The note burns a hole in my pocket. I haven't wanted to risk taking it out when I am close enough to the police that they could see it and confiscate it, but every once in a while, I run my finger-tips over it. I feel the crisp edges, and it calms me, knowing that I will eventually find out something about what happened.

Finally, the police come over to get my statement, and George's. As they begin to speak, more butterflies swirl around me and land on my hands and legs. I try to ignore them and focus on the words coming from the policeman, but it's hard. The insects should be too light to feel, but I do feel them. Every one of their tiny feet are sending electrical pulses through me. I focus as hard as I can on the policeman's words. He asks me to stick around town until tomorrow in case they have any more questions or want to talk to anyone else at the house, but after a preliminary examination of the scene, of his body, they don't suspect foul play.

I want to scoff but sniff and nod instead.

They don't know what's out there.

When we get to the house, the kids are sitting somberly in the living room. I've never seen them so still and quiet.

Eliza picks Tabby up from her playpen and hands her to Rory, pointing to the stairs with a quick bounce of her eyebrows. As he crosses in front of the couches my kids jump a little.

One by one, they turn around to see what changed in the room that prompted Rory to leave. When they realize I'm back, Sammy and Natalie go up on their knees to watch me over the back of the couch. Jessie and Phoebe stand and turn. Jessie's eyes get wide as they scan the sand still clinging to my body and clothes from the crawl I made to my husband. I burst out in fresh sobs when I realize that was the last time that I'll touch him. The kids look at me and all their faces crumble.

They know immediately what I have to tell them. There can be no doubt, not with the state I am in. Jessie and Phoebe hold on to each other, as much to keep each other upright as for the comfort, as sobs shake their bodies and wails escape their throats. Natalie's eyebrows arch up in confusion. She knows but doesn't really understand what it means.

Her face pinches in like she just smelled a pinch of black pepper and is trying to avoid a sneeze, but it's tears that come out instead. Sammy is looking from sister to sister to sister, not knowing what to expect or what to say. He's too young to truly understand what this all means. They're all too young to have to know this pain.

At some point during all this, Benjamin and Joanna appear in the kitchen doorway. Benjamin is in a flour dusted apron. Joanna has her hand over her mouth, trying not to pull attention away from my family's open display of pain. Eliza is still standing near Tabby's play pen, jaw slack.

Eliza doesn't complain when I track sand across her floor and collapse on the couch. The house is silent, except for my sobs that slowly merge with my children's. Jake's children's sobs for the father they no longer have. They join me on the couch or the floor in front of me, all of us touching the rest of us. We have to be one right now. It is the only way we will get through this.

Eliza, Joanna, and the docents leave the room. George and Benjamin talk in the kitchen, but I don't know what they're saying. Everything is a blur.

After some time, things quiet down. I look at my children, who have fallen asleep around me. I wonder what they are dreaming about. I wonder if they are having nightmares about what they've had to endure today, or sweet dreams in which Jake comes home again. I hope it's not the latter. If they dream that then they'll have to suffer the loss all over again when they wake up. I remember the folded-up piece of paper. Slowly and carefully, I extricate myself and drag my feet to the kitchen.

George, Benjamin, and Joanna are on stools at the counter, each with a mug. George jumps up and signals to me to take his stool. Then he prepares a cup of coffee for me. While he's putting the half and half back in the fridge, I slam the note on the counter, making all three of them jump a little.

"What's that?" Joanna asks, breaking the silence.

"It was in Jake's breast pocket. I don't know how it was still crisp when they found him face down in the water. It was almost like magic." I say the last word with a dry sarcasm, my eyes squinting. I know it is something related to being the Guardian, and I'm pissed the fuck off because of it. I stare at the note, angry at its existence. I don't want to have a note, I want to have my husband.

I stare at each of my friends in turn. They look at me with big eyes, as if they're worried I'm cracking up. So am I.

Benjamin reaches out, snatches the piece of paper, and unfolds it. After holding the note at arm's length with his chin tucked to his chest and his eyes squinted, he pulls a pair of reading glasses from his pocket and clears his throat. After a moment though, he changes his mind. "You should read this yourself." He puts the page in front of me. George places my mug of coffee to my side and rests his hand on my shoulder so I know he's there.

I look down at the note and read silently.

> *Guardian,*
>
> *Now your children know how it feels to lose their father. The question is: How long can they keep their mother?*
>
> *See you soon.*

EPILOGUE

This last month has been hard for Miranda and the kids. First losing Jake, in that horrible way, and then, for Miranda, having to read that note and try to figure out what it means.

I don't ever again want to see Miranda the way she was when we found Jake. My stomach churns every time I think about that note. Whatever happened to Jake happened because Miranda is the Guardian. There is no question there. But beyond that, I'm at a loss.

I do have to admit, as hard as he made my job for those few months, he was too good a guy for the ending he got. And too good a father. Those kids needed him, need him. And now, he's not there.

After they laid Jake to rest, I offered for Miranda and the kids to move in with me. I figured it was a win-win-win-win. I have way too many rooms for just me. Miranda wouldn't have to worry about how to pay for the house. I could keep an eye on her and the kids, and they could all train whenever they wanted. Miranda said she'll think about it. I think she'll come around to seeing how much sense it makes soon.

She has been handling all of this with aplomb, which surprises no one. She has been open with all the kids about everything Guardian related and started them training with me, mainly learning self-defense techniques. Miranda wants them to have as much of my attention as possible when they're training, so we don't have everyone here together.

Jessie and Phoebe train together. Similarly, we paired up Natalie and Sammy. It seems to be working well so far.

In a conversation that should not have caught me off guard nearly as much as it did, Jessie and Phoebe expressed some worries and told me in no uncertain terms that they want to learn even more. So now, they're basically learning everything Miranda has learned. And they're good. Better than I could have expected.

Which is what brings me back here, to the League of Docents. Because it is Miranda's role in all of this, even if that's only as the gear around which the rest of us turn, is what led to Jake's murder, she's ready to burn it all to the ground: her birthright, the League, the Guardianship—all of it. And it's my job to try to ensure that doesn't happen. But I still can't let it go completely. Jake deserves better than that.

"Mr. Keating, we understand the question you're posing, but there has simply never been an opportunity for us to test if the powers of The Guardian are genetic. There has never been a child of a Guardian before, so there has never even been a way for us to do so. And because there has never been a child of a Guardian before, there has never been a *reason* to suspect a genetic component."

Perry Fucking Philips, Arch Docent and royal douchebag. I tried to warn him, tried to tell him to find another Guardian. I told him how unfair it would be on Miranda's family. I hate that I was right on this.

Before I speak, I stuff my clenched fists into my pockets and bite the inside of my cheek to keep myself from screaming. "I realize this, Perry. But I am the one training these kids, and I am the one telling you there is something to this. I don't know how we find out more about it, but I think we should. You'd be amazed. It's unbelievable the speed with which Jessie and Phoebe pick up these techniques."

"Mr. Keating, did you ask for permission to train these children? I don't see a record here of such a meeting." Regina Yasmin, the newest member on the League, looks at her notes like she's reading a text book, not a file of a living person's life. She's not much older than I am; therefore, she is much younger than the rest of the League. She probably thinks she has something to prove. Her oily black hair frames her face in lanky tresses. She sits curled in on herself as if she has absolutely no confidence, but when she speaks, her voice is commanding and assured.

Which is how I hope I sound when I answer. "No, ma'am. I didn't. After their father died, they asked—"

"Yes, and about this Jake… He was the last non-Guardian you asked for permission to train, am I correct?" Her brow is furled, head tipped to the side, as if she doesn't already know the answers to all of her obnoxious questions.

I swallow, hard, all the curses I want to sling at her, all the pain I've see Miranda and her kids go through. And I'm the one the League is going to pin it all on. I grit my teeth and try to continue. "I'm sure you understand how much danger the family of The Guardian is inevitably put in and the role we have all been placed in to protect them."

"It just doesn't seem you do a great job at training laymen, if the last one who worked with you is now six feet under. I'm not so sure I'm okay with you working with The Guardian's children." She drops her pen on the stack of papers before her and leans back abruptly. She has said her piece and thinks everyone should, and will, agree with her.

"With all due respect, ma'am, I don't care. I'm going to continue to train Miranda's kids because it is the only thing they are holding onto right now, so they don't lose their minds after finding out their mother is a superhero only to immediately lose their father before they had a chance to even process the information as a family."

This shuts her up, although a ripple of individual conversations works its way down the row of them.

I clear my throat loudly, getting all those eyes back on me before I begin "I came here to implore you to look into the potential genetic component to being The Guardian. I know none of Miranda's children are Chosen. I know the only girl officially in line right now is a toddler, but I am telling you, these kids, at least the older two, are gifted, powerful fighters." I hesitate to make the point that's been ping ponging around in the back of my mind, but I need to share whatever arguments I have for them. "You know Tabby isn't going to be ready to take the mantel before Miranda is too old to keep fighting. We may actually need Jessie and Phoebe."

They stare down at me in a moment of silence, but I won't back down, not like I'm sure they are hoping for.

Finally, Perry speaks. "There is no evidence of there being a genetic piece to any of this. There have never been two Guardians in the same blood line. If you're not mistaken about their abilities, there must be another explanation for what you believe you are witnessing. The League will convene, in a closed meeting, to discuss the matter, and you will be informed of any decisions we make that affect you. You are dismissed."

He bangs his gavel on the long table, and it echoes throughout the room. I'm not sure what I was hoping to accomplish here, but I am unsatisfied with the verdict handed down to me.

I don't care what they say. I know there is something special about Miranda's kids. I'm going to find out what it is. And Miranda and I are going to train them to be the best fucking superheroes yet.

COMING SOON

Miranda's story is still far from over! See how the kids join in on the adventure in the third book of The Guardian Series, due out in Spring 2024.

Be sure to check out Michelle's latest updates; get excerpts, bonus chapters and updates through her newsletter; and connect with her on social media by scanning the code below or visiting msummerswriter. com

ACKNOWLEDGEMENTS

Thank *you*, my reader. Thank you for investing the time and energy to read this chapter in Miranda's story. I hope you loved taking this heart wrenching journey with her, and that come back to see where she goes from here! If you have a moment to click some stars on Amazon it is incredibly helpful for a self-published author.

Thank you to my family: my husband for putting up with my new late night routines and helping me build my new writing spot right in the middle of the family room, my kids who keep trying to steal my books to read because they know they can't until they're much older, my sister for being the ping pong table to bounce my ideas off. My mom, for being my mom.

Thank you to Maria Secoy and Erin P.T. Canning, my editors, for forcing me to stretch into a better writer than I ever thought I could be.

Thank you to Fran and Nicole, my real life Elizas, the ones who know what's behind every word I write.

Thank you to all my friends and supporters, in real life or behind a screen somewhere else. I'd have crawled back into a hole and hidden from the world if it weren't for you!

ABOUT THE AUTHOR

Michelle Summers has been writing since age eight, when she wrote a script that she hoped would be made into a movie staring herself, with Tom Cruise and Meg Ryan as her parents. Michelle has a B.A. in Studio Art and years of experience as a manager in retail. These help her land the prestigious job of an abused executive assistant which she inevitably quit to be a freelance graphic designer, and when that failed, a domestic goddess.

Michelle is most proud of the three little spitfires she is raising, although she sometimes regrets having imbued them with all of her sass and smart-assery.

In her free time—hahaha just kidding. If she *had* free time, she'd enjoy her martial arts training, crocheting, and volunteer work in her community in the suburbs of Metropolitan New York.

Connect with Michelle on Facebook (Michelle Summers – Writer) or Instagram (msummers_80). She loves to hear your feedback and ideas!